**Praise for Christina Skye's
Summer Island series**

"Skye perfectly captures the feel and appeal of
small-town life...[a] sweetly satisfying romance."
—*Booklist* on *The Accidental Bride* (starred review)

"*The Accidental Bride* has something
for every reader—warmth, humor...and chocolate.
I love this book."
—#1 *New York Times* bestselling author
Debbie Macomber on *The Accidental Bride*

"Skye manages to keep her complicated plots
clicking along like busy knitting needles."
—*Publishers Weekly* on *A Home by the Sea*

"A delightful love story with just enough intrigue
and complexity to make it exciting and different."
—*New York Journal of Books* on *A Home by the Sea*

CHRISTINA SKYE

Butterfly Cove

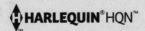

Recycling programs
for this product may
not exist in your area.

ISBN-13: 978-0-373-77785-3

BUTTERFLY COVE

Printed in U.S.A.

Butterfly Cove

PROLOGUE

THE DAY HAD started well enough, with a large iced cinnamon dolce latte with cinnamon sprinkles and a raspberry-walnut scone on the side.

Olivia Sullivan had zipped through morning traffic and was at her drafting desk an hour early. As she finished her scone, she savored the peace and quiet around her. She liked starting her day early. Most of all she liked the quiet time before the hive started to buzz and race with frantic activity.

Twelve minutes after Olivia had finished her newest project, an upscale shopping area and condominium project in a busy Seattle suburb, a man she didn't recognize walked up to her desk and put a small envelope down in front of her. "Olivia Sullivan?"

"That's right."

"This is for you." The man turned around and walked away before she could ask who he was or why he had left an envelope on her desk.

Olivia looked down and rubbed her forehead, feeling a headache begin. But those were nothing new. For months she had been working ten-hour days and she still had no idea whether she'd be kept on after her one-year assessment was done.

She picked up the envelope and turned it over. She saw a woman across the hall glance across at her uncertainly and then look away.

Olivia suddenly knew what was waiting inside that envelope. She frowned and tore open the cheap paper. She saw a check inside, her salary for the last pay period. The amount was prorated to end exactly at noon that day. Beneath the pay stub with her total accrued hours, Olivia saw a letter typed on company letterhead.

Dear Olivia Sullivan,
Notice of termination is hereby given. En-
closed check will serve as final wages due.
Thank you for your services.

Olivia stared at the impersonal, stamped signature of the company's president. *Thank you for your services?*

After eight months of drudgery, this was all she got? *Thank you for your services and a pay stub?*

She folded and unfolded the sheet, feeling the blood drain from her face. Couldn't someone have had the decency to sign her letter himself? Was an actual signature too much to ask? Or even a phone call from someone in Personnel?

With shaking fingers she gathered her reference books and papers and drafting pens. Quickly she slid her framed picture of Summer Island into the knitting bag she kept hidden in the bottom drawer.

Professional women did not knit in public, at least not while at the office. Knitting needles made people uncomfortable, an employment officer had told her quietly. It had to do with the sharp points and the quick movements.

Olivia grabbed the bag and swung it over her shoulder like a flag of angry protest. Maybe some people *ought* to be made uncomfortable.

A security guard showed up two minutes later. When you gave someone the boot, the security guard was there to collect their keys and badges and escort them out of the building. Olivia knew the drill.

She had just never expected to be on the receiving end.

Silently she gathered her other belongings and marched outside with her head held high. She met no one's eyes. She didn't speak on the way down in the elevator or on her angry walk to her car, where she dumped her box and knitting and then sank into the driver's seat.

The guard left. But Olivia sat white-faced and shaking, trying to figure out how her life could possibly get any worse, and what she was going to do to dig herself out of the looming disaster that her father had left behind after his death.

And now she had lost her job. Something burned at her eyelids. She gripped the steering wheel hard and told herself to stay strong.

But it wasn't working. She didn't feel strong. A wave of panic struck and Olivia closed her eyes, knowing what would come next when her anxiety grew into a sickening wave.

She had to get *home*.

She had to find the only place where she had ever felt safe and the friends who had been her anchor through uncertainty and pain. Her hands tightened. Summer Island was waiting for her in the mist, golden in the morning sun.

Olivia had driven the road south many times before, but this was different. This time she was going home.

For good.

Oregon Coast
Late afternoon

THIRTY MILES SOUTH of the Oregon border, the fog appeared. Olivia opened her window and drank in the smells of salt and sea, feeling the wind comb through her hair. The sun was gone and shadows touched the coast. Waves boiled up over black rocks where seals and otters fished in clusters.

A small sign pointed out the turn to the coast road. Her heart kicked up as she saw the misty outline of hills and trees ahead.

Summer Island's only bridge was half-veiled in fog when she turned south and rounded the curve at the top of the island. Olivia looked up, entranced by the big house that glowed in the twilight. Stained glass panels lit the front of the tall Victorian building above the harbor. Freshly painted, the long pier shepherded fishing boats that Olivia knew from childhood.

Princess of Storms.

Sea King.

Bella Luna.

The boats rocked at anchor, secure in the harbor. Warmth touched Olivia at the familiar sight. Summer Island never seemed to change, and she liked that sense of certainty. Slowly she drove along the cobbled streets and turned at the magnificent old building that she and her friends had renovated with loving care.

Imposing in a new coat of paint, the Harbor House gleamed in the twilight, its new windows blazing above the freshly restored porch. Strains of Chopin drifted from the open French doors above the side lawn filled with late-summer roses.

Home.

This beautiful old house with all its vibrant colors and inspiring energy.

Not the big modern house where Olivia had grown up, struggling to make her way through childhood, always too tall and too shy for her critical father. She had never been smart enough to suit her father. He had always expected more and more from her and never showed much real pleasure in any of her accomplishments. He seemed happiest when he was alone, working in his office, a phone in one hand and a keyboard in the other, barking out negotiations for a real estate deal. When he wasn't working, he liked to give big, elegant parties in the house on the cliffs, gathering smart, sophisticated guests who left Olivia feeling awkward and tongue-tied.

No, her safety lay here in the Harbor House. She had always dreamed about restoring the old rooms with her three oldest friends.

And they had done it. A new wrought-iron sign swung in the wind, a cat holding a ball of yarn. Olivia smiled and grabbed her big knitting bag and suitcase, following the steep steps up to the front porch. At the top she was greeted by shelf after shelf of bright yarns, glowing through the front windows. *Island Yarns.*

Her title. Her concept. Her joy. With her job gone, she could finally focus on the new shop. But how long would her money last? And then what would she do, with the employment market for architects so depressed?

The big blue door swung open and her friend Jilly O'Hara looked out. Jilly's big white dog barked in the doorway as she peered over the porch. "Livie? Is that you?"

Olivia walked up through the twilight past bobbing roses and fragrant lavender and boxes of glowing geraniums. "It's me. Everything looks wonderful, Jilly. I love that new sign for the yarn shop."

"Caro and I found it in yesterday's mail. We'd ordered it weeks ago. Walker helped us hang it. We put out another shipment of yarn today, too." Jilly frowned at her friend. "I didn't expect you here until next week. Is everything okay?"

"Just perfect." Olivia forced a smile to hide her worry.

As always, she smiled brightly and stayed calm; the habit was too old to change now. She kept her smile solidly in place as she swung her bag over one shoulder and turned to study the roses above the pier and the restless sea. "I love this place. It always makes me feel so alive, as if everything is possible."

Jilly stood beside her, watching a hummingbird shoot over the roses. "Same for me. Even when the house was a wreck and the garden thick with weeds, this view could sweep me away."

The two women stood for long minutes in the twilight while the sea wind danced through their hair and they savored old memories. Then the hummingbird zipped away and Jilly swung around, frowning at Olivia's big suitcase. "Why so much stuff for a short visit? Did you finally get a vacation from that slave driver you work for in Seattle?"

"In a manner of speaking. We can talk about all that later. Right now I want to see the new English cashmere. And did that angora-silk blend in the muted colors ever arrive?"

"All present and accounted for. Come and see. I'll give you the grand tour." Jilly shot Olivia another thoughtful glance. "After that you can tell me more about this unannounced vacation you've gotten."

"Hmm." Olivia barely heard her friend. The yarn was calling to her, warm in the glow of the antique chandelier she had restored. The whole shop was bathed in golden light when she walked inside.

Her worries seemed to fall away like racing mist. With a sigh she sank into a pink chintz chair near the small counter. Her hands itched for needles and smooth loops sliding into neat rows. But first there was the new yarn to consider.

Olivia glanced from shelf to shelf. "It's nice, isn't it? It's welcoming, just the way we wanted. So people will come. And they'll buy, won't they, Jilly?" Olivia tried to quell the small voices of doubt—the doubt that woke her up at night trembling and gasping for breath. She wouldn't let it ruin her first view of the finished shop filled with beautiful yarn.

Filled with her dreams.

"Of course they'll come, idiot. We'll have to beat them off with big sticks. They'll be *throwing* money at us, begging for our yarn." Jilly pulled Olivia to a corner near the window. "Now explain to me again about this cashmere. If I have to sell it, I need to be convincing, and each of these things costs almost fifty dollars! What kind of person spends fifty dollars for one ball of yarn?"

"I would. So would Caro. You will, too, once you try some."

"Gateway yarn?" Jilly nodded. "That makes sense. So I let them fondle the cashmere for a while. Then I close in for the final sale. Sure—I can do that."

Olivia smiled. She could always count on her friend to be practical and grounded. And that was *exactly* what she needed right now.

CHAPTER ONE

Summer Island
One week later

OLIVIA SULLIVAN HAD no job, not even the remote prospect of a job, but she was holding her worries at bay by staying busy.

In the mornings she helped her friends finish floors, clean walls and sew curtains for the Harbor House. Windows gleamed. Potted flowers beckoned from the new porch and Jilly's new café was in final testing mode.

After almost two years of renovation work, their grand opening was set in three weeks.

So far Jilly had served up mouthwatering double-chocolate brownies, pistachio-raspberry scones and both regular and vegetarian BLTs with her signature chipotle mayonnaise. Once word got out, the café would be thronged with locals, Olivia knew. And in the spring the tourists would be close behind.

But the café had already become a money drain. As a busy, award-winning chef, Jilly needed a high-tech kitchen, but the equipment upgrades had pushed the Harbor House's old pipes to the very limit. Jilly's husband, Walker, had done what he could to improve the plumbing, but a complete overhaul was the only answer.

And a complete overhaul would cost a fortune.

The yarn shop would take time and care to make a profit, too. Olivia planned to work there herself as often as possible, but she wouldn't take a salary until they were on better financial ground. So she needed a real job. And real jobs in architecture weren't falling off trees.

She shoved away the old sense of panic and focused on her current errand instead. She was on her second trip to the hardware store that day. The kitchen drains had backed up again.

Out to sea, gray clouds piled up over gunmetal water. Olivia had heard that a storm was headed inland early the next day, and she wanted all her errands done well before the bad weather hit. As a coastal native, Olivia knew that island storms could never be taken lightly. She had vivid childhood memories of blocked roads, mudslides and flooding along the coast.

As she parked at the main square across from the police station, Olivia waved to Tom Wilkinson, the county sheriff.

He crossed to her car, then leaned down with a tired smile. "Glad to see you back, Olivia. How are things up in Seattle?"

"Fine, Tom. Just fine. I'm glad to see you keeping everyone in line here on the island."

"I try. But these are changing times." He looked away and rubbed his neck as if it hurt. "So you won't be here long? Going back to Seattle next week?"

"Not right away. We've got loads of work yet to finish at the Harbor House. Our grand opening is right around the corner. I hope you'll be there."

"Couldn't keep me away. Especially if Jilly has BLTs and caramel latte macchiatos on the menu."

"You can count on it. She's been making up new recipes all week. You're going to like what she does with chocolate." Olivia found it easy to chat with this man who had been part of the town for three decades. With strangers she became awkward, searching for conversation, ultraselfconscious, but not with Tom. He never seemed to judge her or criticize the way her father's friends did.

"Has the mayor been by to see you yet?"

"No, but I haven't been home very much. Too busy at the Harbor House."

"He said he was looking for you. Wanted you to come over for dinner and drinks, I think."

Olivia was glad she had missed him. She had never felt comfortable with her father's old friend. The current mayor and his wife seemed fixated on the newest model of Italian sports car or the most fashionable jewelry designers in Seattle. Neither was Olivia's style. "I guess I should go." She held up a long handwritten list. "Walker Hale is counting on me to track down snakes and flappers."

"More kitchen leaks? It's a good thing that you

have Walker to help out with the plumbing. Otherwise that old house could get very pricey." The sheriff looked back at the police station. "So you'll be around? Over at the Harbor House mostly?"

"If you want me, that's where you'll find me."

Olivia had a feeling that Tom was going to say something else, but he just nodded. "Better get your errands done soon. That storm looks like it may reach land earlier than predicted. My right knee is aching, so this could be a bad one." He straightened slowly. "I'll tell the mayor where you'll be."

Olivia hesitated and then shook her head. "Tom, would you mind not doing that? I… Well, I'm going to be busy all week. I really shouldn't take time off to socialize."

The sheriff raised an eyebrow. "No time for drinks and chitchat about the mayor's newest sports car?" He laughed dryly. "No problem. Your secret is safe with me. Now get going. The mayor's due across the street for a meeting with the town council any minute."

It was a small act of defiance, but Olivia was glad she had avoided an excruciating night of empty gossip and pointed personal questions. She didn't want to be rude to her father's friends, but she had nothing in common with them.

Frankly, none of her father's friends understood why she was so interested in saving the Harbor House. Several had told her that manual labor was unbecoming to someone in her social set.

Olivia wondered what social set that was. The jobless and nearly broke one?

THE WIND BEGAN to hiss as Olivia crossed the square beneath leaden skies streaked with angry black.

She had already been to the local hardware store half a dozen times in the past week. Right now she suspected the old Harbor House was their best customer, between paint and yard tools and plumbing supplies. The owner looked up and waved as she loaded her cart with washers and flappers and something called a plumbing snake. While she checked out, Olivia kept looking to the west, where the sky was ominously gray. The first drops of rain hit before she reached her car.

Hail followed, hammering her windshield as Olivia turned onto the coast road. It was times like this that she wished the town council had voted to broaden the road, but there had never been enough money—and too many people wanted Summer Island left unchanged.

More hail struck the glass, and Olivia hunched forward, squinting to see the road. A driver in a small truck pulled closer, blared his horn and zoomed around her into the oncoming lane. She gripped the wheel tightly and let him pass. Even if he was a fool, she wouldn't be. A sharp turn lay just ahead.

That caution saved her life.

The driver in the truck hit his accelerator, trying to pass an oncoming SUV, but he was too late.

Olivia heard the awful whine of brakes as he skidded hard and struck the SUV. Both vehicles spun toward the ocean.

Rocks tumbled as the SUV skidded into the mud. Directly in front of her, Olivia saw a minivan with a school logo half buried in another mudslide. Two adults were at the doors, calming the frightened children.

But the stalled school minivan blocked the road.

There was no room in her lane. Olivia had to make a decision, and she had less than a second to do it. Otherwise she would hit the van.

Lights flickered in the oncoming lane. Olivia prayed she would make the right choice.

She hit her brights twice and turned left. Rain hammered down, and more mud washed off the inland hill. She saw the worried face of the school-bus driver as she passed. Olivia hoped they had called for help, but she didn't dare dig in her bag for her cell phone. She needed all her attention to keep from skidding.

Headlights loomed out of the sheeting rain. She heard the shrill cry of a siren as she yanked the wheel right, back into her lane. The siren grew louder.

A car shot out of the fog in front of her. With a sickening crunch, metal hit metal. Olivia felt her tires spin wildly and go into a skid.

She was going to die right here. Right in the middle of the coast highway. It just wasn't fair, because she hadn't even begun to live. She had responsibili-

ties, friends that would miss her. And somewhere,
there might be a man she could love....

Olivia wanted to love someone. She wanted to
feel strong arms around her at night and wake up to
a warm body wrapped around hers.

Light exploded behind her eyes as something
struck her hard from behind. The force of impact
spun her car back into oncoming traffic.

Her head snapped forward and her shoulder
slammed against the wheel. Through a haze of pain,
she saw a police car cut across in front of her. Had
she run into it?

The doors swung open and a man climbed out.

The siren seemed to come from everywhere, shrill
and high. Lights flashed in front of Olivia's eyes,
leaving her nauseous. Her shoulder was on fire and
she couldn't seem to breathe.

Then she fell into a well of endless pain.

OLIVIA OPENED HER eyes to searing torment at her
neck and shoulder.

Someone was pounding on her car door, trying
to get in.

She lifted her hand and even that tiny movement
was excruciating. A blurry figure was pointing
downward and jamming something into the window.

Olivia gritted her teeth, inched forward and gasped
in pain as she managed to unlock the car door. When
it opened, she almost plunged to the ground.

Strong arms caught her.

"Are you okay? That was a bad impact."

The words sounded blurry. They were swallowed up by the banging behind her eyes and the slam of her pulse.

"Need to get you out of this car."

Strong hands released her seat belt. With an odd sense of detachment, she felt the officer touch her neck, then pull back her hair. Searching for signs of trauma, Olivia guessed. If she remembered that, she hadn't lost all her faculties.

"Where does it hurt?"

"My neck. I hit my head." She shivered as rain struck her face. Then Olivia gave a broken laugh. "Everywhere hurts."

"Let's get you somewhere safe. I put up some flares to hold traffic. An ambulance should be here shortly." There was something comforting about his low, husky monotone. It made her feel he wasn't scared. As if he did this all the time, pulling people out of wrecked cars during a major coastal storm.

"Ready to go?"

Olivia half nodded. She tried to see his face, but it was raining too hard.

There was something else. Something about that voice…

But her head was starting to throb and when he tried to lift her, something in her shoulder popped. A bone shifted and then ground against another joint.

She screamed at the sudden, blinding pain.

Dimly she felt him lean her back against the seat.

He crouched beside her and touched her forehead. "You've got a dislocated shoulder. I heard that joint give way and I can see its position. I can set it back into place, and since I don't know how long that ambulance is going to take, I think that would be best—if you agree."

Olivia could barely understand him. Every fiber of her being was screaming madly from the pain in her shoulder.

"Do you understand? It's going to hurt, but you'll feel better. Nod if you hear me and if you agree."

Olivia locked her jaw and managed one sharp nod of assent.

She hadn't known it was possible to feel pain like this. It wiped out all her sanity and logic. She had to make it end.

"Do whatever. Just do it now. Make it s-stop."

"We'll get you through this." He leaned closer, his chest against hers. He pulled off her scarf and opened the top of her sweater, touching her shoulder.

Olivia realized he was being as gentle as he could, taking time.

She didn't want him to be gentle. "Just do it. Do it *now*. Whatever it takes."

"Okay." One strong arm slid around her back and his other hand locked. "This is some heck of a storm. They said to expect rain, but who knew the hillside would collapse. If there's one thing I hate—"

Olivia's mind was screaming for him to stop talking and make the pain go away. But she was following his words, slipping in and out of consciousness as he rotated her arm and then raised it, holding its position tightly. He was gentle, but the pain was excruciating, bone slipping against bone.

Olivia gasped and passed out.

IT WAS GOING to be one of those nights, the new deputy for Summer Island thought.

He got the children off to safety, crowding them into the police cruiser, which he had pulled to the side of the road. Once they and their teacher were safe, he checked on the status of the ambulance and the highway patrol. Neither was due for another six minutes. The first winter storm of the season had left traffic snarled along the coast for forty miles.

Officer Rafe Russo walked to the damaged car and took a deep breath. She looked thinner and more tired than he remembered, but Rafe had recognized her instantly. You never forgot your first love.

He was still shaken at seeing Olivia Sullivan and he was worried about her condition. She was unconscious now. He knew that the pain had been overwhelming. Dislocated shoulders were a bitch, no mistake about it. Rafe had had a few of his own, so he knew what Olivia was going through.

He shrugged out of his sweater and laid it over her for warmth as the temperature dropped. Then he zipped up his jacket and trotted back to the road. At least the flares had done the job. Traffic had slowed to a crawl, and he used another flare to guide cars slowly around the mudslide.

Rain crawled down the neck of his jacket, but Rafe ignored his discomfort. He was used to bad weather, to heat and flies. Afghanistan had taught him to stay focused in all situations.

Off in the distance red lights burned through the rain and he made out the outline of an ambulance. About time. The kids were shaken up. Their teacher was holding it together, but Rafe had learned that she was a diabetic, and she didn't have extra insulin with her. He had already called in that information to the EMT unit so they would have the meds she needed.

Two more cars crawled past. A state police cruiser appeared. The window came down. "Looks like you could use some help here. I'll park and take the other side."

"I'd be glad for it. I've had my hands full with the mudslide." Rafe turned up his collar against the pelting rain. "At least the ambulance is here. I've got somebody in my cruiser with a dislocated shoulder. Possible concussion. She needs to be looked at first."

"I'll pass that on." The cruiser angled forward into a spot right behind Rafe's vehicle.

It was barely 5:15 p.m. on his first day with the Summer Island Police Force.

He had dealt with two accidents. A mudslide. Crank call at the high school and a possible case of identity theft.

It was one helluva homecoming, Rafe thought

grimly. He remembered the sound of the collision. At first he'd been angry. Then he had realized the driver was very brave, choosing the only space left to avoid hitting the van full of stranded children.

She'd kept the collision to minimum impact, despite zero visibility in the storm.

But Rafe wouldn't have expected anything less of Olivia Sullivan. She had always been smart, always been thoughtful and careful. She did the right thing, no matter what. You could count on that.

A flood of other memories returned to haunt him. Rafe's hands clenched. He didn't figure well in most of those memories. They had been very close once. He had let her build up hopes that he couldn't fulfill. In the end he had betrayed her.

Rafe had lived with that guilt every day since.

But now he had a job to do. He couldn't allow Olivia's warm breath or the soft, sweet pressure of her breasts against his shoulder to pull his mind away from all the things he had to do to stabilize the accident scene.

He had screwed up more times than he could count growing up as the town bad boy. He had mocked authority, been a petty thief, played hooky from school as often as he could get away with it and broken more than a few store windows. After one brief season as a football hero, he had given up on sports, too. He didn't care for the male bonding, the authority figures or the relentless schedule.

Which was kind of funny, all things considered,

because Rafe had joined the Marines as soon as he could, and that brought him right back to authority figures and relentless schedules.

But the Marines had given him a home, a focus and a discipline in his life. He would still be over in Afghanistan had it not been for the broken arm and shattered wrist from a fuel explosion that had nearly killed him.

When Tom Wilkinson, the county sheriff, had pitched him the offer of a job, Rafe had simply laughed. He was the last person anyone on Summer Island would expect to wear a uniform. But the sheriff had persisted, and he was a hard man to say no to. At one time, his son and Rafe had been good friends in high school. But Tom's son had been killed in the Sangin Valley, and Tom looked pretty sick these days. Rafe hadn't gotten all the details, but he gathered the diagnosis was inoperable, slow-growing cancer. Tom was signed up for experimental treatments in Portland, but he was getting weaker.

So Rafe had agreed, even though it was the last thing he'd planned to say. Saying yes had brought him here, with traffic snarled around him on a blocked coast road in a driving rain. It had brought him straight into Olivia Sullivan's path on his first day of work.

The ambulance team jumped down and raced toward him. "Where's the patient with the dislocated shoulder? Possible concussion, we were told."

"I called it in. She's right there in the backseat

of my cruiser. I think she's unconscious. I used the Spaso technique to reduce the dislocation."

The two men moved toward the Jeep. "You knew how to do that? You see that kind of thing a lot here on Summer Island?"

"No. I saw it a lot over in Shkin and Kandahar. The Marines give you good field medical training."

The man nodded. "Ex-Marine? Yeah, that would explain it. Nice job. We'll take it from here."

Rafe took a step back as the men stabilized Olivia and lifted her onto a gurney.

She was in good hands now. He told himself he could relax. He'd gotten pretty good dealing with bad traffic over in Afghanistan. At least he could assume that none of the locals were carrying pipe bombs or improvised explosive devices.

As the ambulance faded into the rain, Rafe thought about what Olivia would say when she realized he was back, and whether he could make amends for what he had done to her.

CHAPTER TWO

OLIVIA CAME AWAKE to the sound of rain slapping against windshield wipers. A siren howled. Disoriented, she tried to sit up, only to feel straps holding her in as she jolted back and forth in some kind of truck.

The restraints left her with a feeling of panic and she called out.

"It's okay, ma'am. You were in a car accident. You need to stay still. We don't want any more stress on your shoulder until you can be seen by a surgeon."

Car accident.

Shoulder.

She remembered it all now. Mudslide. The storm. A minivan caught at the side of the road. "The children. Are they okay?" she said hoarsely.

"A-okay. They're upset, but their teacher did a great job. So did you, ma'am. From what the deputy said, you acted fast. Otherwise you would have plowed straight into them."

Olivia wasn't so sure about how fast she had acted or whether it was the best choice. It had been all she could think of.

Her shoulder throbbed, but it was nothing like the agony she had experienced back in her car.

She remembered a man's low voice. Strong arms had leaned close, locked her tight and gently rotated her arm until the joint popped into place. But there was something else...

Olivia remembered those dark eyes. That hard face. He had changed since she saw him last. He was tougher and older and he had an air of command.

But he was still Rafe Russo.

"Did you say *sheriff*?"

"Deputy sheriff. He assessed the trauma and relocated your shoulder. In fact, he did a fine job. I don't think you're going to need surgery." The man looked up at the clock on the ambulance wall. "We just got notice of a six-car pileup. We're going to drop you at the emergency care clinic in town. They'll take care of you."

Olivia barely heard, lost in the past. What were the odds that she would have an accident—and Rafe Russo would respond? It was a crazy way to find him after twelve long years.

An IV swung back and forth above her. They must have given her something for the pain. Drowsiness began to creep over her.

"He looks like...Daniel Craig. Rafe, I mean. Always was too gorgeous for his own good. He could have any girl in town." Olivia frowned. "And he probably did." Her eyes closed.

The woman in the uniform leaned down beside

her and shone a light in her eyes. "No fixed pupils or signs of dilation. She's stable. That deputy did a good job on her shoulder. And she is right about him. He does look a lot like Daniel Craig."

Olivia tried to answer, but instead she fell away into dreams…and restless memories.

HE HAD ALWAYS been a loner, even at nine. Olivia had been fascinated by his sharp eyes and his tough independence. He answered to no one and he was always in or out of a fight. Ever since his father abandoned the family, Rafe had faced life the hard way, rejecting any offer of help. All through junior high and high school he cared for his young brother while his mother worked three jobs, but Rafe's good traits ended at home.

Smart but doesn't apply himself.
Bad attitude.
No respect for authority. No plans for the future.

Olivia knew what his teachers said, but she saw a different side of Rafe, one that was bright and eager and learned new things fast. With encouragement, he could do anything he wanted with his life, and she cheered him on with quiet support and occasional study sessions, carefully hidden from her father.

It was one of those study sessions that had nearly cost Olivia her virginity.

They had parked on the wooded cliffs above Butterfly Cove, arguing about the meaning of an English poem that was a major part of Rafe's senior grade.

When Olivia's book fell, Rafe lunged to catch it, and they had landed in a sprawl against the seat.

One move. One touch.

Rafe whispered her name, and Olivia was swept into a hot, roiling madness that left her shaking and needing more. He had pulled her down across his hard thighs, his fingers sliding beneath her sweater, his lips on her face and then on her suddenly bared breasts.

Caught by desire, Olivia hadn't understood what happened next. Her body had betrayed her and she had fallen into sunlight, while the heat of his mouth marked her burning skin. Then while pleasure still raced and snapped through her, Rafe had stopped abruptly.

Things had gone no further. Resolutely he had pulled away, straightened her clothes and started the engine. His hands shook as he told her that this could never happen again. She had a future too bright to ruin.

Olivia had argued, but he was coldly determined despite everything she said. Regret had left her aching and uncertain, but Rafe had assured her this was best.

Before she knew it he was gone.

Olivia found out he was working in a restaurant in Portland, but no one knew exactly which one. The next thing Olivia heard, he had joined the Marines.

He had never called, had never written to her. He had broken her heart in the process.

The memories sang through her tangled mind now, joy mingling with terrible regret. As she slid back into troubled dreams, Olivia remembered the heat of his mouth on her skin and the blindness of her desire as if it was only yesterday....

"WHY ISN'T SHE BACK? She should have been here half an hour ago." Tall and slender, Caro McNeal paced anxiously.

Lightning cracked overhead. "Maybe there was an accident." Walker looked up from the box of tools next to the kitchen sink. "It's pretty bad out there. She probably got stuck in traffic. That coast road always becomes a mess in a storm."

"But why doesn't she call?" Caro paced some more. "And why doesn't she answer her cell phone? I've tried her half a dozen times."

Jilly gripped Caro's shoulders, slid her into a chair and pressed a steaming cup of herbal tea into her hands. "She'll be fine. You know Olivia. She's got the best mind out there. If there was a problem, she took care of it. If she needed help, she'd tell us. Stop seeing problems that aren't there."

"She should call," Caro muttered, then strode off to the window as an ambulance raced past.

Jilly knelt down next to her husband and slid an arm around his shoulders. "Some way to welcome you back from Colorado, Walker. I'm sorry to toss this plumbing thing into your lap, honey."

"Not a problem. I like to tangle with plumbing

now and again. After renovating that house in the mountains, I know a thing or two about flappers and snakes." He scanned the toolbox and pulled out a long rubber tool. "This should do the job temporarily, but you'll have to replace those gaskets."

Walker watched Caro continue to pace anxiously. He gave a little nod at Jilly. "Why don't you take Caro upstairs to rest. I'll handle things here. I'll keep trying Olivia on her cell phone. Maybe you could knock me out a cappuccino before you go."

"But you've been trying to fix that plumbing for hours, honey."

"And I'm finally making progress." Walker glanced at Caro. "Go on. She needs to rest and I've got to beat some sense into this drain. And you, gorgeous, are distracting me," he said with a low laugh.

AN HOUR PASSED. The storm winds continued to pound the coast, and there was still no word from Olivia. Jilly frowned and then dialed the hardware store.

"Yep, Olivia Sullivan was in here, but that was two hours ago. I hear there's been some kind of mudslide on the coast road. Maybe she got caught in that. Traffic is backed up for miles in both directions. There was a bad accident above Butterfly Cove."

Jilly fought a wave of panic. "What kind of accident? What happened?"

"Don't know. Somebody told me a minivan from school was involved, but that's all they knew."

Jilly tried her friend three more times and got no answer.

Down in the kitchen, Walker was washing his hands at the sink, looking smug, the way a man did when he had just tackled a nasty plumbing problem.

"You did it?"

"That I did, though the supplies Olivia is bringing back will come in handy."

Jilly rose on her toes and kissed him deeply. "My hero. But I'm worried. It's not like Olivia to be out of touch for so long. She's always hyper-responsible. And she left the hardware store hours ago. I called and checked."

She took the cup of coffee Walker held out to her. "I'm going to try her cell phone one more time. Then I'm calling the police."

When Jilly dialed Olivia's number again, the phone rang twice. There was a click and a man answered. The voice was husky and rough, and he sounded tired.

Jilly frowned. "Who is this?"

The man cleared his throat. "This is Officer Russo. Who am I speaking to?"

Jilly gave a muttered oath. "Rafe? Rafe Russo?"

"That's right."

"Well, the party you are speaking to *happens* to be Jilly O'Hara. Olivia's friend. Your friend, too, unless you've forgotten. Now will you kindly tell me where Olivia is?"

"She's been in an accident. She's at the emergency care clinic down on Admiralty Street. But don't get yourself worked up. She's stable and she's going to be fine."

Jilly's hand clenched against her chest. "What— what *kind* of accident? What happened, Rafe?"

"Mudslide on the coast road. She managed to maneuver her car to avoid hitting a minivan full of kids, which was a brave thing to do. In the process, she spun around and slammed into my police cruiser. She got my attention."

Jilly took a deep breath. "And she's *really* okay?"

She squeezed Walker's hand tightly as he stood beside her, giving silent support.

"I'm not lying, Jilly. Olivia is fine. They are going to keep her overnight for observation. She'll have to watch that shoulder for a few weeks. No lifting. No quick movements. I just checked with the doctor, and they gave her something to make her sleep, but I'm going to stick around until she wakes up."

Jilly frowned. Rafe was sticking around, was he? This had promise. Jilly had never found out what had gone wrong between the two of them back in high school, but it looked as if they were going to get a second chance.

"That's great, Rafe. I'll come right over."

"No, you sit tight. The storm is knocking out power lines everywhere. The governor has called an emergency alert. People need to stay off the road tonight so rescue crews can get in and out."

"Then keep me posted, okay? Have Olivia call me when she wakes up in the morning. And Rafe?"

"Yes?"

His voice was cooler, Jilly realized. He sounded about a hundred years older than he had been the last time she had seen him. Probably war did that to you. "Thank you for staying with Livie. And welcome home. I'm glad you're here."

"Hell of a first day back," Rafe said dryly. "But I'll take mudslides over IEDs any day."

CHAPTER THREE

"OLIVIA SULLIVAN? SHE'S right down the hall, Deputy Russo." The harassed clinic nurse looked up from her computer and nodded at Rafe. "But she's still sedated."

"Not a problem. I'll just look in on her for a few minutes." Actually, Rafe was relieved by this news. Seeing Olivia again had left him off balance, unprepared for the wave of emotions that had come in the wake of their meeting. He wasn't sure how she would feel about seeing him again either.

She'd probably throw a shoe at him.

He deserved all that and more.

Rafe opened the door to her room and moved quietly around to her bed. She was still asleep, her breathing slow and regular. An IV line dripped from a bottle over her head and Rafe thought she looked even more beautiful than he remembered.

But tired.

Thinner.

Too pale, and not from the accident.

Why wasn't she glowing with life, married with three kids and a big house overlooking the cliffs?

Rafe frowned as he watched light play over her

pale features. He had thought of her more often than was comfortable since coming back to the States from Afghanistan, but he was a different man from the confused and angry teenager who had run off to join the Marines a decade before. And Olivia had been a huge part of his boyhood. He had trailed home after her in the twilight, curious about the big house where she lived and the important man who was her father. His curiosity had turned into protectiveness when he heard some of the boys say she was tongue-tied and the girls say she was stuck up.

Rafe had figured she was just shy, and he had taken time to draw her out. Over time they had become unlikely friends, arguing over food and books and television shows. And eventually they had become more than friends. . . .

Rafe pushed away the bittersweet memories.

He wasn't here to stir up the past or pick up where they had left off. The new Rafe played by all the rules. That meant making sure he hurt no one, and he figured the best way to avoid hurting Olivia Sullivan was to stay out of her way.

Except staying away became impossible when their cars had crashed together in the storm. She had been brave to choose a possible accident over a certainty of impact with the stalled school minivan.

Brave but crazy, Rafe thought grimly.

Olivia had always taken her responsibilities seriously. Sometimes he had felt as if he had become one of her responsibilities—a mini-crusade to reform the town ne'er-do-well and see him brought into the fold.

Rafe hadn't wanted to join the fold, not on Summer Island or anywhere else. He had accepted Olivia's efforts because for most of his school years he had been crazy in love with her, ready to do anything to get her into bed, with those long, soft legs wrapped around him in blazing passion.

But when the opportunity came, Rafe saw how unprepared she was for sex and the power of her own passion. He had backed off completely. He didn't ruin innocent girls—and he refused to cause Olivia pain.

He had left Summer Island shortly after that.

He had started to call her many times in the years after he left, but each time good sense had stopped him. What did a smart, beautiful, rich girl like Olivia need with an angry screwup like him? She had never seen his dark streak and his anger. Rafe had made sure of that. But the Marines had pulled that part out of him. They had used his anger, honing his traits of independence and command to make him into a valuable weapon. Rafe had been very good at the jobs they gave him in Korea, Iraq and Afghanistan.

He knew that training made him different now. War had marked him deeply, and sometimes he wondered whether he could ever go back to comfortable civilian life after the things he had seen—and done.

Olivia's hand shifted on the bed. Rafe moved back

as she took a rough breath and opened her eyes, staring around the room groggily.

Her eyes moved. She studied the bed, the wall and then looked at his face, seeming confused.

"Rafe? Is that—really you?"

Rafe felt something tighten in his throat at her question. The sound of her voice still had the power to hit him in the chest like a hot fist. "It's me. How do you feel?"

"Sleepy. Strange. Drugged, I guess. You were there in the mudslide? That was you in the car I hit, wasn't it? And then my shoulder—" She closed her eyes, cutting off a sound of pain.

"Take it easy, Livie. You're doing great. There won't be any more pain like that."

"You fixed my shoulder. I remember that." Olivia's hand slid out to grip his. "I thought it was a dream when you walked out of the rain. I'm not dreaming, am I?"

Her eyes were unfocused and Rafe figured she was still half-asleep. She probably didn't have a clue what she was saying. "It's no dream. I'm right here, Livie. Now get some rest."

She smiled sadly. "I missed how you say my name. Say it again?"

"Livie."

"That's nice. I'm glad you're here. Don't go away, Rafe. Not until I wake up. It…might be a while."

Rafe looked down at their fingers linked on the

white hospital bed. He felt a weight at his chest. "I'll be right here."

They were going to have to face their past sometime, he thought. They might as well get it over with as soon as possible.

RAFE WALKED DOWN for a quick cup of coffee and a sandwich from a vending machine. Then he checked in with Tom Wilkinson to be sure things were under control at the station.

Since he was off duty, he figured he would stay with Olivia until one of her friends showed up. Hell, he had nothing better to do.

When he got back to her door, he was surprised to hear the sound of voices from inside the room. Looking in, he saw that she was awake, propped against a pillow, offering knitting tips to three nurses who were admiring a featherlight shawl on her bed.

So she was still a knitter, Rafe thought. Even as a teenager she had been crazy for yarn and fiber. Rafe remembered that she had knit him a hat one year, and it had won a prize at the county fair. He frowned as the rest of the details came back to him. Her father had been angry that she entered the fair without his permission. He had been incendiary when he learned that the hat was a gift for Rafe. But Olivia had refused to relent, determined to give the complex piece of knitting to Rafe. Her father had retaliated by cutting off her allowance and grounding her for a month.

Never one to back down, Jilly had sneaked over at night, climbing up the big oak tree outside Olivia's bedroom, furious at Olivia's punishment.

In a rush, Rafe remembered every sharp detail and regretted that he had made trouble for Olivia with her father. It seemed he had a rare ability to screw up her life.

Just then Olivia looked up and her face filled with color. Rafe could see nothing else but her soft mouth and the way her eyes sparkled.

"Feeling better, I see. But I think you should be resting. Sorry to interrupt, ladies."

The nurses glanced at Rafe curiously, and Olivia introduced him.

The new deputy sheriff.

It still sounded strange to Rafe.

After quick assurances that they would drop by the new yarn shop for lessons with Olivia, the nurses left. Rafe sat down next to the bed and began piling snacks on her tray.

"What's all this?"

"Lemon snack cake. Chocolate cupcakes. Corn chips. Coke. I figured I'd cover all the bases."

Olivia laughed and the sound broke over Rafe like a cool rain after a parched summer. He hadn't realized how much he had missed that laugh.

"You expect me to eat all that?"

"Not immediately. But given the reputation of hospital food, I thought you should stock up."

Olivia reached for the cupcakes, then stopped with

a frown. They had fitted her with a temporary brace, which made using her hand very difficult. "I hate being helpless," she muttered.

Rafe opened the pastry and set it on the plate in front of her. "It's only temporary. Have at it."

"Only if you eat half."

Rafe shook his head. "It's for you. All of it."

"Either we share or I'm not having any." Her mouth set in a line, and Rafe smiled, remembering how stubborn she could be. "Fine. Half and half. So you'll be giving lessons at the Harbor House when it opens?"

"As long as enough people are interested."

"You have three students lined up already. Those nurses were ready to sign up right now."

"The nurses that were here? Oh, they were nice, but they didn't come here to learn about knitting."

"No? It looked that way to me."

Olivia studied his face and smiled slowly. "You really don't know, do you?"

"Know what?" Rafe didn't have a clue what she was talking about.

"They came here to see *you*. Word is out that Rafe Russo is back on the island. They came here to check you out."

Rafe ran a hand over his neck. "That's crazy." He stood up, feeling uncomfortable as he paced the room.

"Not at all." Olivia tilted her head. "You're a high-profile topic, Rafe. You always will be. You stir up strong feelings, whether you want to or not." She started to say something else, then looked away.

Rafe wanted to ask her what it was.

But her face had filled with color again and he didn't want to make her uncomfortable. "Can I get you anything else before I go?"

She shook her head stiffly.

Rafe wondered what he had done to take the joy out of her face.

"Are you sure? I can stay here until one of your friends comes."

"There's no need," she said quickly. "You probably have a lot of things to do. I don't want to keep you. It was…nice of you to come by, though."

Rafe hated this strained formality in her voice. He hated the restless way her good hand picked at the plastic wrapper on her tray.

Most of all, he hated the thought that he had once again done something to hurt her.

THE CLINIC STAYED busy throughout the night following the storm. Rafe helped out when extra stretchers had to be brought inside and an emergency generator needed to be carried up from the basement. As the night passed, he made occasional trips downstairs for coffee or sandwiches. But mostly he sat in the chair beside Olivia's bed, watching her sleep.

Thinking about the past and the ways it could tangle up the future.

During that long night Olivia woke twice, staring around her in confusion until Rafe rested a hand on hers.

Each time she sighed and slid back to sleep as if his touch had assured her that everything would be fine.

WHEN OLIVIA AWOKE around 6:00 a.m, she stared up anxiously. Where was she? And why did her shoulder ache as if it had been hammered?

The storm.

The accident.

Blinking, she glanced across the bed and saw a tall man sitting in the chair nearby. She knew that lean face instantly. So Rafe *was* still here. It hadn't been a dream fueled by the medicine they were giving her for her shoulder.

She swallowed hard, unable to take her eyes off his face.

"Hey. You're awake."

"You stayed here all night?"

He nodded. "Jilly called you and wanted you to call her this morning. I told her what had happened."

"I feel strange. Restless. Medicated."

"How about your shoulder?"

"It's throbbing, but nothing terrible. Not like in the storm." She closed her eyes at the memory.

Rafe stood up slowly, looking uncomfortable. "They'll take good care of you. I don't want to bother you. I'd better go."

Olivia hated how much she wanted him to *stay*.

She glanced up at a knock on the door. "More nurses coming to check out the new deputy? News really does travel fast. *Come in,*" she called.

But Walker Hale opened the door, studying Olivia with concern. "Hey, Livie. How are you doing?"

"Not so bad. I'm still groggy." She frowned down at the brace on her shoulder. "Not much driving or anything else for me right now."

"No worries there. I'm under orders from Jilly to drive you home once your paperwork clears here. We can stop by your house, but Caro and Jilly laid down the law. You're going back to the Harbor House until you feel better."

"That sounds nice." Despite the painkillers and a growing throb at her shoulder, she felt tension fill the room. She glanced from Walker to Rafe. "Sorry. I should have introduced you. Walker, this is Rafe Russo, our new deputy sheriff. He's the one I ran into in the storm last night. And I mean *literally* ran into. Rafe, meet Walker Hale. He and Jilly were married in Colorado after they met at a knitting workshop there. We couldn't have managed all the work on the Harbor House without Walker's help."

Olivia forced a smile and tried to ignore the pain radiating from her neck and shoulder. If she thought the tension would fade after the two men were introduced, she was wrong. The cool, assessing stares went on and on.

She tried to sit up, but Rafe leaned over her with a frown. "Don't *move*. You know what the doctor said. You're not supposed to do anything until they check you out. Tell me what you need, and I'll get it."

"What I *need* is my knitting. Since that's out of the question for now, I would love a drink of water."

Rafe found her glass and held it while she drank.

"Thank you, Rafe." She gave a big yawn. "I guess these painkillers are working." Her eyes drifted over to the window. "Is it still raining, Walker?"

"Afraid so."

"More mudslides?"

"Nothing major," Walker announced. "Most of the big roads are open again."

"That's good." Olivia yawned. "I may slip off now. I can't seem to stay awake…"

She saw Rafe walk to the window. His face was harder than it had been when he left Summer Island. He was lean and controlled in all his movements.

Olivia saw a thin scar above his right eye. "You have a scar," she said sleepily. "I don't remember that."

"Fuel dump exploded," Rafe said tersely. "Go to sleep, Livie."

Olivia had a thousand questions. Had he been happy? Was there a woman in his life?

And the war…

But Olivia was too tired to think straight. Besides, Rafe had cut her out of his life a decade ago with a finality and coldness that still left painful memories. Though he was back, nothing between them had changed.

Olivia had to remember that whatever they'd once had was over.

"Say hi to the nurses," she murmured as her eyes closed.

"There *aren't* any nurses," Rafe said.

"But there will be…there always are. You still don't understand, do you?" Before Rafe could answer, she was asleep.

"WHAT DID SHE mean about nurses?" Walker asked as he closed the door to Olivia's room.

"Nothing."

Walker leaned against the door, sizing Rafe up slowly. "You've known Olivia long?"

"Since I was nine. We had a little history between us."

Walker crossed his arms. "I see." Both men were silent as boundaries were drawn, strengths and weaknesses measured. This was about testosterone and tribe.

Rafe studied Walker. "Marines?"

Walker nodded.

"Same here. I was in the Sangin Valley." *Among other places,* Rafe thought.

"Bad?"

Rafe shrugged. No war was good. The valley had been the scene of a dozen firefights, one of which had left most of his platoon dead. It wasn't the sort of thing you forgot.

Rafe stretched out a callused hand. "So you and Jilly got hitched. That's good. Nice to meet you."

"Jilly says you were all pretty close when you were in school. I figure you could tell a few stories about growing up on the island." Walker gestured toward a vending machine at the end of the hall. "How about some coffee?"

"Sounds good to me."

Walker glanced at Rafe's badge as the two men walked down the hall. "So you're the new deputy. I thought Tom Wilkinson had a hiring freeze in place."

"He did. But he had an unexpected dismissal. I saw him the day I got back, and one thing led to another. Here I am."

"You don't sound too thrilled about it."

"Don't get me wrong. I'm glad to be here. I didn't plan it, but job offers are a little thin on the ground right now. Long-range reconnaissance skills don't add much to a man's résumé. But that's not your question."

Walker palmed quarters into the nearby machine, dialed up a cup of coffee and handed it to Rafe. "So what is my question, Deputy Russo?"

"What happened between Olivia and me. But you'll have to ask her about that." Rafe ran a hand along his neck and frowned. "One thing I can tell you. Nobody expects to see me on the law enforcement side of things. I had a wild and misspent youth on Summer Island."

"The town's bad boy?" Walker bought a cup of

coffee for himself and walked to the window that overlooked the curve of the sea. Up north rain was still hammering the coast. Rescue crews were working hard to reach isolated communities. "Tom Wilkinson strikes me as a coolheaded man. I doubt he would extend an offer unless you were the best man for the job."

"Maybe. Or maybe he was desperate."

Walker's eyes narrowed. "Desperate how?"

Rafe let out a slow breath. "I shouldn't have brought it up. Ask Tom when you see him next." He took a drink of coffee. "Thanks for driving Olivia home. I wanted to take her, but I go on duty in forty-five minutes. This storm has left the whole county in a shambles. It's going to be a busy shift."

"Doesn't look like you had much rest last night either."

"I'll manage. It's not exactly Kandahar." Rafe frowned, staring down at his coffee. "It's still hard to believe I'm actually home. Sometimes I smell the air and wonder what happened to the dust and the burning gasoline."

Walker nodded. "Give it time."

Rafe shrugged. "If you say so. Well, I'd better go."

Walker tossed away his empty coffee cup. "Why don't you drop by for dinner tonight. It won't be fancy. We're down to the wire, trying to finish the renovations on the Harbor House. The grand opening is scheduled in three weeks, and we're not even close."

"Thanks, but I'll be working late."

"Then come late."

Something was happening here, Walker thought. He watched an orderly go into Olivia's room. He noticed the quick way that Rafe turned to assess exactly who was going in and out of that room.

It was clear that Rafe Russo took his responsibilities seriously. That fit with the stories Walker had heard back in Afghanistan about forward recon teams. A man like that carried a lot of baggage. It was written all over Rafe's face.

"Thanks, but I'll pick up something at the diner on the way home. I won't be off shift until ten."

"We'll be up. I've got plumbing repairs to finish."

"I'm pretty good as a second pair of hands on a plumbing job," Rafe said slowly.

"I'll take that as a yes. Jilly's making southwest lasagna with jalapeño corn bread tonight. I put in a request for double-chocolate cake to go with it."

"You make it pretty damn hard to refuse." Rafe hesitated, staring back through the door to Olivia's room, where a nurse had wheeled in a cart full of monitoring equipment.

The frown on his face and the concern in his eyes chased away the last of Walker's reluctance. "Then don't refuse. We'll be up and the food is guaranteed to be good. Jilly's been testing recipes for a new project. She can tell you about it tonight."

"I'll keep it in mind." Rafe gave a little nod and headed down the hall.

He hadn't given a clear answer to the invitation, Walker noticed. There was a whole lot of baggage hidden in those cool, distant eyes.

Walker had heard that recon teams who worked deep behind enemy lines sometimes dug into isolated mountain passes for weeks, forward observers in very dangerous places.

And Walker knew how hard it was to come home from war and try to remember that the world was a good and decent place. The change wasn't easy. At 3:00 a.m., only ghosts and bad memories kept a soldier company.

Rafe Russo looked as if he had more than his share of both.

IT TOOK ALMOST an hour to finish Olivia's paperwork for her release. But she balked at taking a wheelchair. "I don't need one. I can walk perfectly well."

Walker shrugged. "The nurse told me it was hospital policy. Something to do with lawsuits."

Olivia sighed and then sat down carefully. "Fine. My shoulder feels much better already." She hesitated and then scanned the parking lot. "Rafe left, I guess?"

"He had to go on duty. I invited him over for dinner, though."

Olivia's mouth tightened.

"Is that a problem?"

"No. Why should it be?"

"Because he said you two had some history between you."

"We did. Past tense. He's free to do whatever he
wants."

Walker rolled her toward his Jeep. "I'll keep that
in mind," he said thoughtfully. "You know, I dislocated my shoulder when I was thirteen, and I didn't
take time to let it mend the way it should have. I still
have twinges in cold weather. So take my word for it,
follow every instruction. Give yourself time to heal.
You can't cut corners with your health."

"No work and no knitting," Olivia said glumly.
"I'll go crazy *long* before I'm healed."

"More tea? How about another chocolate scone?"

Olivia smiled at Caro and shook her head. "I'm
saving my appetite for lunch. But I could really get
used to all this attention," she joked. She drank in
the wonderful aromas that came from the nearby
kitchen.

Caro straightened Olivia's heating pad and draped
a blanket over her legs. "Jilly's got something special
planned. She's been up cooking since dawn. I don't
know where she gets the energy."

"You know Jilly. She has two speeds—fast-
forward and out of control."

Olivia surveyed the sunny room with quiet pride.
The little café next to the yarn shop was almost finished. The freshly painted walls glowed, the old

wooden floor gleamed and bright new curtains hung at the windows that overlooked the harbor.

No one would have believed how derelict the place had been. Olivia couldn't even believe the change herself.

She tilted her head, caught by the smell of spicy soup and fresh bread. Her stomach gave a loud rumble. "If that's your special chipotle tortilla soup, I promise you my firstborn," Olivia called to Jilly, who was at work in the kitchen. But it was an easy promise to make. Olivia never planned to have any children.

Right on cue Jilly pushed open the pink café doors, a big tray in her hands. "No need to give up your children. You get this for free. It's my new tortilla soup variation, but be careful. Those rolls are fresh from the oven and very hot."

"Be still my beating heart," Olivia murmured. But she quickly discovered that eating soup with her left hand was not going to be easy, especially with her shoulder in a brace.

Jilly frowned at Olivia's clumsiness. "Sorry, I should give you a cup. Then you can just drink it." Jilly carried the big bowl of soup back to the kitchen. "How's that heating pad? Does it help?" she called over her shoulder.

Olivia nodded. She wasn't used to being fussed over. She never asked for help unless she had no other option. Growing up, she had learned that displays of affection were frowned upon. She was expected to excel but to do it quietly, and without any assistance.

The one thing Olivia had wanted most as a girl was to earn her father's love and respect, but that had never happened. She had never measured up to his critical eyes.

Olivia shrugged off dark memories as Jilly breezed back from the kitchen. Steam poured off a big cup of tortilla soup. "So when are you due back in Seattle?"

Olivia winced. She had put off telling her friends that she had been fired. Her job hunt had been going nowhere even before the accident. Once she had learned that no one was hiring locally, she had sent résumés all over the state and turned up two possible openings, but both had been quickly taken. "I have two more weeks. But I may be able to swing some extra time."

Jilly shot a measuring glance at Caro. "How can you do that?"

"I've built up some sick days." Olivia sipped the hot soup slowly. "This is fantastic, Jilly."

"You like it?" Jilly glanced again at Caro. "I— that is, *we* have a question for you. No, let's call it a proposition. Caro and I have been talking, and Grace agrees. We want to hire you."

Olivia frowned. "Hire me for what?"

Jilly sat down beside Olivia. "We want you to build a conservatory on the far side of the Harbor House. Your job would be official. We'd be hiring you as our architect of record. You know how hard it's been to maintain the authentic details of this house during restoration. But with a new conservatory—something bright and welcoming—we could rake in tourists. Then we can add a separate restaurant there, someplace for weekend brunch with a tasteful bar. Every seat would have unmatched views of the coast. With luck, we can book private weddings. That's where serious money comes in. A yarn shop and a café are nice, but the moneymaker would be the restaurant…and the drinks. I've been playing around with recipes, and Grace has already crunched some numbers."

Olivia stiffened. "How long have you three been planning this? You never consulted me." She looked away, hurt at being excluded.

"Hold on." Caro put down her box of cleaning supplies. "You had enough on your plate. Your father's funeral was barely over when we had all those zoning applications to finish. You handled every one so we could focus on the repairs here. We didn't want to bother you again so soon. And I only heard about this conservatory plan last week. No one is sneaking behind your back."

Olivia flushed. "I didn't mean it like that. It's just a surprise."

Caro sat down beside her. "Jilly and Walker had the idea first. Then Grace found a picture of a garden restaurant in Britain that was just perfect. We were going to discuss all this with you yesterday, but there was the storm and you were hurt. So what do you think?"

"It would be a great way to capitalize on revenues. And structure and design fees would be reasonable." The renovations had run to twice the estimates. Olivia figured it would take five years to dig their way out of debt, but the women were willing to work hard. The Harbor House was a key part of Summer Island's history. No way could it be lost, torn down for condominiums or a luxury resort.

And with her job gone, Olivia would have plenty of time to work on a design and then handle the construction plans. "I like the idea. But you don't need to pay me."

"Yes, we do," Jilly said quickly. "You know how the zoning commission puts us through hoops because this is a historic property. It's not going to be easy to find an exterior design that preserves the historic style while also serving a busy restaurant. You're going to earn every penny of your salary."

Olivia knew that was true. Dealing with historical buildings was a huge pain in the neck. They were beautiful outside, but their inner structure was usually a nightmare.

Despite the headaches, Olivia would relish the challenge of the new design. A garden and eating area around the conservatory would be perfect for the coastal location. They could also use the garden plantings to attract the monarch butterflies that migrated south each winter to Pacific Grove and Santa

Cruz. Fewer and fewer could be seen near the coast at Butterfly Cove, as available wild land was built up for expensive shore communities.

"It's a great idea. I'll help any way I can."

"What about your job in Seattle?" Jilly drummed her fingers on the table. "You can't be two places at once. This may be more than we should ask of you, Livie."

"I'll make it work." Olivia took a deep breath. "Now can I have another cup of soup? And this time crank up the heat, will you?"

Jilly gave a wicked smile. "You want hot? I can give you hot."

CHAPTER FOUR

THREE HOURS LATER Olivia had died—and gone straight to heaven. She was surrounded by a mound of cashmere, silk and merino, each yarn color-coded and separated by weight and fiber, to be displayed on rustic wooden shelves. Olivia had always been very organized, and she liked the security of knowing what was around her and how to find it fast.

Olivia had done a big part of the planning for the yarn shop. She had carefully chosen patterns for sale to reflect all ages and all skill levels. Each pattern was carefully inserted in a plastic folder and arranged by garment type. Her own hand-knitted shop samples were displayed on wooden dowels and antique dress forms. She and Caro had chosen the pink toile wallpaper and the curtain fabric. They had found an antique rug at a flea market in Seattle, and Olivia had brought two antique wing chairs of her own down to the shop on loan.

Now the space was bright and cozy, filled with a sense of welcome and inspiration, ready to become part of the community.

She put down the last ball of alpaca yarn and studied her list of invoices, pleased with the neat rows of numbers and check marks. All the yarn was accounted for. All the shop samples were finished. The yarn store would be ready to open on time, even if the plumbing repairs held up Jilly's café opening.

She reached down for the file folder with the shop yarn orders and winced as pain shot through her shoulder. The pain reminded her that she had at least a week of rest before she would feel even close to normal.

"Livie, what's wrong?" Jilly scowled at her. "I told you *not* to lift anything. That's what we're here for. Why didn't you call me?"

"Because I forgot, okay? I was distracted, thinking about the yarn shop and how beautiful it will be. I forgot that I'm a helpless mess."

"You're not helpless and you're not a mess. You did a brave thing in the storm. So stop arguing when we try to help you." Jilly picked up the box of sorted yarn and carried it to the nearby counter. She read each tag and put the ball in its color-coded shelf. "Besides, the lasagna is almost finished. I also think you should sleep here tonight. We have that spare bedroom nearly finished on the second floor. If you have a problem or need anything, you won't be alone." Jilly glanced at her watch. "Now it's almost time for you to take a pain pill."

Olivia rolled her eyes, but secretly enjoyed Jilly's concern. Olivia's role had always been to handle details quietly. She was usually the organized, capable one who worked without drama or attention.

Jilly crossed her arms, ready for a fight. "Well?"

"Well, it's a good idea. I'll stay."

Jilly looked surprised that Olivia hadn't argued. Before she could say anything else, car lights swept across the front porch. Jilly smiled. "It's Walker. Let's get ready to eat."

A second set of car lights swept the front of the Harbor House.

Olivia glanced at the door as footsteps hammered across the porch. Walker opened the door and Olivia saw that he was nearly hidden behind a stack of boxes from the post office. "Mail delivery. I'm guessing this is more yarn. Why you would need more yarn is beyond me."

Olivia stiffened when she saw the tall figure who followed Walker inside, carrying more boxes. She felt heat flood across her face.

Jilly took some boxes from Walker and carried them to the far wall of the yarn shop. "Rafe has been working around the clock. I figured it was our civic duty to feed the new deputy."

Olivia shifted restlessly. It had been one thing when she lay in the hospital, hazy with pain pills. It was another thing entirely to face Rafe now, clear-headed and acutely aware of their tangled past. The whole thing was awkward—and stirred up far too many emotions better left forgotten.

Rafe put down his pile of boxes and turned slowly, studying Olivia's face. "Is my being here a problem?" he asked quietly. "If you'd rather I go…"

"No." Olivia answered in a breathless rush. "It's fine. Why wouldn't it be?"

"You tell me." Rafe's voice was rough. "You're the one who looks like she was just broadsided by a truck."

Did she really look that way? Or was it only Rafe who could see through her?

Somehow he had *always* been able to see through her.

"What makes you think you're so important? I'm hearing a Carly Simon song here."

The corner of Rafe's mouth twitched. He leaned down, his face inches from her mouth. Slowly he picked up the heating pad that had fallen onto the floor at her feet.

"This isn't going to do much good on your feet." The soft fabric curved over her shoulder. Olivia felt the brush of Rafe's fingers.

That simple touch hit her hard, leaving her breathless and off-kilter. It had always been that way. If Rafe was in the same room, she felt it. As a girl, she hadn't understood where that kind of desire could lead.

But Olivia was grown-up now. She knew exactly how passion could dull your logic…and open you to heartbreak.

She pushed away a flood of memories. "Is there something I can do, Jilly?" She ignored Rafe. "Maybe I should get the napkins—"

"You just sit there, rest and entertain Rafe," Jilly

called. "Tell him all about the yarn shop. I'm sure he'll be fascinated by the fiber density and staple count of merino in comparison to alpaca," Jilly said dryly.

Then she vanished back into the kitchen, rattling pans and laughing with Walker.

Olivia looked down at her hands. She couldn't think of anything to say. Once she could have spoken about any subject with him.

She cleared her throat. "You must be exhausted from dealing with this storm."

Rafe rubbed his neck. "One day normal, the next day traffic pileup and roads closed. This one storm could drain half the state's total winter-road budget." He walked to the window, studying the sweeping green lawns that led down to the rugged coast. "You four have really made something remarkable here. All I remember about this place is boarded-up windows, weeds in the grass and graffiti on the sidewalk. But you four always did have great vision, didn't you? You saw what this place could become. That takes guts."

Olivia felt her jangling nerves relax slightly. "It hasn't come cheap. The house was in worse shape than any of us realized. Given its historical designation, we've been limited in the materials and kind of improvements that we can make. Jilly just told me that she wants to add a conservatory on the south side of the house so she can cater private weddings and have upscale brunches in the summer. It's a fantastic idea—but it will be difficult to get zoning approval. The neighbors may object to the noise. There are groundwater issues to consider with a new business, and we need to maintain the house's historic look. It will all be complicated."

"If anybody can smooth-talk the bureaucrats, it's you," Rafe said gravely. "You were always the one to talk your friends out of trouble. You always knew the right words to say."

Olivia stiffened. For some reason his description made her angry. "You mean, I was the town *good* girl, so no one could say no to me."

"That's not what I meant. I—"

Olivia cut him off. "Isn't it? Well, let's get this straight. I did my share of bad things growing up. Jilly wasn't the only one who got into trouble. You make me sound like a sleazy manipulator."

Rafe shook his head. "I didn't mean to. It was a compliment, believe me. It takes skill to calm people down. As I recall, you always had that skill."

Olivia couldn't find anything to argue with there. But arguing seemed much safer than letting down her guard. "So what are your plans? I expect you'll move on to more exciting places like South America or Asia. You always said you wanted to see the world."

Rafe looked at her gravely. "You remember that?" His voice hardened. "Then you should also remember that I wanted to go to those places with you. That never happened, did it?"

Olivia took a sharp breath. Suddenly the room was filled with memories and unspoken emotions.

"Not through any fault of mine." Olivia stopped right there. The last thing she wanted was to open up old wounds. They couldn't go back.

Rafe had made that decision over a decade before.

He rested an arm on the windowsill and studied her, eyes narrowed. "What about you, Livie? Did you ever see the world? I seem to recall that Italy was on the top of your list."

"I got to Italy. It was everything I'd expected. If things had been different…I might have stayed. There was an old olive mill that would have made an amazing bed-and-breakfast. I could have started a lavender farm and maybe raised some sheep." She stopped, angry at how easy it was for him to draw her out.

"So what happened?" Rafe frowned. "Why aren't you in Italy right now raising those sheep?"

"Because I have responsibilities. Because I made a promise to my friends and to myself. We're going to get the Harbor House on its feet as a stable, long-term business. And because—"

She looked away grimly. Her father's financial choices had crippled her own plans for the future, and she didn't have all the details yet.

"What else?"

Why was it a surprise that he could read her so easily and knew there was much more that she had not told him? That had always been one of his skills. "My father died earlier this year. You might not have heard. I have his legal affairs to settle. Between that and the Harbor House opening, I won't be free for any travel for the next couple of years. Pretty boring, isn't it?"

"Not boring. Not with the right person. With the right person, a little patch of mud can be heaven."

Olivia caught a breath. Was this the same Rafe talking? He had always been the first to get into trouble. The first to take a dare.

And the first one to leave town, looking for new adventures.

"I guess that's the problem. Finding the right person isn't easy."

Rafe stood up and walked to the row of black-and-white photographs that lined the walls outside the yarn shop. "This looks like Milan. Did you take these?"

Olivia had forgotten about these photographs from her Italian trip. She didn't want to discuss them with Rafe. There was too much of her heart captured on those carefully processed papers. "They're mine. Something to remember my trip by."

"You loved it there, didn't you?"

Olivia simply nodded.

"I can see it in the light and the way you captured the buildings." Rafe ran a finger slowly along a photograph of the Piazza San Marco. "I hope you get back one day. I hope that life brings you everything you wished for, Livie. If anyone deserves it, you do."

Olivia was trying to muster an answer when Jilly emerged from the kitchen with a steaming platter of lasagna. "Come on and eat, you two. Everything is ready. Rafe, help Olivia, will you?" Jilly's eyes narrowed. "She won't admit it, but her shoulder is hurting again and she won't ask for help."

CHAPTER FIVE

THE CONVERSATION FLOWED, punctuated by laughter and occasional arguing. Olivia had to admit that Rafe fit right in. Somehow they gathered up the threads of town gossip and old memories easily; Walker had to laugh more than once at their stories.

She tried hard to relax, but it was impossible. His leg kept bumping against hers and their hands brushed as he poured water for her. Even those small contacts were excruciating to Olivia.

"I was trying to tell Livie how good her photographs of Italy were. She shrugged it off." Rafe finished a third piece of lasagna and pushed away his plate. He turned around, gesturing at a black-and-white photograph next to the table in the unfinished café. "I'd say that's the bridge over the Arno."

"Have you been to Italy, Rafe?" Jilly poured more wine in Walker's glass and then topped off Rafe's. "I never knew Italy was on your to-do list."

"Oh, I had a *very* long to-do list in those days. I've narrowed it down quite a bit since then." He glanced at Olivia. "I got to Italy once. It was only for a few days, but I managed to work in my own little Roman-history tour."

Olivia couldn't process this. Rafe and Roman history? When did that start? "When were you there?"

"After my first tour in Afghanistan, I wanted to kick the dust off my feet. I hit Italy and France. Then a few stops in Asia. I didn't have anything holding me, so I figured I might as well travel." There was something hard in his voice. Olivia glanced at Jilly and saw that she had heard it, too.

"Try this, Rafe." Jilly held out a piece of chocolate-espresso cake with whipped cream.

"Haven't you heard about high cholesterol?" He shook his head. "Thanks for the offer, but I'd better check in with the station. We're understaffed right now. The lasagna was great, Jilly, but I should get going."

"You don't want cake?" Jilly looked stunned.

Rafe shook his head. "Thanks just the same." He turned his hat in his hands. "You've done a great job here with the house. I'm sure you'll make a big success of it. It strikes me that anything you four ladies agree on turns into a success. You always did stick together."

He glanced around the room for a moment and Olivia had the odd sense that he was memorizing the details as if he wanted to save them.

But his eyes were cool and distant when he picked up his jacket and strode to the door, and he did not look back.

JILLY KEPT STARING at the door, confusion on her face. "Was it my cake? Does he have something against chocolate? Who refuses fresh chocolate cake?"

Despite Jilly's joking tone, the abruptness of Rafe's departure left them all a little stunned.

"Maybe he was tired." Walker passed a slice of cake to Olivia and then cut two more pieces. "You heard what he said about being short staffed after the storm."

Jilly drummed her fingers on the table. "I don't think that's it. Didn't you see how his face changed? He was looking around, measuring everything. I can't figure out what happened."

Walker smiled and slid a hand over Jilly's. "Then don't try. You don't have to be responsible for everyone. You don't have to figure them out or straighten them out. He's a grown man, honey."

Jilly huffed out a little breath. "Just as long it wasn't my cake that sent him off. When people walk out on my food, I get grouchy."

Walker leaned down and kissed her gently. "If it makes you feel better, I'll eat mine and his, too."

Jilly gave a muffled laugh and ran her hands through his hair, whispering softly.

Olivia looked away, happy for them yet embarrassed to be the third wheel. But she figured she ought to get used to it. Being the third wheel would probably be a major part of her future.

MUCH LATER, AFTER she had awkwardly made her way upstairs, undressed and slid under the covers, Olivia allowed herself to think about Rafe.

Jilly had insisted she take her last pain pill and

now she was drifting somewhere between present and past, listening to rain patter on the window.

She couldn't lie to herself. She still felt the same sensual pull for Rafe. Time had not changed that chemistry. Several times that evening, when they had been talking, Olivia had the sense that Rafe was trying hard to sort out his own memories.

She let her mind drift on, comforted by the murmur of the rain and the sound of the breakers beyond the point.

Olivia told herself that she and Rafe might as well be strangers, but her body did not believe her.

THE SOUND OF hammering woke her early the next morning. She sat up abruptly and winced in pain from her shoulder.

Slow down, she reminded herself. *Displaced joint and torn ligaments, remember?*

She blinked as the noise outside grew louder. With small movements she stood up and moved to the window.

A lean body in a black T-shirt and worn jeans perched at the end of a ladder, hammering a shutter in place right outside her window.

Olivia couldn't look away as the taut muscles at his shoulders rippled. Sweet heaven, he had always had an amazing body. Now it was harder and stronger than ever.

Olivia watched Rafe work, every movement slow and controlled. His palm smoothed the new shutter and eased the wood into place. His broad hands were powerful and confident. Suddenly heat swirled in hidden, warm places that Olivia had almost forgotten.

She forced her eyes away. There was nothing going on between them. Nothing was *going* to take place between them. She wouldn't make another mistake in her life.

No matter how tempting it might be.

As if aware of her thoughts, Rafe turned around on the ladder. His cheeks were red from exercise and the cold wind, and Olivia thought he looked younger and less distant than he had the night before.

When he went back to work, she found herself watching him again. Every one of his movements was smooth and methodical, as if he had done this kind of repair before. She had always wondered what he had done after leaving Summer Island. Town gossip had it that he had gone straight into the Marines, but now Olivia wasn't so sure.

She ran a hand through her hair and winced. Even that small movement sent pain radiating through her shoulder.

There was a knock at her door. Paws raced along the corridor. "Duffy, stay. Are you up, Livie?"

"Sure. Come on in."

The door opened, and Jilly's big white dog bounded straight toward Olivia. She put up a hand, afraid he would knock her over, but Jilly's loud order made the Samoyed freeze in his tracks.

"Duffy, sit."

Amazingly, the command worked. Clearly, Jilly and Walker had been doing intensive work with obedience training.

Another furry body appeared at the door. Walker's trained service dog, Winslow, trotted across the room and sat down next to Duffy. Winslow was controlled and well behaved, while Duffy shivered with energy, eager to get up.

The interaction seemed good for both of them. Duffy was learning control, while Winslow got a high-octane friend for long runs on the beach.

Olivia reached down and rubbed Winslow's ears carefully, then gave the same treatment to Duffy. She was finally starting to feel comfortable around the dogs. "Is your shoulder better?" Jilly looked anxious. "The doctor at the emergency care center said that I should call if the pain got worse. You're not to lift anything for two weeks. They'll reassess you after that."

Two weeks.

Olivia was going to become a lunatic if she didn't find something to keep herself occupied.

"I'm fine." Olivia forced her eyes away from the window as Rafe continued to work on the shutter.

"He's good with a hammer, isn't he?" Jilly glanced out the window. "He volunteered to fix that banging shutter. No way was I saying no." Jilly blew out a breath. "So where were we?"

"With me being bored to death for two weeks while my shoulder heals," Olivia said dryly.

"Why don't you take your camera and shoot some photographs of the Harbor House. I know you've been wanting to make an architectural record of the site, and Rafe was right. Your photographs are amazing, Livie. I think we should blow them up and frame them for the café. They would make a wonderful portrait of the house."

Olivia couldn't seem to process the idea. Photography was a fun hobby that she picked up when she had a spare moment, but she'd never taken lessons or worked with any professional.

"Why? I'm not trained."

"So what? You're good. And if your shots are bad, you can just erase them. That is the beauty of a digital camera. At least it will keep you busy."

"My camera is at home. I may not be able to find it."

Jilly gave a guilty laugh. "Walker and I went over this morning. I grabbed some clean clothes for you, the book on your nightstand and your camera bag from the closet. I almost got your knitting bag, but I figured that would be cruel and unusual punishment, seeing as how knitting is off-limits for at least another week."

"How can I go without knitting?"

"Stay busy. Use your small digital camera. It's so light you won't have any problems." Jilly continued in a rush, "The nurse at the emergency care center is a knitter. She knew exactly how you feel, but she warned me that it would be a bad mistake. Knitting uses small movements, but it involves your whole upper body. Why risk a setback?"

Olivia sighed. "You're right. Fine, I'll try some photos. But I make no promises."

Olivia listened to the sound of Rafe working at the window next door. "Maybe I'll go sit on the porch."

"Perfect. I'll bring you out a cup of tea and some chocolate scones. Maybe Rafe will be done with the window by then," Jilly murmured.

WHEN OLIVIA OPENED her case, the camera battery was charged. She was methodical that way. She put things away clean and ready to use.

The little camera felt good in her hands, and if she was careful the movements caused no pain. Still sitting, she took a dozen surreptitious shots of Rafe as he moved up and down the ladder. Then she forced her attention down to the beach, where the storm surge had deposited chunks of driftwood and dead crabs and fallen seabirds.

Her camera wasn't high-tech. It fit nicely in the palm of her hand, without big lenses, and it was easy to hold.

The German lenses were very good and Olivia captured the cove in sun and in shadow, with seabirds hovering at the end of the pier and a group of seals riding the surf out beyond the harbor. She liked to work like this, sliding into the zone, unaware of anything around her, becoming an extension of the lens. When she recorded the messy, chaotic, beautiful flow of life around her, Olivia felt safe. She wasn't sure why, but probably it came from the way she had grown up, working hard but never feeling her father loved or even cared much about her. But behind her camera, Olivia was alive. She defined her world and forced it into clarity. At her drafting table, making complex architectural designs, she felt the same way.

Rafe had moved to the far side of the house now, his hammering muted. According to Jilly, they had lost several shutters and a dozen or so roof tiles in the storm. Given the damage farther up the coast, this was nothing. They had been very lucky.

Olivia felt a pang at her shoulder, but she ignored it. Caro would be over in an hour and Olivia was going to help her organize the new knitting patterns in big binders so all the designs were easy to find and beautifully displayed.

Olivia had taken pictures of some beautiful sweaters while she was in Italy. She wondered how they would look blown up and framed. Or maybe even as sketches for the yarn shop walls.

Then she discarded the idea.

She had no training or special skills, after all. Probably the photos would turn out to be ugly.

"Finish your tea and stop frowning." Jilly stood at the door to the porch, hands on her hips, frowning. "I hate it when you get *that* look on your face, wistful and worried. You always looked that way after your father yelled at you for doing something wrong. Except you never did anything wrong. He was just blowing off for no reason." Jilly caught back a breath and shook her head. They had had this argument before. It never solved or changed anything. Jilly hadn't liked Olivia's father.

"I'm perfectly happy. The weather is beautiful and I'm enjoying my camera. For the record, I'm not frowning or looking wistful about anything," she said flatly.

"If you say so." Jilly leaned closer. "Rafe looks pretty good in that tight black T-shirt. If I didn't have Walker, I could be very tempted."

Olivia rolled her eyes. Jilly was never subtle about anything, even when she made a joke. "It's nice of him to come and help Walker. Any new problems?"

"The upstairs back bathtub is leaking now. Walker went to get caulking and some kind of rubber gaskets this morning. Frankly, I think we should invest in a hardware store of our own."

Rafe walked up the stairway below the porch, pulling off his black T-shirt as he spoke. "Jilly, can I take Duffy for a run on the beach? I'm pretty sweaty here, despite the chill. I think the two of us need a swim."

Sweat glistened on his bare chest and slid slowly down his powerful biceps, and Olivia strangled a sigh at the sight of that tanned, rugged body.

The man was drop-dead gorgeous. Didn't he realize that?

Olivia could hear the sudden drum of her heart. Rafe had always been good to look at. But now, after hard years of exercise and fieldwork, he had a dangerous, lean body that left Olivia wondering what it would be like to set a match to all that hot, dangerous energy and feel it explode.

She coughed hard, angry at the direction her thoughts had taken.

Rafe stared at the two women. *"What?"*

"What what?" Jilly muttered.

"Why are you staring at me?" Rafe tossed his T-shirt over his shoulder. "Do I have grease all over me? I wouldn't be surprised. I don't think those shutters have been cleaned in fifty years."

"Nope. No grease. Not a speck." Jilly shot a covert glance at Olivia. "Go take Duffy for that run. He'll love it. Watch the current, though. This time of year that riptide can be dangerous."

"You think I'd forget that? When I was twelve I almost drowned out there," Rafe said quietly.

Olivia hadn't known that story. The tides could change quickly out beyond the cove, and there were danger signs posted all around the island, but occasionally swimmers got cocky. Usually they were vacationing tourists, too excited to be near the water to pay attention to the warnings.

"What happened?" Olivia kept her eyes on his

face even though they kept trying to drift south to that hard-muscled chest.

"Usual thing. I thought the signs were for everybody else. Lucky thing a fishing boat picked me up about a mile out. Otherwise my body would have floated all the way to Mexico."

Olivia shivered. It wasn't remotely a joke. Knowing Rafe, he had been swimming alone, without telling anyone of his plans. He might have lost consciousness and drifted off, then never been seen again.

Her hands clenched.

"Hey, no worries. I'm fine. It taught me a good lesson. I always read the signs now," he said with a grin. She felt the warmth of his skin and the heady scent of wind and man and sea.

She tried to pull away, but their fingers brushed when he turned a page of her notebook. "You did these? That one looks like Venice. Is that one a sweater? What are all those crisscross lines?"

Olivia had to clear her throat twice before she could talk. "Cables. It's a sweater. A sweater pattern. I'm designing it. From memory. It's something I saw in Venice."

She bit back the jerky explanations. How did he manage to unravel her this way?

Rafe leaned closer. Olivia saw the glistening line of his shoulder close enough to touch. She smelled his skin, and she wanted to run her hands along that curve of muscle and then her tongue.

"Oh, I get it now. That's the sleeve. And that top thing is the collar."

Olivia couldn't answer. It was taking all her will-power not to lean over and touch his glistening skin.

Jilly cut through the haze of Olivia's sensual distraction. "I've never seen that pattern before, Livie. When did you make it?"

"New one. Took the picture in Italy." Olivia closed her eyes, summoning up her calm and control. She *wasn't* going to allow Rafe Russo to get under her skin like this.

Not *again*.

"Have a nice swim, Rafe," she said tightly. "I'd better get back to work while my imagination is hot."

She winced at the word choice. When she tried to avoid his gaze, her eyes fell, trailing across the muscled lines of his chest and the sculpted abs that ran lower, disappearing beneath his worn jeans. The sight made her pulse skip and flutter.

"Have a nice time. Down at the beach. You and Duffy," she rasped.

"Yes, go on, Rafe. You're disgusting and sweaty. You and Duffy go clean yourselves up and I'll have chili ready by the time you get back." Jilly waved a warning finger at him. "And take care of my dog. Don't let Duffy get into any trouble down there."

"Aye, aye, sir." Rafe gave a mock two-finger salute, shoved his T-shirt into his waistband and called for Duffy. Then the two of them raced toward the beach.

"I think maybe we need to call 911." Jilly blew out a slow breath. "I forgot how he was built."

"So did I." Olivia didn't bother to lie. When you knew a friend as long as she had known Jilly, lies were generally pointless anyway. "He does look great. I had no idea about that crazy swimming story he told. What if he hadn't been picked up? He could have died."

Jilly shook her head. "He's told me about a few of his crazy adventures. Some of them were worse than that."

Olivia frowned. "Worse than getting pulled out to sea?"

Jilly gave a rueful smile. "That's right. But if you want details, you'll have to ask him yourself." She turned to search Olivia's face. "You look like you're feeling better. The sun and wind have put some color back into your cheeks. Or maybe…it wasn't just the weather," Jilly said astutely. "No need to get up. You keep an eye on Rafe and Duffy. I'm going to organize lunch."

CHAPTER SIX

MAYBE IT WAS the sunny weather after long days of rain. Maybe it was the need for distraction. Either way, Olivia found her pencil flowing in sketch after sketch while Rafe and Duffy ran along the beach. By the time Jilly came out with a small table and lemonade, Olivia had completed four different sweater designs.

She looked down as Duffy was dashing over the sand, chasing the stick that Rafe had thrown through the air. Both of them looked happy and soaking wet from a quick swim in the ocean.

But Jilly was far more interested in Olivia's sketches then her dog's antics. "These patterns are great, Livie. I really like that little shrug thing."

"It looks complicated, but actually it's totally easy. I think I'll write that one up first with a chart. Do you think anyone would buy it?"

"If you knit up samples in three different colors and sizes, I'm sure we could get five dollars for the pattern." Jilly frowned. "Make more designs like these. Things that are simple but elegant, just the way you always look. In fact, maybe we should set you up with a website. We can put it right under the

Harbor House site. I've been thinking of offering a few specialty foods for sale through the website, too." Jilly drummed her hands on the porch railing. "We could hook you into that big knitting site that you love so much. You could post your sketches and your photographs from Italy. How cool would that be!"

"I don't know, Jilly." Olivia was comfortable writing a few informal patterns to sell in their yarn shop, but she wasn't ready to share them at a huge knitting website. She had no kind of formal training, after all. "No, I don't think they would be good enough."

"Just consider it, okay? I'm not pushing you to anything you don't want to do." Jilly flipped a dish towel over her shoulder and glanced down to the cove. "I see the two males are bonding over sweat and sticks down on the beach. I'm glad Rafe is giving Duffy a good run. Walker has been distracted with this plumbing work, and I just don't have time to run Duffy the way I should."

Olivia didn't answer. She was too distracted by the sight of Rafe pulling on his T-shirt and sweater as Duffy charged up the slope, then raced back toward the water.

Something about the sight of Rafe and the racing dog looked exuberant and primal. Every movement held raw energy, which for some reason made Olivia aware of how long it had been since she'd been involved with a man.

She was fascinated by the way Duffy and Rafe charged in mad circles, lost in the pure joy of movement. She smiled at Rafe's bark of laughter drifting on the wind.

"Earth to Mars. Are you here?"

Olivia looked up, surprised to see Jilly smoothing a white linen cloth over the table. "I've been asking what you want to drink. That is, if you can tear yourself away from watching Rafe."

Olivia flushed. "I don't know what you're talking about. And iced tea would be fine."

Jilly glanced back and waved to Rafe. "Keep him entertained, will you? I'll have lunch out here in a minute. Walker should be down by then."

Rafe trotted up the front steps with Duffy close behind. He toweled Duffy off and let him inside and then sat down on the railing, one leg dangling. He looked tired but relaxed.

"Duffy was in dog heaven down there."

"He's got way too much energy. I doubt I could have kept up with him much longer. I'm glad Jilly has a great dog like that." He cocked his head, sniffing the air. "Is that what I think it is?"

Olivia smiled. "Cowboy chili. Jilly's special Southwest recipe. Pull up a chair. She's bringing the food out here so we can eat on the porch, since it's so sunny today." Olivia started to stand up. "I should go help her."

"Forget it. Stay right there and keep on doing whatever you were doing." Rafe leaned over Olivia's shoulder. "Are you designing clothes now? Sweaters? I thought you were an architect. Did you change careers while I was gone?"

No, she had just *lost* one career. Olivia swept the papers up and turned them over. "I was just… doodling. I'm still an architect. I just happen to be an *unemployed* one right now." Olivia frowned. She hadn't meant to tell anyone about that yet.

"Sorry to hear it. You'll bounce back."

Olivia didn't know what to say. She couldn't manage small talk with Rafe, and every important topic made her uncomfortable. She cleared her throat. "Walker is working upstairs. He should be down any minute, and then we can eat."

Rafe frowned, brushing sand off his feet. "Is this hard for you, Livie? Do I make you uncomfortable? If so, I'll leave."

"Uncomfortable? Me? What makes you think I'm uncomfortable? That's ridiculous," she sputtered.

Rafe slipped on his old sneakers. "Right now your leg is banging up and down, and you keep opening and closing your hands. You're definitely uncomfortable and I'd like to know why."

"I'm *fine*. Jilly invited you and that's that. Go help her with the food. Bring me the napkins and silverware while you're at it."

But Rafe didn't move. His eyes lingered on her face. "Are you sure, Livie? Because I didn't come back here to pick up where we left off. I want you to know that. There's no point in opening old wounds."

Olivia looked up and felt how intensely he

watched her, as if she was the only thing that mattered at that moment. She fell down into the darkness of his eyes, into the cold strength of his face. But the joy was gone. It was a stranger's face now.

"That's just the way I want it, too. After all this time, who could remember the things we said to each other anyway?" Olivia gave a shrug, ignoring the pain that bit into her shoulder.

It was nothing close to the cold regret that settled over her heart.

"You're sure about that?"

"Absolutely. Now—go and help Jilly, will you?"

There was nothing more for them to say. They couldn't go back.

Life had taught Olivia how to live with pain and distance. In a way, she was glad for that now. And as she looked at Rafe's face, she was certain that the grim reality of war had taught Rafe that same lesson.

CHAPTER SEVEN

JILLY'S COWBOY CHILI vanished in less than four minutes, attacked by two hungry men with a little help from Olivia. When Jilly produced a double-chocolate cake, Rafe found room to put away two pieces before his self-control returned.

"I'm glad I don't eat this way every day. I'd have to go to the gym and work it off at a punching bag."

"You?" Jilly sniffed. "You'll never be fat. You've got that metabolism that never stops burning. I hate people like you," she said dryly. "Duffy, let's go for a run." Jilly brushed off her hands and then raced down to the front lawn, chasing the big white dog while he barked with a puppy's enthusiasm.

"Jilly always had a way with pets." Rafe leaned back, watching the two race in a mock charge toward the pier. "And your dog is a service dog, is that right?"

Walker nodded. "He has a Congressional Medal of Honor," he said with quiet pride. "He saved my skin more than once."

Rafe looked down, toying with the last crumbs of his cake. "I seem to recall hearing something about that dog of yours. It was back during my first tour of duty in Afghanistan."

Walker didn't answer. Rafe caught the little glance he angled at Olivia. Clearly, the man didn't choose to talk about those days.

Rafe understood perfectly.

"Any luck with the plumbing imbroglio? I don't go on duty until midnight, so I'm open to lend a hand."

"Finish your cake. Jilly will kill me if I disturb your dessert. But once you're done, I'll show you the problem." Walker drummed his hands on the table and glanced at Olivia, one eyebrow raised. "Unless you two had something planned for the afternoon?"

"No. Not me. Nothing planned at all," Olivia said quickly. "I'm just going to sit here on the porch and sketch. You two go off and work."

Rafe stood up slowly, searching her face. "How about I bring you some lemonade or iced tea before we go? Jilly will be out to check on you, but you may be thirsty."

He didn't wait for her to answer. Olivia kept her gaze lowered. She could feel the damning heat swirl through her cheeks.

When was she going to get over being close to this man? "Thank you. That…that would be nice."

She had planned to clear away some of the dishes, but even that job was taken away as Walker and Rafe stacked up the plates and flatware and carried them back to the kitchen.

Wind blew up from the harbor, playing at her hair

and cooling the heat in Olivia's cheeks. She pulled out her sketches and pencil, focusing on the patterns that were still singing in her head.

Around the back she heard a screen door slam, Jilly going inside the back way. She looked up quickly as Rafe set a pitcher with iced tea and a fresh glass in front of her. "Jilly says she'll be out in a few minutes." Rafe's eyes darkened. "And I meant what I said before. I didn't come back to dig at old wounds or complicate your life, Livie. That's one thing you don't need to worry about," he said roughly.

SHE DIDN'T SEE Rafe for three hours. He and Walker vanished into the basement, pounding water pipes and arguing about flow variables. Olivia had heard them move around the side of the house, discussing how to upgrade the whole plumbing system in the old house without breaking the bank account. Olivia picked up something about *sweat equity* and smiled. Walker was persuasive, all right. And what he couldn't manage to do, Jilly could. She was pretty sure that they would talk Rafe into helping out with the long-term repairs.

Olivia realized that meant she would be seeing Rafe a lot more than she expected or wanted. And she wasn't ready to be around him with any sort of calm.

So what? She would simply make a note of his schedule and arrange to be gone whenever he was around. She wasn't sure how mature that plan was, but it was practical and it would save them both a whole lot of discomfort.

She felt movement at her feet. Duffy was curled up on the little rug, his body warm in the afternoon sunlight. After his run with Rafe, he was enjoying a long nap. He looked at Olivia, banged his tail once and gave a little sigh of contentment. Then he put his head across her feet and settled back to sleep.

Olivia stiffened. She was afraid of dogs. She had been afraid for a long time. And Duffy was a big dog.

But she told herself that he was her friend. He would never do anything to hurt her. And though she wanted to slide her feet out from under his head and put some distance between them, the sight of his warm, drowsy face made her stop. *You can't let anxiety destroy your future.* A therapist had told her that several years ago. Olivia was trying hard to remember that.

Back in the kitchen, a pan fell suddenly, the sound echoing like a gunshot. Olivia jerked upright. "Jilly, are you okay?"

Another pan hit the floor.

There was no answer.

Olivia anchored her papers under the iced tea glass and then pushed awkwardly to her feet. The sounds from the kitchen had already woken Duffy, who was scratching madly at the screen door. Olivia let him in, walking slowly as her shoulder began to ache.

"Jilly, what happened? Where are you?"

"Back here. The kitchen." Jilly's voice sounded low and muffled. Duffy began to bark hard.

When Olivia reached the door to the kitchen, she froze in panic. Jilly was bent over the counter next to the sink, her arm wrapped in a dishcloth, Olivia smelled smoke from the nearby gas range. "What happened, Jilly?"

"You shouldn't have come in. I'm fine." Jilly was cradling her left hand, her eyes closed. "It's just a little burn. I wasn't paying attention when I was melting chocolate."

"Let me see it." Olivia leaned over her friend and sucked in a breath when she saw the red welt and the blister rising across Jilly's thumb. "Did you put anything on it? We need ice. Or butter. I can't remember what you're supposed to do for a burn," Olivia said anxiously.

"Neither one. I have salve. It's in that little glass jar beside the sink. I can't reach it."

Olivia handed the jar to Jilly. "Are you sure about this? Maybe you need to go to the emergency care center? What if it's infected?"

"It's not. I cleaned it." Jilly took a long, shaky breath. She unscrewed the jar with clumsy fingers and smoothed clear cream over the welt. "Stop worrying, Livie. This will take care of it. It's my master cream for cuts and burns. I couldn't have gotten through cooking school without this stuff."

She winced a little, but continued to smooth cream in place until the whole wound was covered. "It was stupid. I wasn't paying attention. And then the handle slipped." She closed her eyes and her mouth settled in a tense line. "There's so much to do, and I'm worried about opening on time. I'm worried about Caro and why she looks so tired. I'm worried about you, too, Livie. And I'm wondering if—" Jilly shook her head and stopped.

"You're wondering what?"

Jilly looked away. "It doesn't matter. I'm being stupid. Everybody's got worries. There's no reason to let them take over." Jilly forced an awkward smile. "I'm sorry you had to get up." She reached down to calm Duffy, who was pressing hard against her leg, sniffing the air anxiously. "I think I'll take a rain check on the chocolate cream truffle recipe I was working on. I need a cup of herbal tea to calm down."

Olivia hid a smile. This person was nothing like the high-strung, Energizer Bunny that Olivia had grown up with. But it was good to see Jilly creating balance in her life. She had been dangerously ill, diagnosed with a heart condition, and that had forced her to cut back on her stressful lifestyle.

Olivia was smart enough to know that a good part of Jilly's new balance came from Walker's strong, calming presence. "Shall I go get Walker? Is there something you need?"

"Good heavens, don't call Walker. He'll hover and want to give me Tylenol and wrap my hand up in a bandage and make me take the rest of the afternoon off."

Olivia stared at her friend. "How often do you hurt yourself like this, Jilly? That's a bad burn. You can't be telling me that that happens often." She knew that cooking could be dangerous, but she hated the thought of Jilly maiming herself on a regular basis.

"Oh, stop looking so worried. I get cut or burned once a week. It's no big deal. I had friends who lost fingers when I was working back in Arizona. This is *nothing*."

"No wonder Walker's inclined to hover. You have to be more careful, Jilly. Not just about yourself. This old house—well, we almost have it cobbled together, but you know how old the wiring is. It wouldn't take an awful lot to send this building up in smoke."

Jilly's bravado vanished. "I've been thinking about that. It scares the living daylights out of me. I put in an order for half a dozen fire extinguishers, along with special high-sensitivity smoke alarms in all the downstairs rooms. When Grace gets back, we're going to consult with a company in California who has new smoke-sensing technology. Believe me, I'm not taking the threat of fire lightly."

"I'm glad to hear it." Olivia slid an arm around her friend's shoulders. "I can't stand the thought of anything happening to you—or to this house."

Olivia could feel the tension in Jilly's shoulders. She realized that despite her friend's bravado, she was deeply worried, too. They had sunk so much of their time, resources and savings into this house, yet it remained a dangerous gamble.

"I thought I heard pans crashing. What's going on?" Walker peered through the back door, frowning at Jilly, who quickly shoved her bandaged hand behind her back. "Is everything okay?"

"Fine. Wonderful." Jilly's voice took on her usual enthusiasm. "Olivia and I were just catching up on girl talk. We don't need you around. You should go keep Rafe company."

"Are you sure?" Walker glanced around the kitchen, frowning. "I could have sworn I heard something fall in here. And then yelling."

"Nope. Must be your imagination." Jilly glanced over her shoulder at Rafe. "So now that you've done your guy check and made sure the helpless women are fine, you can go back to working with grease and wrenches."

Walker shook his head. "It sounds boring when you put it that way. But I'm actually enjoying going mano a mano with this plumbing. Rafe and I are cooking up a pretty good plan. I'd better get back to work."

"Have a great time," Jilly said with a cheery smile.

As soon as the door closed, she leaned against the kitchen counter and looked down at her hand. The welt was much bigger, bright red, streaked with deep purple. There was a second blister forming at the base of her wrist.

"Jilly, I don't know. That looks really bad. I think you should have someone look at it."

Jilly rolled her shoulders, grimacing. "Like I've

already told you, this is not the first burn I've had, Livie. I'll be fine. Stop arguing with me and go out on the porch. I'm going to make us some tea. Then I want to look at those new sketches you made."

JILLY ANALYZED EVERY one of Olivia's designs, picking them apart by ease of knitting, cost and general practicality. Jilly was, after all, a consummate pragmatist in life as well as in her clothing choices.

On the aesthetic front, there were no problems. Olivia was pleased with what she had created so far. In each pattern, she had sketched an architectural background that reflected the design. One captured the medieval stone bridge over the Arno in Florence. One sketch held the drama of the Piazza San Marco in Venice. Another sketch caught the unforgettable grace of the Trevi Fountain in Rome. In keeping with the architecture, each design was classic and beautifully structured. From Jilly's excitement, Olivia knew she was onto something. "You like them?"

"Livie, these are *amazing.* We are going to sell out of these in a week. Plus, we'll get Caro's grandmother to model them. You know how dramatic she can be. I don't know what made you think of this, but get back to work. Make more sketches. Fast projects would be great. Gloves. Hats. A narrow shawl. Or an infinity cowl. Things that people can make fast."

Olivia had been thinking the same thing. A quick investment in time and money would make a more attractive project. She couldn't wait to get started on knitted samples. She was aching for the feel of smooth wool and soft alpaca between her fingers as she tested lace and cable patterns. She glanced through the window at the bright colors on the shelves of the yarn shop, considering possibilities, choosing her first yarn.

Unfortunately, Jilly figured out her secret plan.

"Oh no you don't. No knitting for *you*. Not for another week at least. That was what the doctor said."

Olivia looked down and muttered beneath her breath.

"I heard that. No cursing allowed. Cursing is what I do. But I have a compromise. I'll go choose some yarn if you tell me which ones you want. At least you can hold them and squeeze them. I get the whole thing about squeezing yarn now. It took me a while but my knitting-camp experience was a breakthrough."

"Holding is good, even if it's not as good as knitting." Olivia studied the colors that she could see through the front window. Then she rattled off a list of six yarns in classic colors.

At least she had something to focus on other than shoulder pain and her bleak financial outlook. Olivia was also determined to use this time to find out what was stressing Jilly out.

Before the weekend was over, Olivia swore to have all the answers.

YARN GLOWED IN the light of the setting sun, mirrored by the jeweled colors of the Harbor House's stained glass windows. Olivia and Jilly had bickered about keeping yarn projects for the new shop simple and low cost. But even Jilly was swept into the beauty of Olivia's designs, imagining gloves with long cables and tiny buttons up the inside of the cuff. Dreaming of berets with textured stitches and warm, snuggly ribbing around the face, Olivia made more sketches. After her third glass of herbal tea, she yawned. It had been a full day. The sea air had left her tired suddenly. She tried to hide another yawn.

"That's the second time you've yawned. You need to rest. The guys are nearly done with that back plumbing line, so they shouldn't be banging on the pipes." Jilly stood up and stretched. "And just for the record, these are wonderful designs. Grace and Caro can help you work out numbers and the row-by-row directions for your patterns. I really think you're onto something here, Livie. I'll get going on that website design tonight."

Olivia wasn't so sure. She had no training in art or fashion, but she didn't want to spoil Jilly's excitement. "I should probably go home."

"You're going nowhere, my friend. Walker and I will take care of you right here. You can go home after two more days, once we're certain that you're better."

Olivia glared. "Are you *hovering?*"

"Damn straight I am." Jilly gave a wicked laugh as she swept up the sketches from the table, grabbed their teacups and headed inside. "Go take a nap. I'm going to clean up a few things in the kitchen and then check on the status of the plumbing."

Hearing the sound of footsteps, Duffy charged around the corner, tail banging. Jilly expertly cut him off before he slammed into Olivia.

"Are you sure you can get up the stairs okay? I can help if you want," she said.

Olivia shot Jilly an irritated look. "I dislocated my shoulder. I *didn't* break my leg. I'll be fine. Stop worrying. Go take that big ferocious dog of yours for a run on the beach so I can rest."

DESPITE HER FIRM assurances to Jilly, it was harder for Olivia to walk up the stairs then she had expected. Every movement put pressure on her shoulder, and pressure meant pain. She found she had to learn a whole new way of walking.

She was exhausted by the time she sat down on the big bed in the cheerful lavender room that faced the ocean. Jilly had plans of opening a bed-and-breakfast here eventually, but for now, the rooms were open for family or friends.

Olivia was glad she had not struggled her way back to her own house. Right now driving a car was out of the question.

She yawned, lulled by the sound of the breakers out on the cove and the tapping of a branch against the big picture window. She drove away all thoughts of Rafe, sweaty and tanned as he worked outside.

It was over between them. He had made that absolutely plain.

Isn't that what she wanted?

But the past wasn't easy to put aside. It drifted, somewhere beneath the surface, out of sight but always ready to emerge when you least expected it. And now memories returned in vivid waves as Olivia slid down into sleep.

THE IMAGES DRIFTED up through her dreams, carried on currents of emotion. Half forgotten, the colors and sounds mingled in a restless dance.

Olivia had just turned thirteen. Rafe was almost sixteen.

It had been a bad time for Olivia. She hated the German class her father insisted she take. The sounds were rough and harsh and the grammar defied all logic. Her heart had been set on Italian, a language of beauty and architecture. She had even begun studying it on her own. But her father had scoffed and put his foot down.

German it would be. German was important for science and math and business.

In the end Olivia had yielded.

But that year her father had turned more distant, trusting her less and less. Every day he questioned her about where she went after school and who her friends were and why she didn't study harder so she could make a success of herself. Olivia already spent four out of five school nights at home studying. Usu-

ally she spent Saturday mornings studying, too. But it never seemed to be enough for her father.

In desperation, she announced that she had been invited to join an advanced-study group. Since the others were children of her father's closest friends, he gave complete approval. And so Thursday nights were spent at the library with people she hated. Olivia had suffered through the gossip, the competition and the cutting comments for one reason only.

She knew that Rafe would be waiting at her back fence, silent in the shadows, when she walked home. And for fifteen minutes every Thursday night, there beneath the big apple tree in her backyard, Olivia felt alive, filled with dreams and colors, determined that she could find a future that she chose, not her father.

Rafe was different there in the quiet of night, with the chirp of crickets the only sound. When he was alone with Olivia he was quiet and thoughtful. He listened to everything she said and gave careful answers that Olivia knew she could trust.

But there was more than listening there in the darkness.

There was restless tension and heated skin. When their hands met, she felt her face flame. She remembered that heat, the way her skin flushed and her throat felt dry and her body stirred with need. The heat was part of her memory, but there was joy and adventure and a sense of deep connection, too. She believed in Rafe and drank up his words when he talked about places he meant to see when he was a little older and he left Summer Island.

There had never been any doubt that he would leave Summer Island.

Where? Olivia wanted to know. What would he see first?

The Loire Valley.

Machu Picchu.

Umbria in spring.

Olivia drank in the names, wanting to go with him, wanting adventure and discovery and all the restless, hot, physical desire that he stirred in her blood.

Sometimes they kissed. As wind whispered through the trees, the brush of their mouths was gentle and tentative. Olivia knew there could be far more to a kiss. She knew Rafe could have explored her aching, sensitive skin and pushed that experience to a different place. Olivia would never have stopped him.

But he didn't. He took a hard breath and whispered her name and then moved away to lean against the shadowed fence.

Their time always ended too soon. In ten minutes or in twelve, the lights would come on in the kitchen and Olivia knew that her father was there waiting for her, frowning as he checked his watch. And Olivia's dreams died every night when Rafe squeezed her hand and then handed Olivia her nearly forgotten book bag.

He always made certain that her hair was smooth and her sweater was straight.

Because her father would check for that, too.

When she looked back through the quiet darkness, he raised his hand once and then slid into the shadows. Olivia wondered if her life would ever change and if she would be ground down by her father's rules and expectations. All through that year and the next, when she was thirteen and then fourteen and her world felt grim and the anxiety attacks began to grow more frequent, Olivia shut everything away except Rafe and the dream of spices in a hot wind and the sound of bells in a mountain valley.

Umbria in spring.

Machu Picchu.

The Loire Valley.

Those dreams kept her whole when everything felt gray and bleak. Olivia swore to herself on the day Rafe left Summer Island, she would go with him.

She would go without a backward glance.

She already had a suitcase packed, hidden inside an old trunk up in the attic. She would go no matter what her father or anyone else said. She would see all those places that Rafe could take her.

Now, years later, caught in sleep, Olivia moved restlessly, her hands tense. She made a low sound of pain and loss.

Because in the end, it hadn't turned out that way. Not even close. Her father had won after all.

OLIVIA WOKE UP to noisy banging on her door. She blinked, shaking away tangled dreams of Rafe and the old apple tree in her backyard.

When she sat up sharply, pain dug into her shoulder. Olivia winced and looked around her. No one was banging on the door. The sound was coming from the window, where a dry branch scraped hard against the glass. Even then the tangled heat of her restless dreams seemed to linger. Rafe had been in those dreams. She remembered him standing in the shadows, touching her hair.

Olivia blew out an irritated breath and shook her head. No more dreams. She looked down and checked her watch. She had been asleep for almost two hours, and now it was nearly dark outside.

Delicious smells drifted up from the kitchen. Olivia sniffed and decided it had to be Jilly's amazing Southwest lasagna and some kind of chocolate dessert.

Right on cue, her stomach grumbled.

But first Olivia needed to clean up. Her hair was a wreck and she would have loved a shower, but that would have to wait. Struggling in and out of her clothes would be an ordeal, and she simply refused to ask Jilly for help undressing and getting dressed again. A splash of water and a quick brushing of her hair would be as much as she could manage.

When she opened the door to the little adjoining bathroom, she saw Jilly's handwritten note taped to the sink, written in big block letters. *PLUMBING UNDER REPAIR. DO NOT USE.*

Rolling her eyes, Olivia pulled on her sweater and shoes and made her way slowly downstairs to the small ground-floor bathroom at the back of the house. She was still feeling the effects of the pain pill she had taken before her nap. She didn't handle medicine well, and these pills had been strong.

She shoved back her hair and glanced outside, hearing Jilly's laughter and the sound of Duffy's barking. Walker said something about a new invoice from the hardware store. Olivia frowned, trying to listen, but she couldn't pick up the details.

The worry returned, heavier than before. She had no job and her savings were limited. There was no way she could help out until she found a job or until she managed to straighten out the mess of her father's business accounts.

Distracted, she pushed at the bathroom door. It caught a little, as if something was stuck, but Olivia knew all the old house's secrets. Half-asleep, she turned the knob backward. With a gentle tug, she lifted the handle slightly while turning the knob in the same motion.

The door swung open.

Warm air brushed her face. Jilly had probably taken a shower here recently. The way they had all been working on the repairs, this had become a second home for all of them.

She shot a quick glance in the mirror, frowning at

the chaos of her hair. She wished she had a different set of clothes, something better than the old cotton sweater she wore while working.

Maybe she would ask—

Every thought flashed out of her mind as Rafe emerged through the steaming air from the alcove beside the shower. Olivia stood rooted to the spot, her heart pounding.

He was naked, and she couldn't take her eyes off the tanned, muscular sweep of his powerful body.

CHAPTER EIGHT

HOT STEAM DRIFTED around Olivia's face. Warm air brushed her cheeks and shoulders. She couldn't seem to move, fascinated by the little beads of water running down Rafe's tanned chest. There was a scar at the base of his right shoulder. Another one criss-crossed his collarbone. Olivia swallowed hard, thinking about Rafe in Afghanistan, wondering what had put those scars there. Or had they come long before Afghanistan, in some scrappy fight or mishap right here in Oregon?

She didn't know how or why, but her finger rose. Gently she traced the scar that crossed his collarbone. When their skin touched, he seemed to stiffen. She saw his jaw clench.

She shouldn't be here. She definitely shouldn't be touching him this way. But none of that seemed to matter. Her finger tracked another little scar up the edge of his jaw to the side of his cheek.

"What happened?" Olivia asked, her voice low and raw with emotion.

Rafe reached up. His callused fingers curled around her wrist. "Olivia, you should go."

"I want to know, Rafe. Can you answer one simple question?"

He muttered as her fingers moved, feathering over the locked line of his jaw. He blew out an angry breath. "What happened? Fighting. Angry men in angry places. Some of them were in a distant country, but not all of them. Men fight wherever they are," Rafe said grimly.

"I'm sorry," Olivia whispered. She brushed another scar along his wrist. "So sorry."

"Why? You're the last one who has to apologize. You were the only one who never hurt me, Livie. The only one who showed me…" Rafe shook his head, his eyes dark and troubled. "You were the only one who showed me that things didn't always have to hurt. You could always reach me. You seemed to know exactly how."

Olivia rose and kissed his jaw gently. "I'm glad," she whispered.

A shudder ran through him. His fingers opened on her wrist. He slid their hands together and worked his fingers through hers. His skin was rough, warm; this slow touch brought back dangerously intimate memories.

Desire bloomed, racing blindly through Olivia's chest, until every part of her was suddenly alive. Aware.

Needing more.

Olivia caught a long breath. She wasn't sixteen

anymore. She knew where this could lead. Once before they had come too close.

Her gaze locked with Rafe's. The air seemed charged, heavy with old memories and emotions too powerful to face.

Rafe closed his eyes, leaning back against the tile wall, Olivia's hands still caught between his fingers. "I should have come to say goodbye that night, Livie. But there were reasons—"

"I don't care. It's over, Rafe. This isn't about the past."

"Then what *is* it about?" His voice was harsh.

"I don't have a clue. Not one single clue," Olivia said hoarsely.

It was time to go. It was time to stop this dangerous thread of wishing things could be different, wondering whether they could go back. She blew out an angry breath and pulled her hand from his, needing to be anywhere but here, anyplace where the warm steamy air didn't betray all her hard-won self-control. Olivia pressed a shaky hand against the corner linen closet and the door popped open, towels raining down on her head and shoulders. An old metal towel rack shoved in a corner spilled out and struck her head and she caught back a sharp sound of pain.

With a curse Rafe grabbed the long piece of metal. Carefully he lifted Olivia's damp hair back from her cheek. "Are you okay? There's a cut above your eye, Livie. I think you should—"

"What I should do is leave." She elbowed him in the ribs with her good arm, blinking away tears. What had made her think she could go back? What had made her dream that anything could be different between them? "Let me go, damn it."

Rafe took a slow step back. Distance filled his face. "I'm not holding you, Livie. And I've never meant to cause you pain."

"But you did. I thought we had the same plans and hopes, when we weren't even close. I guess I should thank you, though. You made me grow up a lot sooner than I might have," she said roughly. "And I have one more thing to tell you. I don't think we should see each other. Not ever. When I see you walking on the street, I'm going to cross to the other side. I'd appreciate it if you'd do the same," she said coldly.

After a long time, Rafe nodded. "You're right. You usually are. Fine. I'll keep out of your way."

He reached down and his long fingers locked at the top of the towel that was wrapped around his waist. Olivia looked away, determined not to study that strong, rangy body or the hard line of his chest and the powerful muscles that vanished below the edge of the towel.

If she looked there, if she let down her control, she would be lost.

Just the way she had been lost as a girl.

She turned her back to Rafe. She felt cold air

brush her neck and then the sound of his feet moving to the door.

"I'll keep out of your way. I only wish I'd been able to keep out of your way all those years ago."

Olivia felt steam brush her face, followed by cool air as the door closed.

And then he was gone.

She put one hand on her chest to soothe her pounding heart. The sense of loneliness was crushing. Closing her eyes, she leaned back, feeling the cold tile at her neck as she began to tremble, caught by anger and hurt and years of regret.

And even then she wanted him.

"EVERYTHING OKAY, RAFE?"

Jilly was in the kitchen, her face flushed from cooking. "I thought you had two more hours before work?"

"Got a call. Somebody's sick and they need me early." If only that had been a lie. If only he hadn't been showering in that spare bathroom he might have missed Olivia. He didn't want to remember her surprise—or the way desire had flared into her expressive face. Rafe could always read that face.

But he couldn't afford to be irresponsible or take advantage of the passion she had not been able to hide.

"Sorry to hear that. But this is a small force. If somebody gets sick, it puts a strain on the whole department." She reached for a paper bag, then took out a box of aluminum foil. "This should get you started. Chocolate cake. Leftover lasagna. I'll put a hot double cappuccino in a thermos. Looks as if it might rain again tonight. I figure this should help."

Rafe frowned. "Hell, Jilly, I don't want to eat up all your leftovers. Why don't you keep them for Walker?"

"Walker will be fed just fine, pal. Take the food and shut up. Now get going. Go drink some coffee and then protect and defend. We're all glad to have you back here on Summer Island. I know it's a little awkward for you. I also know that there are people with long memories who may not be too welcoming. But give them time. You could make a good life for yourself here, Rafe."

Then Jilly shook her head, looking embarrassed. "Who am I to be giving advice? I've been the biggest screwup on Summer Island for years. So forget what I just said. You can make your own decisions just fine." She frowned, glancing toward the stairs. "By the way, did you see Livie? Or is she still asleep?"

Rafe picked up his coat. "Nope, didn't see her. She's probably still resting." The lie came too easily. But at one time Rafe had been a very good liar. "Thanks again for the food, Jilly. It was a good day." He frowned and looked back at her. "I'm going to be pretty busy over the next month. I've got two training sessions in Portland, and I'll be working double shifts for a while. I think—well, I won't be around very much. I'll call you if I get some time off. Then

I could help Walker finish his work. But it won't be for a few weeks. Tell him…I'm sorry about that."

Jilly crossed her arms slowly. "This seems a little hasty. Is everything okay?"

"Just fine. The new duty schedule was changed, that's all. I don't want to make promises and have you counting on me," he said quietly.

The words seemed to hang.

Rafe felt the weight of them—and the shame. When he was younger, he had made promises. People had counted on him, and he'd let them down.

He was never going back to that way of life.

CHAPTER NINE

As THE DAYS passed, Olivia's enforced rest felt like torture. She found distraction in her pattern sketches and the task of helping Jilly to catalogue the last of the yarn shipments for the new shop. But anything strenuous was still impossible.

Her one bright light in the day was the afternoon Harvest Fair, one of the most popular events on the island. In addition to a chili cook-off, there were contests for home-brewed cider and molded-gelatin desserts, along with a pie-eating contest (all entries made using local apples, of course).

Olivia was scheduled to judge the wildly popular book-costume contest. All costume entries had to be based on children's books that had won either the prestigious Newbery or Caldecott medals. Olivia was to choose a winning costume based on originality, design and authenticity to the original book.

Olivia thought that Jilly seemed distracted as they drove back to her house before the fair. When they pulled up to the front door, Olivia frowned to see a dozen boxes and containers stacked on the porch.

"I haven't ordered anything." Olivia carefully walked up the front steps and stared at the plastic containers. Each one held food—chocolate cupcakes, handmade bread and walnut scones. Each container was marked with a different label and different hand-writing.

Olivia didn't move, feeling a lump press at her throat. She realized that this was a way of saying thank you, offered by people whose lives had been affected by her moment of courage in the storm. They had responded by dropping off what they could share to show their thanks.

She picked up a loaf of bread wrapped in cellophane and tied with red ribbons. There were no names on any of the containers. All she found were simple, handwritten notes of thanks for the thing that she had done.

Jilly stood beside her and rested a hand on her shoulder. "I'm glad they did this, Livie. They owe you. We all do. Don't ever downplay how much courage that took."

Olivia forced a crooked smile. "It was mostly desperation. But this is way more food than I can eat. Why don't you and Walker take the cupcakes? You can share them with Grace. She and Noah are supposed to be back tonight from San Francisco, aren't they?"

"It will probably be very late. Grace emailed me that she wanted to see you as soon as she could. I'd hoped they would be back for the Harvest Fair, but they won't be."

When Olivia pushed open the heavy wooden door,

the house felt cold and unwelcoming. This house had never really felt like a home. Growing up, she had spent as many hours as she could at Caro's house or with Jilly. On the weekends the group had spent time with Grace, working at her grandfather's animal clinic. By silent agreement, the friends had never gone to her house. It had never been comfortable.

Her father had seen to that.

But Sawyer Sullivan was dead and there would be no way to find out what had made him so cold and judgmental to his only child. Maybe it was the desertion of his wife while Olivia had been so young—or maybe some other disappointment she would never know.

Right now the only thing she needed to focus on was healing her own life.

She walked slowly through the silent house, her heels tapping on the expensive wooden floor. Jilly followed her, piling the boxes in the kitchen.

"I'll take half of the cupcakes for Walker. The man does love chocolate. I'll take half the loaf of bread, if you want. In exchange, you have to come over for breakfast for the rest of the week. It's that or no deal."

"You always drive a hard bargain. Fine, it's a deal. But let's sort this out fast. I don't want to be late for the judging."

Once all the food cartons had been split between them, Olivia ran a hand through her hair. "Thanks again for everything, Jilly. I really do appreciate—"

They both jumped at a sharp beep. Frowning, Olivia dug out her cell phone. "Voice mail? The phone didn't even ring. All my calls have been going right through to voice mail lately." Olivia frowned at the number. "It's my father's lawyer."

Olivia listened to the message twice. The lawyer needed to speak to her as soon as possible in connection with her father's estate. Judging by his voice, the news was not going to be good. Olivia listened to the terse message one more time, wishing he had left her more information.

"Don't brood. It's a waste of time. Call him right now and find out what it is. If you need to go see him, I'll drive you over there," Jilly said flatly.

Olivia forced a smile. "He probably just needs more signatures. I've had to sign at least twenty documents already."

When Olivia called the lawyer back, she didn't beat around the bush. "I got your message, Harrison. What have you found out?"

"I'm afraid my news is not very good, Olivia. We haven't found any other accounts in your father's name."

"None? You went through all my father's banking records and his business papers?"

"We did, and everything that you wrote down is accounted for. As I understand it, there were two savings accounts set up for you as a legacy from your grandmother. There was also a bequest and items of a sentimental nature from your grandmother that

were left for you in an additional safe-deposit box."
He cleared his throat, sounding uncomfortable. "So
far we have not found any of those accounts."

"My grandmother's legacy is gone, too?" Olivia
swallowed hard. She had hoped to use her grandmother's bequest to meet her expenses until she
found a job. How did you manage to make fifty thousand dollars disappear?

"Isn't there some way to track those things? Don't
banks keep a list of depositors? I thought that was a
security requirement after 9/11?"

"In the case of very large cash deposits, yes. But
not in the matter of safe-deposit boxes. The contents
are not examined or recorded by the bank. Privacy
is respected." Harrison Monroe cleared his throat.
"I'm afraid I've done everything I can. Of course,
you might consider other measures. Possibly you
can check your father's personal letters. If that is
unsuccessful, I would suggest you hire a private investigator."

"To find what? My father wasn't a criminal. He
was the mayor for two terms. His real estate business was in solid shape and he paid all his bills on
time. What would an investigator do to help me?"

"An investigator might find details of accounts
that we cannot trace. He might locate the transfer
and/or sale of any items that are missing. He might
determine business partners that your father never
mentioned or other people who had access to your
father's account. As I understand it, your father was

fairly disorganized at the end of his life. His records appear to be incomplete."

Disorganized? Olivia knew now that her father had been in the early stages of dementia. He had good days that could fool her and all his friends, but in the end his decline had come with shocking speed. If only he had asked Olivia for help...

But of course that was out of the question. Sawyer Sullivan would *never* stoop to ask for help from his daughter.

Olivia refocused her thoughts with an effort. "So how much money is left?"

The lawyer cleared his throat again. "There is one account. Its balance is thirty-four dollars."

"That's *all?* Everything else is...gone?"

"I'm afraid so."

"This won't even pay your own bill." Olivia felt angry. Even worse, she felt helpless. "Thank you for your help. I will pay your bill in installments, if that is acceptable. As you know, my finances are very thin right now," she said stiffly.

"I'm certain we can work out a delayed-payment plan. I'll have someone from our accounting department call you."

Olivia's face reddened. She hated to be in anyone's debt. Growing up, she had always known her father was highly respected, a key figure in Summer Island's hierarchy. No important decision was made on Summer Island without his participation.

How had he left her this kind of financial disaster?

She hung up and then said nothing, crossing to pour herself a glass of water. Leaning against the counter, she drank it slowly.

"You look white, Livie. What is it?"

"Nothing. Everything's fine." But the words came as a rush, too fast and too flat. Olivia looked through the window, watching the flow of cars and bikes and kids and families headed to the Harvest Fair.

In the distance she could see blue cruisers pull into the police station and wondered if Rafe was driving one of them.

"Now try telling me the truth," Jilly said quietly.

"Okay. You may as well know. I didn't get a vacation—I was fired." Tears backed up, burning her eyes. "And now I find my father took all his money and most of mine, but we can't find any of the accounts. So I'm broke." Olivia closed her eyes, fighting her embarrassment and anger, but somehow relieved to share the truth with her friend. "Everything is gone. All except for thirty-four dollars."

Jilly just stared at her in shock. "That's all?"

"Afraid so. Aren't you going to tell me it was my bad management or my decadent lifestyle?" Olivia gave a hoarse laugh. "I guess it was all those trips I made to Ibiza and Monte Carlo and that month I spent in Paris."

Except Olivia had done none of those things. She had never taken a break beyond a long-dreamed of trip to Italy. Beyond that, her life had been pure work. Architecture school. Internship and then two high-pressure jobs in Oregon. She had loved architecture—right up to the day she had been fired without preamble or explanation.

She didn't regret the long years of graduate study and the internships, but she hated that she couldn't pull her weight now, when the Harbor House was so close to opening.

"Livie, I don't understand. We all assumed that you and your father were in good financial shape. I mean, this house has to be worth a lot. And he always had great cars. Everything new for Sawyer Sullivan."

Olivia gave a grim laugh. "Yes, he always loved a grand lifestyle. And the house should be worth a good amount. But my father didn't keep up with the repairs. I didn't realize until the end how confused he had become. He took money out of one account and put it in another account. He had at least a dozen different bank accounts, and he didn't keep good records. The lawyer and I have been going through his papers, trying to figure things out, but it doesn't look good."

"When you said thirty-four dollars, you meant that he spent all his money? *Yours, too?*" Jilly blurted out.

"It looks that way." Olivia rubbed her neck as pain radiated along her shoulder. "If I had known he was so confused and that things were in such chaos, I would have demanded answers from him. But there's nothing I can do about it now. He hid everything from me. He was always good at that." Olivia looked out the window at the gray line of the sea, where white breakers hammered against the cove.

"We'll help you. You know that," Jilly said fiercely.

"Thanks for the offer, but I'll manage. First off, I'm going to fix the house up and sell it. It's way too big for me anyway."

Jilly studied the big ornate staircase that climbed in a dramatic spiral up two flights. "I always liked this house. It was always so perfect, so well organized and clean. Even the floors gleamed like mirrors. Growing up, I told myself I'd have a house like this of my own one day." Jilly gave an embarrassed laugh. "Surprised?"

"Trust me, the *last* thing you want is a house like this. It's a terrible money drain." There was no point in telling Jilly that a place like this was also filled with loneliness. Too pristine ever to be comfortable. "But," she continued slowly, "if you like it so much, you and Walker should buy it," Olivia said firmly. "I'm putting it up for sale next week."

Jilly stared at her in shock. "You're really going through with this?"

"Absolutely. The real truth is, I *hate* this house. It's about time that I started making some changes, and I may as well start right here. A place this size should go to someone who will use every room and fill the whole house with children." This was something that Olivia never meant to do. "Until I'm solvent again, I need to be very careful about my expenses, Jilly. That means I can't pull my weight at the Harbor House. I only wish—"

"You've *always* pulled your weight, Livie. You just do it in different ways. And we'll help with this place. We'll clean it until it glows, so you get the best offer available, and that will help you back on your feet. Until then, forget about the Harbor House. After selling my restaurant in Arizona, I have a nice nest egg put aside, and it's going into renovations. Walker and I have discussed all this."

Olivia wanted to argue with Jilly, but there was nothing more she could say. Her friends could cover the costs temporarily while Olivia dug her way out from under the mess that her father had left. Then she would find a job and pick up her end of the expenses. She had to stay positive.

Jilly stared down at the restless gray ocean. "I know your grandmother left you a legacy. What about that?"

Olivia picked at her nail. "Gone. They can't find any of it." She forced down her pain and bitterness. "Everything is lost—my grandmother's old letters and photographs from Paris in the twenties. Her vintage scarves and lace gloves. I loved those things."

The despair must have shown on her face because Jilly rested a hand on her arm. "The miserable weasel," she muttered. Olivia heard it, but she pretended not to. "How could he *do* that to you?"

Olivia was thinking pretty much the same thing, but she had given up trying to understand her father.

He had never discussed business with her or anything else financial.

The two of them sat unmoving while seabirds circled overhead. Somewhere in the back of the house a clock chimed noon. It was less than a mile down to the sea, Olivia knew. Less than a mile to fresh wind and a deserted cove where she could walk facing the water, where no one was watching her.

But the cove would have to wait. Right now the Harvest Fair was about to begin up on the hill. Olivia refused to let this bad news spoil that for her.

CHAPTER TEN

"THIS IS A bad idea." Jilly trailed after Olivia down the hall. "I think you should stay here and rest. Let someone else do the judging today."

"I've been resting for a week already and I'm going *crazy* from resting." Olivia slid her keys into her pocket and grabbed her scarf. "I wouldn't miss the Harvest Fair for anything. If you don't want to take me, I'll walk. It's just up the hill."

"I *know* exactly where it is," Jilly grumbled. "It's in the same spot it's always been for the last seventy-five years. Were you always this stubborn or is it getting worse?"

"That's the pot calling the kettle black. Can we hurry? I need time to see all the costumes. You know what a madhouse it can be."

"I certainly do. That's why you should stay home. Okay, okay, fine. I'll drive you." Jilly walked out onto the porch. "Remember last year? There were two fistfights, as I recall. Will Rafe be there to keep the peace?"

"I have no idea what Rafe's plans are." Olivia's mouth tightened. "You'll have to ask him for details."

Jilly shook her head and muttered the word *stub-*

born a few times as she started the car, but she kept any other comments to herself.

The big meadow near the old oak was already crowded with tables and tents when the two women arrived. Olivia wandered through the crowd with Jilly, smiling at old friends and stopping to talk with neighbors. Someone was roasting poblano chiles over an open grill and the smoke was fragrant and intense as it drifted over the hillside. That smell always caught Olivia, making her remember dozens of other festivals that had taken place here on this big field full of wildflowers above the ocean.

But so far there had been no butterflies. It seemed that every year fewer and fewer made their way to Summer Island. Olivia knew it was because wild space was being lost to development. She hated the idea of losing a part of the island's natural beauty and wildlife.

"Almost ready?" The mayor and his wife bustled up, disturbing Olivia's revelry. "The judging is about to start and you're late."

"Actually, I'm right on time." Olivia was finding the conversation irritating and she'd barely been in the couple's presence for five seconds. "I think, if you check, you're early."

The mayor cleared his throat. "I suppose that might be possible. But never mind. This is going to be a hot event. We have nine *Jumanji* contestants already, plus several Madelines, an *Owl Moon* father and daughter, all kinds of Dr. Seuss and a whole bunch of Wild Things."

"That's Maurice Sendak," the mayor's wife added. "They're monsters."

"I think I knew that already," Olivia murmured. But she tried to keep her good mood even though her shoulder throbbed just a little. She smiled at the crowd of excited children and parents who were united in their love of wonderful and inspiring books. "Well, I think there's a Wild Thing headed right toward us. Let's go."

"OLIVIA LOOKS LIKE she is enjoying this." Tom Wilkinson finished off his third chocolate donut and handed a cup of hot apple cider to Rafe. "You want some of that cherry-gelatin mold?" the county sheriff asked him.

"Think I'll pass," Rafe said dryly.

"You know how seriously everyone takes the contest. Olivia will have some hard choices."

"Why is Olivia the only judge? I still don't get that part."

"Oh, her father did it for years. After he died, it seemed right that Olivia should carry on the tradition as his only child."

Rafe studied the children dressed as Sendak monsters or owls or *Jumanji* animals and rubbed his neck. "She always did know how to calm people down. She knows how to listen, too. But her shoulder isn't healed yet, Tom."

The sheriff nodded. "Then you'd better head on over and see that she wraps up the judging as fast as possible. Because you can count on it that the mayor and his wife will drag this out as long as they can. It makes them feel important," the sheriff said dryly.

"Me? You want me to tell the mayor to back off and hurry Olivia up?" Rafe cleared his throat. "Why me?"

"Because you're on duty right now, Russo. I'm off. Plus, Olivia will listen to you."

"Like hell she will," Rafe muttered. Smoke drifted up from barbecue grills and hot-dog counters and popcorn tents and suddenly Rafe was back in Afghanistan, caught by the acrid smell of burning garbage and cordite. "Look, Tom—maybe you should send someone else. None of those people up there want to see yours truly wading into the middle of their fun. I'm still the bad kid on the block as far as most of these people are concerned."

"Then show them you've changed," the sheriff said dryly. "They'll forget if you give them a reason to."

"Forgetting isn't easy. I try all the time," Rafe said slowly. "Right now I'm back in Afghanistan and that sound I hear is gunfire, not firecrackers." Rafe glanced at his old friend, a man he had looked up to since he was fifteen. "When does it get better and actually start to feel normal to be a civilian again? I keep hoping, but frankly it hasn't happened yet."

The sheriff tossed his empty cup into a garbage

bin. "Two men in zebra costumes are about to duke it out with a Dr. Seuss bird in red cowboy boots while their wives shout encouragement. On what level do you consider that to be *normal?*" the sheriff said. "Now go on over there and rescue Olivia so we can get this contest finished. I don't want any book characters spilling blood on my watch."

THE PROBLEM WAS that Olivia didn't want to be rescued, Rafe discovered. He watched her, his expression grim as he cut through clusters of costumed contestants and eager family members trailing after Olivia.

When she saw him, she stood her ground. She waved off his suggestions that she should sit down and take a break. She told him stiffly that she didn't need any help and that she could handle her duties as a judge just fine. She wasn't going home until she was done.

But the faint lines of strain around her eyes told Rafe that she was in pain, no matter what she said. And when the *Jumanji* zebra decided to tackle one of the Wild Things and then two angry fathers knocked over a table filled with Summer Island book contest T-shirts, Rafe decided enough was enough. He broke up the fight, sent both angry fathers off to different food tents for ten minutes to cool off, and then he steered Olivia over to the booth where Jilly and Walker were giving out free hot cider and newsletters about Harbor House.

"Make her sit down and rest, will you? Her shoulder is hurting again."

"It is not," Olivia said stiffly.

Rafe ignored her. "It's been hurting for the past ten minutes and she needs a break. Get her some of that hot cider, okay? I'm going to round up the contestants and the mayor so he can announce the winners. There's no reason to drag this out."

Jilly was already steering Olivia to a chair. "He's right, Livie. You do look pale."

"I can manage a little longer." Olivia smiled gratefully as she accepted cider from her friend. "But everybody is getting too upset. And if there are any more fistfights…"

"There won't be." Rafe's voice was hard. "Because the next father who even looks like he's planning something stupid is going to get tossed right into my cruiser." He motioned curtly to the mayor and stalked off.

"When did he get so bossy?" Olivia said, watching him stride off.

"I'd say he was taking charge. I'm glad to see it. These contests keep getting out of control." Jilly frowned at the milling crowd next to the mayor and his wife. "So who *is* the winner?"

Olivia took a deep breath. "It's close. But *Jumanji* just got edged out by Dr. Seuss. How do you argue with a Tizzle-Topped Tufted Mazurka bird wearing red cowboy boots? Father and son in the same costume."

"You gotta love this town," Jilly said, beaming.

OLIVIA WAS GLAD when the mayor finally stopped talking and she could announce the winner in the Harvest Fair Book Costume event. There was a burst of hooting and loud clapping, and she waited while the prizes were handed out, and then turned to go back to the Harbor House tent.

But the mayor and his wife called out loudly to her, cutting her off. "We were just going to try some barbecue over on the other side of the hill, Olivia. You should join us. I think that your father's lawyer is over there and we can all have a nice talk. I know that he's been wanting to speak with you."

"I'm a little tired right now," Olivia said flatly. The last person she wanted to see was Harrison Monroe. "I'll have to take a rain check."

"But you can't—"

"Yes, she *can.*"

Olivia looked up, surprised to feel strong fingers open on her back.

Rafe glared at the mayor. "Sorry, but Olivia is going with me." He was already guiding her through the crowd.

"Going where?" The mayor blinked angrily at him.

"Tom Wilkinson wants to talk to Olivia."

"About what?" the mayor persisted.

"He wants to ask her about some design flaws in the new annex for the police station. He said to bring her right over."

Olivia felt hot and breathless, acutely aware of

the pressure of Rafe's thigh against her hip and his hard shoulder against her arm as they walked away. "Is that true? Are there design flaws in the annex plans?" she said anxiously.

"Hell, no. I just wanted to get you out of there. That seemed like the fastest way." Rafe steered her through the crowd, his face unreadable. "Why didn't you just leave? You didn't have to stay and shake everyone's hands."

"I didn't want to disappoint them. Those people had prepared for months for this event. It's only fair—"

"Fair? Don't talk to me about fair. Right now you're sheet-white, and you wince every time someone bumps into you. No, don't bother to deny it. I have eyes, so don't tell me I'm crazy."

Olivia opened her mouth to argue and then closed it again. "Okay. I won't try to deny it. My shoulder is hurting again."

"Good. Honesty is a start." Rafe guided her up the grassy slope. "Now get into the car." He walked to the gravel driveway and held open the door of his cruiser.

"Why?"

"Because, Livie, I'm driving you home. I'm doing it right now and I don't want an argument. Are we clear on that?"

Olivia took a deep breath. "I'm not arguing." She slid into the seat of his car and sat stiffly, looking forward.

Anywhere but into Rafe's dark eyes.

"You could have fooled me." Rafe shut her door and then walked around, sliding behind the wheel. "I forgot how stubborn you could be."

"I was just…pointing out that I didn't want to disappoint people who have made so many plans and care so much."

"What about you? Who's checking to see that you aren't disappointed?" Rafe turned on the engine and drove slowly through the edge of the crowd, up the winding road to a flat spot on the cliffs. He parked on a piece of grass that overlooked the ocean. "Maybe you can answer that for me." His hands tightened on the wheel.

Olivia blinked at the anger in his voice. She didn't understand it. "No one's checking on me. I'm all grown-up, Rafe. I don't need anyone to take care of me." The words were stiff and they sounded a little bitter, so Olivia tried to smile and hide the moment of pain she had felt. "I've been taking care of myself for a long time, you know. It doesn't bother me."

"Maybe it should bother you. Maybe you should expect a lot more," Rafe said roughly. "Hell, I'm just trying to help."

"Could have fooled me," Olivia said dryly.

Rafe let out a slow breath. "Okay, point taken. I'm a little cranky today. I guess I'm not used to all this *normalcy*." He leaned over and picked up Olivia's knitted shawl, slipping it around her shoulders.

How odd, she thought. She hadn't even realized

that the shawl had dropped to the floor. But maybe it wasn't odd after all, because all Olivia could think about was the tension snapping between them and the way Rafe's callused fingers locked on the wheel of the car as sunlight glinted off his brown hair and brushed the little scar above his right eyebrow.

Suddenly Olivia wanted to touch that scar gently. She wanted to ask him how he had gotten hurt and where he had been and whether he had ever thought about her in the years since he had left Summer Island.

The curiosity and emotions welled up inside her and threatened to spill over until Olivia had to fight to hold them back. There wasn't any point in asking questions. Whatever there had been between them was done.

WHEN THEY REACHED her house, Rafe insisted on walking her up to the front door. But he stopped when he saw more boxes in plastic containers in a neat stack on her porch. "What's all this stuff?" He leaned down and picked up a round plastic container tied with a bright blue ribbon.

"Oh, it's nothing. Probably Jilly came by." Olivia reached down quickly, trying to gather up the anonymous food gifts that had been left that afternoon. Brownies, cupcakes and peanut brittle in this batch, she saw.

"Jilly left you all this?" Rafe moved around her

and picked up two plastic containers, frowning. "There are too many."

Olivia didn't answer. Her shoulder had begun to throb more than ever and she wanted to sit down, preferably with a cup of hot tea and a heating pad on her shoulder.

"Oh. I get it." Rafe stood in the clear afternoon sunlight, his arms full of food containers, an arrested look on his face. "You don't know who sent them. You don't need to know. It's just their way of saying thank you. It's because of what you did with that bus and the schoolkids. This is some town," Rafe said slowly. "It may be crazy, but it's never boring."

After Olivia unlocked the front door, he held it open and followed her to the kitchen, stacking the food in a neat pile. "Nice room." He looked around slowly. "I can see you cooking in here. I can see you keeping everything organized and straight." He cleared his throat. "Not that it's any of my business. Is there anything else I can do before I go?"

"You can do me a favor and take some of those food cartons. I can't possibly eat all this."

"They didn't make that food for me, Olivia."

"But it will go to waste. Besides, I think you could use it. You're too busy to cook." Olivia moved around him and found a paper bag. She packed half the food inside it. "I'm keeping the caramel apples. They happen to be a secret vice. I think I may have one for dinner. Actually, I'm probably going to have two or three."

"Live dangerously," he said dryly. "That's probably your only vice," Rafe muttered. He looked around the room and frowned. "It feels cold in here. Why don't I start a fire in the living room. Do you still keep wood out on the back porch?"

"Yes, but—"

Rafe walked past her and vanished down the hall. "Fine. Go sit down and put your feet up," he called. "I'll get a fire going and then I'll be out of your hair."

Olivia frowned, listening to the back door open and the sound of Rafe stacking wood on the porch. Why did he think she needed to be *handled?* She was recovering perfectly well and he didn't need to babysit her. It was demeaning, she thought irritably.

When Rafe stamped past her, half-hidden by a stack of logs, she followed him to the living room. Her anger was growing by the second. "You don't need to do that."

"When did you last have a fire in here? You need to be sure that everything is in good working order." Rafe sank down before the fireplace and began stacking the logs expertly.

"I know that," Olivia answered. "I had it checked three months ago. But I don't bother to use it very often."

"Well, you're going to use it today. You'll feel better. Go on, sit down and relax. I don't need you hovering while I build this fire."

"Me? Hovering?" This was the last straw. Olivia shoved her hands into her pockets, feeling her face flush. "What about you? You tear me away from the Harvest Fair early, saying that I'm pale and weak. You—you force me into your car and then you insist on bustling around and making a fire so I won't be cold, even though I'm *not* cold, not at all, and I'm perfectly comfortable here and I hate it—I just hate it when people want to *handle* me," she said in an angry, breathless rush.

"Do you think I'm handling you?" Rafe knelt on one knee before the fire. "I'd say it's just being friendly. I'm sorry if it annoys you, but too bad. You're going to have a fire and a cup of tea and a blanket and a good book before I go," he said roughly.

It was hard for her to stay angry at him, Olivia thought. He was so calm. So damnably confident. Nothing seemed to bother him. Probably that was what had made her so angry before, because she so rarely felt calm and confident herself. She'd been working hard on that, practicing relaxation and meditation techniques, but the results seemed minimal.

Still, that was no reason for her to be angry at Rafe. That was her problem, not his.

She blew out a breath and sat down on the couch. He had offered her simple friendship, and there was no reason for her to be so stirred up about it. "Okay. I'm sorry if I was…short-tempered and rude like that. I guess my shoulder is taking longer to heal than I thought and it makes me angry. I hate being dependent and asking for favors."

"Actually, you didn't ask. I just did it anyway.

So don't feel bad about it." Rafe looked up from the growing fire and gave a cocky grin. "As for rude—attack away. You don't have to put on an act with me, Livie. I figure we've seen each other at our best and at our worst. No lies or pretenses are necessary. If it makes you feel better to rant at me, go right ahead."

"I wasn't *ranting*." Olivia started to snap at him again, but the idiocy of her outburst caught her and she laughed instead. "Okay, maybe I was ranting. Just a little. But you do stir me up. And it makes me crazy when you take charge in that cool way of yours and start moving people around like they're chess pieces."

Rafe didn't answer, staring at the fire. "I've gotten used to giving orders," he said quietly. "It comes with the territory and the job I had to do. It's going to take me a long time to change, I think." His eyes narrowed on the fire and Olivia sensed he was a million miles away, back in the dust and noise of a war zone.

As the fire caught, light flickered over the room, casting his hard face into sharp lines and dark angles. Olivia wondered what he had seen and done and whether there had been a woman's soft arms and willing body to soothe his nights.

Dangerous thoughts.

"Did you mean that, Rafe? About no lies and pretense necessary between us?" Olivia knew she shouldn't pursue this topic. It was too personal, and emotionally charged. But she couldn't seem to let it go.

"I meant it. You always did put other people first, and you're still doing it. That makes me angry. I say it's time you put yourself first. You'll feel a lot better."

"Thank you for the therapy." Olivia frowned. "As it happens, I am seeing someone about…coping. She said pretty much the same thing you just did."

Rafe nodded and added another log on the fire. "I'm glad to hear you're talking to someone. Talking is good." He stood up and looked down at the dancing flames. "We used to talk about everything, you and me. Any topic at all. Or maybe that's just my imagination and it wasn't really like that." He turned then, his expression thoughtful. "I've imagined a lot of things since I've been gone, but distance can distort memories." He handed Olivia a blanket from a nearby ottoman and then glanced at the wall clock. "I'd better get moving. Tom may want me back at the fair to keep an eye on things. Anything else you need before I go?"

There were a lot of things she needed, Olivia realized. She could use a friend to talk to, someone who wouldn't judge her or expect pretenses—just the way Rafe had described. Olivia loved her friends and cherished their support…but having Rafe to bounce ideas off would give her an entirely different perspective on her problems.

Yet Olivia knew better than to get close to him. He wouldn't be staying here, and she'd made that mistake once before.

So Olivia summoned up a friendly smile that neither asked for nor offered anything personal. "No, I'm fine. Thanks for…everything. And I'm sorry I was snappy with you."

"Forget about it." Rafe smiled slowly. "By the way, I should be thanking you. You made me fifty bucks today."

"Me?"

"Tom and I had a bet going about who you would choose as the winner. He figured you for *Polar Express,* because it had all that emotion and drama, but it kept bringing things right back to home and family. He said that you cared about those things most."

"You don't agree?"

"No. You're all about tradition and you've got an amazing imagination. I was holding out for Dr. Seuss." Rafe smiled at her. "As soon as I saw that father and his kid dressed up as wacky birds, I knew they were going to win."

"Because I'm traditional and predictable," Olivia said stiffly.

"That's *not* what I said. Because you believe in tradition. But you have the imagination to look beyond it. That's a very powerful combination."

Olivia thought about that. She didn't feel very imaginative. Her job had ground her down with office competition and politics and uncertainty about her future. Though she loved the abstraction of designing buildings, Olivia wasn't so sure she enjoyed the thousand details like feasibility reports, water usage and materials assessments.

"I guess you know me better than I thought," she said slowly.

"I remember a lot of things. I remember that big apple tree in spring and the way pink flowers fell on your hair after you walked back from the library. I remember the way your eyes always seemed to shine when you talked about Italy. I'm glad you got to go there. I hope it was all you dreamed it would be."

"It was. The food. The architecture and its sense of age. Everything was so…civilized. I loved all of it." Olivia flushed, remembering her embarrassing near encounter with an attractive Frenchman she had met in a bookstore in Florence. "I never got to Umbria in spring, though."

"There's time. You're young."

"Did you…go to those places you mentioned? Machu Picchu? The Loire Valley?"

"Some of them. I still have a list."

"I guess you'll be leaving soon. Going to see the rest of the places on your list."

"That depends." Rafe's eyes hardened. "Since I got back, you've never asked me what happened that night I was supposed to take you to the prom. The night I never showed up," he added slowly.

Olivia had buried those memories. She had tried to bury the hurt, too. "Since you didn't come, I figured you had a good reason."

"Oh, there was a good reason," Rafe said grimly.

"But I'm sorry I hurt you, Livie. You had everything planned—your dress. A necklace. I know your father was furious and he tried to keep you from accepting."

"He kept expecting that I would give in. When I didn't, it made him furious. But at the least, I should have been able to go to my junior prom with the person I wanted. And that was you." Olivia studied Rafe's face in the firelight. "Was he involved somehow? Did you go away because of something he said?"

"No." Rafe's voice was flat. "I went away because of something stupid. I was stupid most of the time back then. I hurt people that I shouldn't have." He took a rough breath. "I hurt you that night. I hope you didn't hate me after that."

"I could never hate you," Oliva said softly. "Growing up, the only time I felt alive was when you were there."

A muscle moved at Rafe's jaw. "I'd probably say the same."

Olivia moved restlessly, afraid of the emotions stirring to life inside her. She winced a little as her shoulder began to ache again.

"Sorry. You're tired, so I'll shove off. Do you want some tea first?"

"No, I'm good. I think I might just nap right here." She managed a little smile. "If I'm lucky, I'll dream of the Loire Valley. Or Umbria in the spring," she said quietly. "Because someway or another I'm going to get to those places."

After Rafe left, she watched the flames dance. She thought about why Rafe had left Summer Island and where he would go next. But her dreams, when they came, were closer to home.

She walked into the velvet darkness and saw a big apple tree raining pink petals in spring, while Rafe walked toward her from the shadows.

CHAPTER ELEVEN

OLIVIA'S SHOULDER CONTINUED to heal, but her brace had to stay on for another week. Its removal was her one bright spot, signaling that she could finally knit again. Even if her shoulder was stiff and her movements clumsy, Olivia delighted in every slow stitch she finished.

During that week, she and Jilly interviewed four different private detectives. The options ranged from laughable to far beyond Olivia's price range. Two of them had been personable and experienced. They advised her that she didn't need a private detective for this kind of work. What she really needed was a good financial forensic expert with lots of access. They also advised her to tap into her father's email.

Did he have email? Olivia had no idea. That was another thing they had never discussed.

She was trying to make sense of this advice as she sat in her big, quiet kitchen overlooking the ocean. She figured she might as well spend as much time as possible cleaning the house so she could sell it.

An hour earlier, Jilly had arrived to help her sort out food from the big pantry.

"I've been thinking, Jilly. I want to call Walker's

sister for a consultation. Maybe she could tell me where I should be looking. I think I should be given more time to pay the bills my father left. A lawyer would know how to arrange that, right?"

Jilly nodded. "She's not licensed in Oregon, as far as I know. Legal requirements are different from state to state, but I'm certain she could tell you how to start. She would make the necessary calls, too. I think Walker invited her for a visit next month." Jilly looked away, hesitating.

"What's wrong, Jilly?"

Jilly shrugged. "It's…complicated and I don't really want to go into it now." She tossed an old box of soup into the garbage. "This one says 2009. Your dad was really slipping."

Olivia wondered what was bothering Jilly. Her friend seemed very distracted. "Is there a problem with this new specialty-food line you're working on?"

Jilly tossed an expired box of cereal into the garbage. "Nothing I didn't expect. No, I'm thinking about Gage coming home. I also want to make a special menu for Noah and Grace tomorrow night. If you ask me, there's going to be a wedding announcement from them soon.

"They need to put their problems behind them and start a life together. After everything that happened to her, Grace is very cautious, but Noah's the one. Anyone can see how she feels. How he feels about her, too."

"They definitely act like they're in love. But you never know. Things can simmer below the surface."

"Are you speaking from personal experience, Livie? You're not involved with anyone, are you?" Jilly frowned. "I got the impression that you weren't seeing anyone, and that there hadn't been anyone important in your life for a while. Actually, not since…"

Olivia's cheeks filled with color. "Since Rafe. Go on and say it. Everyone assumes that. Unfortunately, it's pretty close to the truth. There were a few near misses, one in Italy. But there is *nothing* going on between Rafe and me. I'd appreciate it if you would remember that. And don't start matchmaking. It will only make it harder for both of us," Olivia said firmly.

Even Jilly, stubborn as she was, could hear the cold determination in those words.

But Jilly also heard the pain Olivia thought she could conceal.

"Fine." Jilly threw up her hands in surrender. "No matchmaking, I promise. It's just that—Rafe's a good man, Livie. He had his wild days, but he's grown up. He's…different now. I think he may actually stay here on Summer Island. I don't think this is a temporary job for him."

Olivia gave a little jerk. The jar of blueberry preserves dropped from her hands and exploded against the floor. She didn't move, staring at the shattered pieces of glass buried in dark fruit.

Quietly Jilly began picking up pieces of broken

glass. "You want to tell me what's *really* going on, Livie? You're both so tense when you're together that the air seethes. And when you look at each other— forget it. It could be lightning and ozone snapping. Do you want to explain that?"

"No," Olivia said flatly. "So mind your own business."

Jilly kept working with slow, careful movements. "Walker's asked Rafe to work on the plumbing. You're bound to see each other at the house."

That was the last thing Olivia wanted to hear. But she managed to keep her voice calm and give Jilly a brief answer. "It's...very uncomfortable. Both of us are remembering things that we wish we hadn't said or done. It's better if we keep our distance. I'm counting on you to help make that happen, Jilly."

Jilly finished cleaning up the mess, her head averted. "I'll do whatever I can. If you're sure?"

"I'm sure. This is important, Jilly." Olivia squared her shoulders. "Rafe and I talked it over. This is what we both want. Just please give us some distance."

Jilly sighed. "Sure. Whatever. It's your choice." But she didn't sound as if she believed it, not for a second.

AFTER JILLY LEFT, Olivia climbed up two floors to the big attic, where her father had stored old clothes, schoolbooks and broken toys. Frugal by nature, Sawyer Sullivan had never been one to give away anything. All their memories were stored up here. It was the last place where Olivia could find answers about what had happened at the end of his life. There was so much she didn't understand.

Shadows fell through the long room, brushing the dusty shelves with old dresses, rabbits with torn ears and Olivia's forgotten childhood tea set. Each thing she touched tugged at her heart. It had been too long since she had faced the past, too long since she had accepted her mother's abandonment of the family. The news of her death the following year was a wound that had never quite healed.

Olivia stood for long moments, listening to the silence and the creaks of the lonely old house. She told herself this was the past. She couldn't change it. All she could do was embrace it.

Olivia crossed to the nearest box, sneezing as she opened the lid. Inside she found old photographs of her father's expensive cars, which he had replaced every year like clockwork.

Beneath the photos Olivia found all her school yearbooks, the bronze desk set that her father had been given by the town when he retired as mayor for a second term and an old diary that she had kept for one month in fourth grade.

It pained her to see that even then, Rafe had figured in most of her entries. She hadn't realized that she had been crazy about him for so long.

She snapped the diary shut and tossed it into a nearby box. Enough thinking about Rafe and his insidious charm.

She had to concentrate on her survival.

She kept searching, hoping for a document or letter to explain her father's state of mind the last months of his life, when he had made such a dismal mess of his finances and the finances of his daughter. With one or two clues, Walker's sister might be able to trace the missing accounts that no one else could locate.

Olivia hated to ask for help. It went totally against her nature and upbringing. But Jilly was right. When Jilly had faced the worst news of her life, her friends had been right beside her. They had all learned something from that process.

Olivia closed the last box and turned, staring down through the narrow oriel window at the gray cove. Now *she* would have to swallow her pride and allow her friends to help.

JILLY STACKED SPICES in the new canisters she had found in Colorado, enjoying the bright colors against her stainless-steel counters. She was still thinking about all that Olivia had told her.

She jumped as Walker pulled her into his arms and kissed the soft line of her neck. "Everything going well on your negotiations for a distributor? Didn't you talk to two people today?"

Jilly tried to focus. It was impossible when Walker's hands opened on her waist and then slid up higher. She swallowed as her sweater rose slowly. "I think I found the right person. He wants a larger cut than I'd hoped, but his references are solid. I would be his smallest customer, but he understands my concept. For the long-term it's the best choice. Unfortunately, for the short-term…it means my cash flow will be tighter than I wanted."

Walker kissed the line of Jilly's jaw. "My offer still goes. You know how I feel. Everything I have is yours, honey. I'm more than willing to write you a check for a temporary loan. If it were my choice, I would make it an outright gift, but I know what you'll say to that. If Rafe and I could hire a helper, we could finish all the work on the house by next week. Then we can help you with the detail work inside."

Jilly closed her eyes, seduced as always by the offer of finances from this tough, amazing man who had come into her life at its very worst moment. "I don't want to lean on you, Walker. We've discussed this before."

"You won't be leaning on me. You're the woman I love, Jilly, the woman I intend to spend every moment of the rest of my life with. It's called a helping hand." He sounded a little exasperated.

Jilly wasn't surprised. They had had this discussion far too often in the past two months since the Harbor House repair bills had shot out of control.

"I'll think about it. I appreciate the offer, Walker. You know that, right?"

His hands opened and he angled her body against his. His eyes darkened. "I'm glad you appreciate it. But I'd rather think that you trusted me enough to accept my gift. There are no strings attached, Jilly. There never will be. What I have is yours."

She made a broken little sound and closed her eyes. As always, this man overwhelmed her. Jilly didn't have a clue what she had done to deserve him in her life. She sighed as his hands curved over her breasts. Desire left her throat dry and her knees weak. "I don't know how you do this to me," she whispered. "But I hope you never stop."

He lifted her, letting their bodies slide together. Jilly reached for his belt, her eyes hot with welcome.

They weren't going to make the bedroom. They probably wouldn't even make it to the little couch in the back office, Jilly thought dimly.

AN HOUR LATER they staggered up the stairs, clothes gripped in hands that were weak from sharing, touching and giving freely. Jilly stumbled and Walker managed to catch her, dropping most of his clothes in the process.

She gave a throaty laugh. Her hands slid along the muscles at his hip. "Have I told you that I love you lately?"

"That's an affirmative, ma'am. Three times, if my memory serves. Each time you said it right before you cried out my name," he said gruffly.

Even now Jilly flushed. Walker was her best friend and the rock-solid anchor of her life. She still couldn't believe the level of passion they shared— and the trust that never wavered.

He opened the door to the big bedroom that they had renovated first, to use while they stayed on Summer Island. He caught Jilly and carried her to the bed, toppling down with her against his chest. "Something is bothering you, Jilly. If you have any problems, you know you can bring them to me."

Her fingers threaded through his. She brought their linked hands to her mouth and kissed his palm. "I know that. It's still hard for me to trust anyone, but I do trust you, Walker. It's just that I'm worried about Olivia. She's got money problems and her father messed up all their finances. I'm also worried about Rafe coming back. He hurt her badly when he left for the Marines without even saying goodbye. Olivia never talks about it, but I know the pain is there. She told me that she and Rafe are going to keep their distance. Olivia swears it's for the best."

"And you're not sure about that?" Walker brushed a strand of hair from Jilly's cheek. "So instead of keeping clear of it, you intend to throw them together every chance you get." He traced the curve of her lips. "Let's have it."

"From the first moment I set eyes on you in the airport in Lost Creek, you could read me. I still can't get over that."

"Call it a gift."

"I do. It's just that…" Abruptly Jilly looked away. She rolled to one side and sat up slowly. "I think I need a shower."

AS THE HOT spray from the shower beat down on Jilly's shoulders, she closed her eyes and sank forward, her face to the cold tiles. She was scared. She had been scared before in her life, but never like *this*.

She stiffened when she felt cool air brush her shoulder and then the pressure of Walker's rugged body. He reached up, working shampoo into her hair, scrubbing the spots at her neck and behind her ears exactly the way she liked best.

"I figured we could save money. Showering together is an ecologically sound choice, don't you think?"

Jilly bit back a shaky laugh. "You just don't believe in privacy, do you?"

He finished shampooing her hair and then tilted her face, rinsing away the suds. "It never seemed to bother you before. I wonder why it does now." His hands were gentle, but his shoulders were stiff. "I think it's time you told me what's bothering you, Jilly."

"I can't. Just—leave it alone, will you?"

She wanted to tell him. Her whole body shook with the need to explain. But the wrong word could shatter everything, destroying the joy that Jilly had come to rely on more than breathing.

No, she couldn't risk it. The chance for loss was too great.

Shaking, she pulled free and wrenched open the shower door, nearly stumbling as she lunged from the room.

WALKER DIDN'T MOVE. His heart pounded, and anger came first. But it was swallowed up by the uncertainty that had been growing in him over the past weeks.

Something was wrong. And if they weren't very careful, they were going to lose everything that mattered.

CHAPTER TWELVE

JILLY TRIED TO pull on her old terry-cloth robe, but her fingers shook too hard and the sleeve kept falling, tangling around her hands, blocking her movements.

She owed Walker the truth. She knew that. But the truth terrified her.

She heard a quick footstep and then her robe was torn from her fingers. Walker swung her around, his eyes hard and distant. "We need to talk. We're going to do it now, Jilly. I'm tired of seeing the distance in your eyes, damn it."

Before she could grab a breath, he swept her naked body up into his arms and stalked to the big wing chair that overlooked the harbor. She struggled, shoving at his chest, but he refused to free her.

"Did anybody ever tell you that you fight like a girl?"

She muttered angrily, elbowing him in the ribs.

Walker was tempted to make another joke, but he didn't want to let either of them off the hook. This was serious. This had to be faced. Life had taught him that delaying hard decisions and hiding painful truths destroyed the things you most wanted to protect.

He pulled a blanket around her shoulders, sliding his hands around her waist so their bodies met intimately. It was a reminder to both of them what they had found and how hard it would be to give it up.

Jilly's eyes closed. She bit back a sound of pain and worry.

"What is it, Jilly? Did you hear something from the doctor? Have you changed your mind about a future with me and my seriously dysfunctional family? Is there another man?" he said grimly.

Her eyes flashed open in anger. "There's *not* another man! How could you ask a thing like that?"

Walker felt a dizzying wave of relief. He hadn't really suspected this was the problem, but Jilly was a complicated person and she had a colorful past. It didn't bother him a bit, but he was realistic enough to know that her past might have reemerged. He didn't think he could compete with a billionaire Arizona real estate developer or the colorful California rock star she had once told him about.

Yes, Walker definitely felt a wave of relief. But then the fear crept back, darker than ever. "Then tell me what's wrong, Jilly. Are you getting cold feet about my family coming here and our wedding vows being repeated?"

Her hands opened and closed and her body filled with tension. "It's not about our vows. At least it's only a little about that. Although your family scares the hell out of me."

"They scare the hell out of me, too, honey. That's

why I'm counting on having you around. Between the two of us, we'll battle them back."

Jilly didn't want to, but she laughed. He could always make her laugh, even at the worst of times. It had been her first clue that she was in love with him.

"I'm scared, Walker. Really scared," she whispered.

He ran a hand through her hair, hating what she would say next but knowing that there was no more time to delay. "Then tell me. Did the doctor tell you something? Your lab tests and cardio scans…"

Walker prayed her heart condition had not worsened. They had both been rigorous, following all the doctor's orders. But he knew Jilly had been stressed over the repairs of the Harbor House and worrying about her friend.

He was furious that he had not seen the signs earlier. "Tell me," he said roughly.

"I'm not sure I can. I never thought…" She closed her eyes and then her hands clenched on his shoulders. She blinked back tears. "This is a different test. I went to see the doctor last week, but not about arrhythmias or problems with my blood pressure," she said in a voice that shook.

Walker felt another blinding wave of relief. If it wasn't her heart, they could deal with it. They could pull through anything. He wasn't going to let her escape from the future he had planned for both of them and the joy he was going to bring her.

But he gave her time to tell the story in her own

way. She was stubborn and independent; Walker wouldn't have it any other way.

Jilly looked up, meeting his gaze with eyes that shimmered from unshed tears. "Okay, here it is. I didn't want to screw this up. But I think I did." She gnawed her lip mercilessly, never looking away from Walker's face. "Because this test that I took left no question. I'm pregnant."

WALKER DIDN'T MOVE. His body seemed frozen. Jilly couldn't pick up any expression in his face.

This was bad, she thought. Really bad. He was as shocked as she had been.

Panic hit her in a wave and she shoved hard at his chest, desperate to be free. Desperate to avoid the rejection and the disapproval at this huge change in their relationship.

Walker's hands curved around her wrists and tightened. "You're...pregnant?" He shook his head a little. "You're going to have a baby?"

"That's what the word means. When you're pregnant a baby is involved," she snapped. She gave another angry twist, elbowing him in the chest.

Walker didn't even seem to notice. He frowned, staring at her face. One eyebrow rose. "I don't understand. We've been careful about that. We both agreed this wasn't the right time."

Jilly closed her eyes, trying to stay calm. "Yes, we've been careful. All except that one time in Santa Barbara. We went up so I could look for new produce sources, and we stayed at that little bed-and-breakfast near the beach. It was romantic. Secluded." She looked away, her voice flat. "And I screwed up."

"You screwed up how?"

"It was supposed to be the last day of my cycle. You know how they mark those pill boxes?"

"Not exactly. But I know you always take one. What went wrong?" He sounded confused, in a fog.

"What went wrong was I thought I'd taken one, but it had jiggled loose somehow. I found it today in the bottom of my purse. One pill that I missed. Oh, Lord, I can't believe this is happening," she whispered.

"We missed one pill. Now you're pregnant." Walker took a long, rough breath. "We're pregnant," he said slowly. "With a baby." His voice broke.

Jilly looked up, stunned to see the emotions that filled his eyes. He turned her wrists in his hands and brought them up to his mouth, kissing the line of burns of her latest kitchen mishap. "Do you have any idea how this makes me feel?"

"Angry? Worried? Betrayed by a calculating female who wants her hands on your money?"

Walker's fingers slid over her mouth, stopping the anxious flow of words. "Overwhelmed. Amazed. Delirious," he said. The confusion was vanishing from his face.

Jilly was pretty sure she saw unmistakable joy replacing the confusion. "You're not angry or worried?"

"Hell, no, I'm not angry. I'm dazed. I feel like a tank just ran over me and then backed up and ran over me again. But I should be used to that by now. Living with you, I feel like a tank runs over me at least once a week."

Any other woman would have been angry at the reference, but Jilly gave in to laughter. To tell the truth, she found the reference flattering. "And you don't blame me? You don't think this is some kind of weird manipulative thing I'm doing to get you tied up with access to all that money your family has?" It was only partly a jest. Other people had whispered those things within her hearing. Jilly had to face the possibility, for both of them.

"That does get me mad. You can do a lot better than me. You had an offer from a billionaire, as I recall."

"It wasn't an offer of marriage," Jilly said dryly.

Walker shrugged. "Pretty close. And as for all our so-called Hale billions, the money is so tangled up in trust funds that you'd have to be a very patient woman to want me for financial gain."

"So you're not mad?" Jilly persisted, needing to hear him say the words. Otherwise she wouldn't be free of the terrible fear that had hit her at the first symptoms of pregnancy. "I need to be completely sure, Walker. If you have any second thoughts—"

His laughter cut her off. He gripped her hard and swung her round the room, their bodies locked tightly. "I don't have a single second thought, honey," he said roughly, kissing her neck and then her mouth. "In fact, I take it as a sign. This is where we're meant to be. We've been so careful. If this could still happen, I think somebody way more important than we are had a hand in it."

Jilly smiled slowly. "You mean your old commanding officer? Or maybe your father?"

"Not either of them, and you damn well know it. The only thing that makes me angry is your waiting to tell me. Because you thought I would be angry at the news." He lifted her face to his. "I'm over the moon. We'll say our vows again whenever you want. A small, official ceremony, just between you and me. We don't even need to tell anyone. We can have our reception that we promised my family after that. That way you can delay all the planning."

"Technically, we're already married. Remember?"

"But I want to do it again, Jilly. For real, fully committed to the decision. I think you'd like your close friends to be there this time, too."

Jilly laughed quietly, sliding her face against his warm chest. He knew her so well. And now she knew he was holding back nothing. He really was thrilled by the idea of a child.

She swung around, frowning. "But there's another problem, Walker. I'll make the world's worst mother. I don't have a nurturing bone in my body. I'll mess up playdates and teach this baby bad language. I'm going to screw this all up," she said, closing her eyes, feeling the burden of a thousand worries and insecurities.

Wise man that he was, Walker didn't laugh. He simply slid his hands into her hair and held her. "Whatever problems that come, we'll tackle them together, honey. We'll make it work. We'll make it work amazingly well."

He looked down at her, frowning. "Are you sick? Any nausea—that morning thing?" He looked uncomfortable.

Jilly snorted. "Not a bit of it. I'm eating like a horse. That was the first thing that cued me something was up. In fact, I've got a ravenous desire for lasagna right now."

"Whatever happened to pickles and ice cream?"

"I'm thinking jalapeños and ice cream." Jilly's eyes brightened. "Actually, I'm thinking of a whole line of specialty items for pregnant women. Healthy food that won't upset their stomachs. Something they can eat even if they don't feel like it."

"Jalapeños?" he said dryly.

"That's for *me,* not for the public. You know how I love peppers." Her hand opened, gently cradling the line of her slender stomach as if she could already imagine the new life growing there. "Something tells me this child is going to love chiles as much as I do. But I'm thinking low-fat recipes with high fiber and lots of taste."

"I'll go heat up some lasagna for you." Then his eyes darkened as Jilly's fingers slid down his chest and opened the snap of his jeans. He was half-soaked, his pants wet from when he had followed her into the shower.

And there was no mistaking the hunger in Jilly's eyes as she slid her fingers under the wet denim and found his hard response.

"The lasagna can wait," she whispered. Her fingers circled and traced. "I want you right here. I want us to remember this."

He cut back an oath as Jilly's fingers tightened, overwhelming his reason and control.

The way she always did.

They fell in a sprawl of hot, hungry skin and linked fingers, reason swept away by need. Walker tried to wait, but Jilly wouldn't let him, pressing her body to his. Around them the old Harbor House seemed to sigh, creaking with age and memories and something that might have been peace.

CHAPTER THIRTEEN

OLIVIA BARELY SAW her friends over the next week. Jilly was busy testing new recipes, and Caro was preparing for her husband's return from Afghanistan. Grace and Noah were back in town but had barely spoken to anyone. Noah had three more days before he had to return to work in San Francisco, and it was clear they were hoarding every minute together. Grace's friends wouldn't have considered intruding on their privacy. Meanwhile, Olivia continued to search through her father's boxes, papers and closets, as the last private detective had advised her.

She had called the management office of the condominium Sawyer Sullivan had maintained in Seattle, but there had been almost nothing in the condominium when it was sold three months before his death.

There had been no record of any storage units, bank accounts or deposit boxes in Seattle despite all her searching.

Another dead end.

She tried all the local banks along the coast, thinking he might have had accounts in several places.

Again it was a dead end.

She had checked the local post office to see if he had rented a postal box. No luck there either.

With her options running out, she turned her focus to the house itself. There were dozens of possible hiding spaces in a big building like this one. Olivia checked each wall, searching for signs of new paint or repaired wood that might conceal a recent addition to cover a wall safe or hiding place.

She didn't know why she was following this train of thought, but instinct whispered that if there was any answer, it would be here, in the grand house her father had loved so much.

For Sawyer Sullivan this house had always represented status, power and security. In her search, Olivia found a tangle of old documents that gave her clear signs her father had been failing in the last year of his life. But there was no record of any new bank accounts or any sign of the items missing from her grandmother's estate.

Olivia knew she couldn't keep the sad state of her finances hidden much longer. There were taxes to pay and her car payment was due. Worst of all, her father's banker told her that a number of people in town had approached him discreetly, indicating that Sawyer Sullivan had owed them money.

It was all turning worse than Olivia had thought possible.

As the days passed, she opened every box in the attic and even checked for storage spaces under the floorboards. Something told her that she needed to understand her father's state of mind in those last months of his life. He hadn't been clear in his mind and he might have been becoming a little paranoid.

Olivia almost felt sorry for him; the letters no longer showed an aloof, confident businessman. In these pages Olivia saw an old man fighting to stay in control, afraid of something.

She sank into a pool of sunlight in the dusty attic, watching the breakers roll in far out at sea, thinking about growing up on this island she had always loved.

As she was growing up, Sawyer Sullivan had always made it clear he had wanted a son, not a daughter, and if he had to have a daughter, she should have been smarter and prettier than Olivia could ever be. And one thing was painfully clear. He had never trusted Rafe and never wanted him around Olivia.

He had never suspected how close the two had become.

But that was old history. Olivia shoved away the past and turned her thoughts to the present. She had begun to put her life back together with the help of a therapist that Caro had recommended. Olivia accepted that her insecurities came from losing her mother very young and having a father who was both distant and demanding.

She refused to be a victim. She was moving on, whether she found the answers about her father or not.

Something glinted on the floor near her feet.

Frowning, she leaned down and picked up a pile of old library books, stamped for resale. Her father must have purchased them after one of the fund-raising sales for the local library. They were a mix of Dickens, British history and modern paperback thrillers. Nothing significant there. Beside them was a stack of DVDs that he had never returned. When she shoved the DVDs aside, she saw a piece of metal caught in the molding at the bottom of the wall.

Why was a key pushed into the wood? It couldn't have fallen, not back in a corner.

Her fingers shook a little as she dug at the key, which was wedged down into a crack in the molding. Olivia held it up into the light and read the number.

Summer Island Bank. Number 192.

A safe-deposit box?

Her father's banker had told Olivia that he had an account there. After the funeral, she had filled out paperwork and they had opened the box.

All they had found were an old coin set and tax returns dating back ten years. Olivia was almost certain that the box number they had opened was different from this one. She frowned, thinking about what to do next. She needed to know if this box was current. If so, had it belonged to her father?

She stood for a long time in the silent attic, feeling the cold outline of the key dig into her fingers. It dug in harder and harder until she gritted her teeth and felt the pain grow, but even then Olivia couldn't relax her grip.

Something felt wrong.

She walked downstairs, back to the sunny kitchen and her handbag with the cell phone. She dialed.

"Summer Island Bank. May I help you?"

"I hope you can. I have a safe-deposit box at the bank. I wanted to check your banking hours today."

"Today is our late day. You can come until seven forty-five. Be sure to bring your key. If you don't have your key, we can't open the vault."

"Oh, I have my key." Olivia hesitated. "It's been a while, so I can't remember your sign-in process. Do I need identification?"

"You'll have to sign in and show an ID. Your signature will have to match the signature card, too. This will be done in the presence of a bank representative. After that, you have as much time to access your box as you require."

This was bad news. Olivia knew she wasn't a signatory, so they wouldn't let her in to open the box. There had to be a perfectly normal reason that the account had never turned up before this. Probably her father had just forgotten. Probably the bank records were incomplete.

But as she hung up the phone, a little voice kept whispering that banks do not make mistakes and that her father had not made a mistake either. He had meant to keep this box secret.

For the life of her, Olivia couldn't figure out why.

She sat in the quiet kitchen, the key cold in her fingers. She heard the sound of her pulse and the beat of her heart. She told herself to stay calm, that there had to be a good reason her father had never mentioned this key or the box.

Fortunately, one person might have answers for her. She dialed the number of Sawyer Sullivan's longtime business adviser, Martin Eaglewood, an island native who had been a friend of her father's as long as Olivia could remember.

He answered the phone on the first ring. "Livie, how are you doing? I haven't heard from you in weeks. I'm hoping you're calling to take me up on that offer of lunch. It's been too long."

"Lunch would be wonderful, Martin." Olivia kept her voice calm and upbeat. "You name the date. We're fairly busy with the final repairs on the Harbor House, but I can work around my schedule."

"Everything okay there? Al at the hardware store says you've spent a lot of money on repairs."

No secrets in a small town, Olivia thought. "Everything is on schedule. Actually, I was calling about my father's financial records."

"Of course. What can I do to help?"

"I just wondered if you had found any indication that he had additional accounts? Or maybe he had a safe-deposit box somewhere? Is there anything that has not shown up before now?"

"I'm afraid not. I've been through all our correspondence and all the documents that we found at the bank. He had one safe-deposit box at the bank, and you were there when we cleared it out. Why do you ask?"

Olivia squeezed the key, hearing the loud hammer of her pulse. She felt like a traitor, but she couldn't seem to trust her father's executor or anyone else right now. "I always thought there were more documents somewhere. I figured I should ask you."

"Well, I'm glad you got that off your chest. But there are no other accounts or bank boxes. You can be very certain that if I had found anything I would have contacted you immediately." The silence stretched out for long moments. "When you were going through the house, did you find any papers or things that your father had left for you?"

It was such an innocent question. There was no reason for Olivia to feel wary in answering it. "No, nothing at all, Martin."

Her father's adviser cleared his throat.

"Is there something else I need to know?"

"I'm afraid…your father owed people money. Only four. It's nothing major, Olivia. There was a grocery account. He had a small tab running at the café downtown. He was also making payments on a boat that he was renting."

"A boat? He never mentioned that to me."

"I just heard about it this week. I was going to call you. I thought you and I might go over and have a look. Maybe—well, he might have left something there."

Olivia felt the cold pressure of the key in her fingers. Would Martin have really called her? Or would he have gone to check the boat himself?

Olivia hated the way her thoughts were running, but she couldn't stop seeing shadows. "That sounds like a good idea. If you're free, why don't we go there first thing tomorrow. Where is it?"

"I'll have my secretary email you all the information. It's about a half hour up the coast. I'll check and see when they open. We can meet there. Then perhaps you'll let me take you to breakfast after that?"

"Of course. I'll watch for the email. I'm busy later in the day, so I'd like to do it as early as possible."

After he hung up, Olivia saw the email from his office and checked the location of the dock, which was about thirty miles to the north. She dialed the management office to check the hours.

Martin had said that he would meet her there at eight-thirty, but Olivia found out that the office opened at seven-thirty. It was probably nothing, but she wanted to be there when the office first opened.

A sudden growling in her stomach reminded Olivia that she hadn't eaten anything all day. Though she had no real appetite, she went down to the kitchen and heated some soup in the microwave. But when the timer went off, she made no move to eat. She simply stood at the big kitchen window, looking out at the harbor.

The house seemed too big and too quiet. Loneliness clung to every room. She looked down at the key she had found and wondered if there was some way to work around normal channels to view the contents of the box. At this point she didn't even know if it belonged to her father. She doubted it belonged to a prior owner of the house, since her father had lived here for almost forty years. And that narrowed down the list of possibilities.

She wanted to pick up the phone and call Grace or Caro or Jilly, laying out the new developments and asking for their advice. But they were all too busy with their own lives and problems.

Olivia turned away, her soup forgotten. She had no appetite. She wanted to crawl into bed and pull the blankets over her head, but the worries grew and Olivia recognized the first stages of the old attacks that had crippled her since elementary school.

The sudden cold sweats. The shaking hands.

The looming sense of failure, impossible to escape.

Olivia closed her eyes and locked her hands together, holding back the bad memories and the fear and all the ways that she could fail in the future. She had been plagued by panic attacks since she was fourteen. Now she was learning to understand their patterns and to deal with them.

She took slow breaths, forcing out the bad memories. She repeated out loud all the things she loved in her life and all the things she had to be grateful for. She summoned up memories of her friends and pictures of the beautiful yarn shop and new café at the Harbor House. She pictured a full parking lot and happy shoppers.

It was all going to be fine, she told herself, sinking into a chair at the kitchen table. The key fell onto the table in front of her, glinting in the sunlight, but Olivia felt stronger now, able to beat back the demons of fear.

Sharp knocking at the back door made her jump. She glanced back to see who was there.

A lanky figure was shadowed against the stained glass door. Olivia knew only one man who was that tall.

And because she was so relieved to see him, because she wanted badly to discuss what she had found and ask for help, Olivia forced herself to stay right where she was. "Go away, Rafe."

CHAPTER FOURTEEN

THERE WAS NO sign of apology in Rafe's eyes as he stood in the doorway, only concern. "Jilly gave me the key. She said I should swing by."

Olivia shrugged. "There was no need. I—I'm fine. Just busy."

Rafe crossed the room slowly, looking around the kitchen. "You're sure everything is okay?"

"Everything is *fine*." Olivia shoved her hands in her pockets, praying for him to leave. "But I'm cooking."

"You are?"

"That's right." Olivia backed away. She knew her face was pale and she could feel the sweat on her forehead as the anxiety began to return in slow, insidious waves. "I'm—okay, Rafe. But I'm busy. Cooking. I think you need to go."

"I don't smell anything cooking. There's just a single bowl of soup on the counter and I'm pretty sure that came from a can because it's what I have every night."

"Stop it, Rafe. Just leave." Olivia pressed a shaking hand to the wall, needing the support. Why wouldn't he go away? She needed to focus before she was caught by a full-blown anxiety attack.

"You don't look so good. Why don't you sit down? I'll make you a cup of tea."

When he walked toward her, lean and tall in his uniform, sunlight struck the badge at his chest. Olivia heard the creak of leather at his belt and knew that he was carrying a service weapon.

And though it was the last thing she wanted, Olivia was comforted by his presence, anchored by his quiet strength.

"Okay, you're right. I'm not feeling very well." She spoke stiffly. "I have a pill I should take when this…happens." Her hands shook slightly as she leaned over the counter for her bag. She hadn't really told anyone about the panic attacks—and the medication she had started taking to help deal with them.

Rafe's fingers curved around hers. He held her shoulders gently and guided her to the chair at the window. "I'll get the bag and the water. I'll put hot water on for tea. Shouldn't you eat something when you take medicine?"

Food was so far from Olivia's mind that she laughed. "Maybe later. But tea sounds good. It's in the red canister next to the teapot."

"Got it." He moved with quiet efficiency, and though the kitchen was not his own, he seemed to be at ease. While the water bubbled, Olivia focused on her breathing exercises and watched gray waves rise lazily and then crash on the beach.

She began to feel better. Her hands slowly unclenched. The thunder of her heartbeat grew quieter. She hadn't even taken her pill yet, and she had held back the attack. The knowledge made her stronger than a whole bottle of pills.

"Tea's ready. I found something called Raspberry Herbal Zinger." Rafe smiled wryly. "Here's your water and the bottle I found in your purse." He pulled out a chair and sat beside her. There was no judgment or curiosity in his face. He was simply calm. Simply a friend helping a friend in difficulty.

Olivia remembered that he had always known how to keep his head in the middle of a storm, even as a boy. People remembered Rafe for his misbehavior and his bad-boy charm, but she remembered him for his strength. He had always been a good listener when few other people in her life bothered.

She took the pill and then added two spoonfuls of sugar to her tea. "My other vice, along with the caramel apples. I love dark sweet tea." She cut off her nervous chatter and then faced him directly. "You're not going to ask?"

They both knew that she was referring to whatever it was that left her white-faced and sweating, her hands clenched on the table.

Rafe frowned at Olivia's tense fingers. "No, I'm not going to ask. I figured I would just make you tea and we could sit here. If we talk, that's fine. If we don't talk, that's fine, too."

The way he said it, Olivia knew he meant it. He

was comfortable in his own skin. He could sit here in the quiet house and say nothing and it wouldn't bother him a bit. How many men could you say that about?

The fact that he didn't barrage her with questions gave her the strength to face him. To really see him.

And to allow him to really see her.

"I get them. Anxiety attacks. I've had them... since I was fourteen. Nobody knows," she said slowly. "Not even Jilly. My father sent me to a psychiatrist up in Seattle. All he wanted to do was give me medication. I took the pills for a week and flushed the rest down the toilet. They didn't help the anxiety. All they did was make me feel weird and disconnected. I told the doctor that, but he didn't seem to care."

Rafe sat silently for long moments. "And so you dealt with it yourself. You've been dealing with this yourself all these years?"

Olivia nodded. "I never told my father they were worse. It wouldn't have made any difference."

Rafe poured his own cup of tea. "I'm not saying you shouldn't take them if you need them and if they help you. But it doesn't sound like that particular set of pills was doing you any good." He added sugar to his tea, not looking at Olivia. "Jilly says sugar and lemon ruin Earl Gray. But I can't break the habit. When I was over there in the field, I could be gone for days. And I always thought about hot tea. Good tea, made with lemon and sugar, just like this. It seemed like an impossible luxury, but I kept it in my mind, telling myself I would get through everything and then I would have tea anytime I wanted. No more shouting. No more bullets or IEDs." His eyes darkened. "Strange what we fixate on to get us through hard times," he said quietly.

Olivia watched him squeeze more lemon into the tea and stir it slowly. His fingers were long and agile. He moved them slowly back and forth over the rim of the teacup, and the sight made something flutter in her chest.

She cleared her throat. "You're in uniform. Aren't you supposed to be on duty?"

"I am on duty. I just swung by to make sure everything was okay here."

"Why wouldn't it be? I didn't call in with any problems."

"Serve and protect, Livie. Jilly told me to check in on you. I try to drive down every street in town at least once a day. You know Mrs. Granger over by the bank? I found her trying to climb a tree to get her cat down. She's eighty if she's a day. She could have broken every bone in her body. I finally got the cat down—and I still have the claw marks to show for it," he said dryly.

"A dangerous assignment."

"You're damn right. Yesterday I drove by the old beach road and found four high school kids down there drinking and necking. One of the girls' fathers showed up and he was carrying a gun. That wasn't so amusing. I managed to talk them all out of doing something they would regret. Gave them the name of a family therapist, and I told them the visit wasn't optional. They would all go or they would be looking at the inside of a jail cell."

Olivia watched his long fingers cradle the teacup, listening to the gravity of his voice. "That should help them more than time in a cell."

Rafe shrugged. "You can only do what you can do. That's another thing I've learned." He looked up and then he reached through the sunlight, his hands sliding down over hers. "You want to tell me what's going on? And why your panic attacks are getting worse?"

"Who said they're getting worse?"

"You did. Not in words. Because you seemed surprised and you look like you're struggling to keep that surprise out of sight, from yourself as well as from me. That means something's changed. You want to tell me about that?" he said quietly.

"No. I don't want to tell you."

He chuckled slightly and shook his head. "Tough. I'm not going away until I hear the whole story. So I'm staying here, and I'm going to continue to sit here until you talk to me. You know I can be a very patient man, Livie." He glanced at the clock. "I'm off duty in ten minutes. I'm going to call Tom and have him clock me out early. So don't think you're getting rid of me."

Olivia looked away, squeezing her eyes together

tightly. The tea was working, warming her up, and she could feel the steady pressure of Rafe's hands on hers, strong and warm.

And because he didn't press her but only sat calmly, one hand on hers while he drank his tea, Olivia took a deep breath and began to talk. The words she had never said before seemed to well up from deep inside her. First she gave him the facts, like the dizziness and the shortness of breath, the nausea and the sweating. She told him what happened next, the way her brain seemed to get stuck, caught in repeating circles until she couldn't escape from the fear. But she was coming to understand herself and the triggers that started a cascade of anxiety. She told him about that, too, along with the relaxation exercises and the journaling exercises that she was practicing.

Rafe listened to all of it without expression or questions. He simply nodded now and then, as if he understood. Because she felt calm, Olivia told him about the situation with her father—how he had lost his clarity at the end of his life and along with that had managed to lose everything but this house.

Rafe looked stunned. "There's nothing left? I don't know much about your father, but he always struck me as being very careful. He didn't seem like a gambler or a big risk taker where money was concerned. So what happened?"

"Not a clue. His banker and his executor have both been through all the papers. There's no sign of other bank accounts. But he was losing his faculties at the end of his life. He could have done anything with his accounts…" She frowned down at the tea, growing cold on the table in front of her. "A little while ago I found this up in the attic."

Olivia pushed the dusty key across the table toward Rafe. "It's from the bank. But I can't get into the vault because I was never listed as one of his agents or cosigners. There's no way to know what's inside or even if the box was *his*. I could get a court order and have the box opened, couldn't I?"

"As long as it's registered in your father's name, and you're one of his heirs, it shouldn't be too hard to arrange." Rafe picked up the key and studied it. "He never told you about this?"

She shook her head. "He had another box at the bank. When we opened it, all it had was old tax records and a few other documents. But this is a different box. He never mentioned it to anyone that I know of." Olivia blew out a breath. "And then there's his boat. I just heard about that from his business manager. Tomorrow I'm going to meet Martin Eaglewood there and check the boat out. You remember him, don't you?"

Rafe nodded, but his eyes were narrowed. "I'm off tomorrow. Why don't I tag along?"

She managed a smile. "What do you think I'm going to find, old *Playboy* magazines? Laundered drug money?"

"Knowing your father, I doubt that. But that's

the problem. You don't know what you're going to find. That's why I don't want you to go there alone." Rafe refilled the teapot carefully, and Olivia had the sense that he was choosing every word he said. "If you don't want me along, ask Jilly and Walker to go with you. How well do you know this business adviser of his?"

"Martin? He's handled my father's affairs forever. At least thirty years." Olivia frowned. "If Martin Eaglewood is crooked, then Santa Claus is crooked, too. I simply refuse to believe there's any problem like that."

Rafe rubbed his neck. "Probably it's nothing. You'll take a look and clean out whatever he left behind. All the same, it wouldn't hurt to talk to some of the neighbors. Ask a few questions and see if any other people had visited the boat with him."

Olivia sat up very straight. "What do you mean, other people? You think someone was there with him?"

"I don't think anything. I'm just saying that it would be a good idea." Rafe took a sip of tea and looked out over the harbor. "It's better to be prepared. That's what I'm saying. I can be here to pick you up whenever you want."

Olivia didn't plan to say yes, but the words tumbled out. If Rafe wanted to spend his day on a wildgoose chase with her, who was she to complain? The hard thing was separating her anxiety issues from the general mess of her father's financial affairs. She told herself it was nothing, and he had simply forgotten to mention the boat to her.

When Olivia looked up, she realized that Rafe was staring at her. "What's wrong?"

"I just asked you a question. Twice, as a matter of fact. I haven't eaten anything since breakfast, and I thought you might have dinner with me."

"Dinner?" Olivia cleared her throat. "Now?"

"That's right. Two people. One table. A lot of food. It's a fairly civilized process," he said dryly.

"I know what dinner means," she snapped. "It's just that I…" What excuse could she make that didn't sound ridiculous? "I was going to call it a night. I'm tired and we've been working hard finishing up at the Harbor House."

Rafe didn't move.

"I'm not just brushing you off, Rafe. I'd like to have dinner with you. Really." She looked away, feeling uncomfortable.

"Then do it. Tonight. Right now," he said flatly. "We'll just share a little conversation and some good food. What's there to be afraid of in that?"

"I'm not afraid of having dinner with you," Olivia shot back.

She was cut off by a loud knocking over her head. She froze as another loud thump echoed from the attic near the side of the house. Her eyes flashed to Rafe's.

He put a finger over his lips, shaking his head, warning her against making any noise. When he looked around the kitchen, Olivia realized he was trying to remember the layout of the house and the fastest way upstairs.

She crossed the room silently and pointed to the back stairway that led to the attic. Rafe nodded. Olivia noticed that his hand reached behind him. He slid something leather away from his holster that held his service weapon.

Olivia drew in a slow breath, chilled by that single movement. When Rafe reached the bottom step he stopped, listening intently.

Olivia heard a low hum.

And then the lights went out.

CHAPTER FIFTEEN

IN THE SUDDEN darkness, every sound seemed magnified. The main thing that Olivia noticed was the hammering of her heart. She heard a soft creak.

Rafe's hands rose, touching her shoulder. "I'm going up." His voice was low, cold. "Stay here."

Olivia didn't even think of arguing. If someone was in the attic, he would be far better equipped to deal with it. But she knew one thing that he would need.

Olivia slid her hand into her pocket and pulled out her cell phone. Carefully she triggered the application that changed it into a flashlight. "Take this," she whispered. "Touch the center button for the light."

"Thanks," he said. "My service flashlight is out in the car." His strong fingers brushed against hers. "Stay here. I don't want to be wondering where you are in the dark if anything happens."

"I won't go up. But if you yell or I hear a gunshot— let me know what happened. I don't want to sit here worrying about you."

"Don't worry about me. Worry for whoever made that sound," Rafe said grimly.

Olivia heard a faint rustle of clothing in the darkness and then he was gone.

OLIVIA STOOD NEAR the base of the stairs, one hand on the wall as the seconds crept past. She heard no sounds from the attic. The power was still off.

She turned to the big kitchen window and glanced over the hillside toward town. A few lights were on, but all the houses near hers were dark. Maybe there was a problem with the power line that serviced the hillside. That happened occasionally after a storm or mudslide.

She looked out at the houses with power and tried to figure out where they were, but it was hard to know. She was too distracted, worrying about Rafe.

Something hit her shoulders and she swung around, striking blindly with her fists.

"Hey." Rafe gave a muffled oath. "I'm friendly." The light came on from her cell phone.

It felt as if he had been gone an hour. "Did you find anything?"

"Nobody up there. I found a few nuts by a window that was open a crack. That might have been the sound we heard, maybe from squirrels. When was the last time you checked the windows up there?"

Olivia paced the kitchen. "Earlier this afternoon. That's when I found the key I told you about. But I'm almost certain all the windows were closed. No one else was in the house after that."

"Are you sure all the windows were closed? Did you check them?"

"I didn't smell outside air. Nothing looked touched. But if you mean did I actually lean down and check each window, the answer is no."

Rafe didn't look riled by her answer. He nodded slowly. "One of them might have been opened. A squirrel can squeeze through a pretty small crack."

Olivia's hands twisted back and forth. She bit back her fear and focused instead on anger at the thought that this might be a prank. "How can I be sure? How am I going to sleep, wondering...what made that noise?"

Rafe glanced down the hill at the line of houses. "I'm going to check in at the station. I want to see if there's been a power outage reported, and you're going to come with me while I do that." He took her hand and turned her around, heading toward the back door. "After we have a sitrep, we'll decide what to do next."

Olivia cleared her throat. She felt a little light-headed. "Sitrep?"

"It's a military term. A field situation report. And don't bother arguing with me." His voice hardened. "Because there's no way in hell that you're staying here alone tonight, Livie."

RAFE CHECKED IN at the station. There was a power outage, all right. It covered part of the hillside, but it didn't cover the street near Olivia's house.

That meant something else had cut off her power.

Rafe didn't lie to her. He laid out the possibilities, keeping his voice neutral and calm. He saw her struggle with anxiety. After what she had told him, he realized that this whole situation was harder for her than he had thought.

So he changed clothes, logged off duty and then guided her out to his car. No matter what she said, they were going to have dinner.

Rafe tried not to think about what would happen after that.

SITTING IN THE old downtown diner was uncomfortable, to say the least. Everyone in town recognized Rafe by now. There was open curiosity when Olivia walked in with him. When they sat down to eat, more than a few disapproving glances were sent their way. People in Summer Island clearly remembered Rafe Russo's more outrageous antics growing up. A number of people in the room made it obvious they did not care for the idea of Rafe and Olivia being involved.

Even if it was only for a leisurely dinner.

That thought left Olivia furious. Rafe had served his country bravely and now he was serving the community in law enforcement. Nobody in this town had *any* right to look down on him. He had changed and they needed to see that.

In her anger about his treatment, Olivia laughed a little louder and sat a little closer than she might have. If it gave Rafe the wrong impression, Olivia decided she would explain later.

After the smiling waitress took their order, she returned moments later and handed Rafe a huge plate of French fries even though it had not been on the order. "Fries are on the house. I know that you like them because you order them whenever you come in. I figured maybe you forgot, seeing how you might be distracted and all." The waitress shot a meaningful glance at Olivia.

"Thanks, Sallyann." Rafe reached for the salt and the ketchup, grinning. "I never could get decent fries when I was away. After another year of eating them every day, I may actually get tired of them."

The waitress crossed her arms. "You mean while you were over in Afghanistan, I take it. Well, we all thank you for your service there. Just because *some* people in town are all fuss and bother doesn't mean the rest of us don't appreciate it. Tom Wilkinson happens to be an old friend of mine. I heard a few stories about the things you did over there," she said quietly.

Rafe frowned. "All exaggerated, I assure you." Before she could say anything else, he picked up the menu. "How about adding some root beer to the order? I'm thinking Olivia and I should split a root-beer float." He glanced at Olivia and raised an eyebrow. "What do you say?"

Olivia nodded, remembering the few times that she had shared a float with him on Saturday afternoons in junior high. They hadn't done it often.

It had raised too many eyebrows.

As soon as the waitress had gone, she leaned closer. "You want to explain that?"

"Not particularly. I've put all that behind me. Let's just have a nice meal, okay?"

Olivia saw the wife of the mayor glance their way and frown. The daughter of the town librarian was sitting off to their right. She frowned at Rafe, too. Clearly their night out was being noted.

And because there were so many disapproving looks, Olivia took Rafe's hand between hers. "Thank you for your service in Afghanistan, Rafe. Sallyann was right. We do value it."

Rafe looked down at his hands, gripped inside Olivia's. He cleared his throat. "I believed in it. I still believe in it. But you don't have to hold my hands, Livie. Although it's nice." He glanced around the crowded diner and smiled a little. "But I get it. I've seen the looks, too. You're just making a statement. After all, once the town bad boy always the town bad boy," he said dryly.

It was true; that had been her original intention. But when he put it that way, Olivia realized she needed to be honest. There was something more going on.

"The day two people can't go out for dinner and not be frowned at is the day I leave this town," she said coldly. She followed up the words with a glare at the mayor and his wife.

To her fury, they answered with little waves and

a smile. But the smile was only for her, not Rafe. How could people be so stupid and close-minded?

Sallyann brought back a huge root-beer float and Olivia attacked it with a straw and a big spoon. She suddenly realized how hungry she was.

"Hey, slow down. You won't have any room for dinner," Rafe said quietly.

"I could eat a horse. Jilly sent me lasagna a few days back, but it's all gone. I've been too busy to bother cooking."

Rafe smiled. When he saw that the mayor and his companions were watching them, he reached across the table and slid an arm around Olivia. Then he leaned down and kissed her lightly on the cheek. "That was in the spirit of making a public statement, too."

Olivia looked around the room and saw more disapproving looks.

"The hell with that," she muttered. Leaning forward, she gripped the front of Rafe's shirt and slowly pulled him toward her.

This kiss was neither light nor casual, but slow and searching. It held heat and memories, along with an edge of recklessness. And for the space of long heartbeats, Olivia forgot that it was just supposed to be an act.

When they came up for air, she could have sworn the room around them was silent. She could feel eyes burning into her back, but she didn't care.

Rafe cleared his throat, looking a little bit overwhelmed. "That was some statement you just made, honey."

"I certainly hope so. Let the small minds talk about that, since they're so determined to gossip," she said angrily.

"I'm sorry to intrude on your meal." A tall gray-haired lady in a scarlet scarf moved to the table and held out her hand. "I'm Andrea Moore. Andi to my friends. I live around the corner from you, Olivia. You may not remember me, but I knew your father for many years."

The two shook hands, and then the older woman glanced around the room. "Everyone is watching you, but I guess you know that."

"It's hard to ignore. Do you want to sit down, Ms. Moore?"

"Oh, call me Andi. And thank you, but I just finished my dinner. Best fries outside of L.A. I only came by to introduce myself and leave my card. I handle real estate on the island, and I specialize in high-end properties." She hesitated. "I hope you'll forgive me…but I noticed that your rain gutters are clogged and in need of repair. I had mentioned it to your father a few years ago, but he felt the repairs could wait. The thing is, you shouldn't ignore a roof. It can cause all kinds of problems."

Olivia looked down at the business card and frowned. "I'm glad to know about this. I plan to put the house up for sale and I was hoping to find a real estate agent to give me an estimate on what would be necessary first. I could also use a price comparison of other homes that have sold in the area."

The real estate agent's eyes widened. "You're selling your house? Your father was always so proud of it, especially your view to the sea. Are you sure you want to do something so drastic?"

"I'm sure. But if you aren't interested in the business, I understand."

"Oh, I'm *definitely* interested. There's no house on the island that can compare with yours. With the right touches in place and all repairs done, I could sell it in a second. Of course, the economy is a little slow, but I'm sure I could do very well for you."

Olivia nodded, her mind made up. "Then we should talk. I'll call to set up a time. I'd like to get a repair estimate as soon as possible."

A muscular teenager stood up at the adjoining table. He waved to the real estate agent and pointed to his watch.

"Oh, sorry. My son is finished and he's getting bored. I'd better go. He has a gymnastics event tomorrow, and he needs his rest. Meanwhile, I hope you enjoy your dinner. I look forward to walking the house with you, Olivia."

Olivia stopped her as she turned away. "Andi, this may be odd…but I have something to ask you. You said you knew my father for many years. Did you know that he had a boat up north?"

The real estate agent shook her head. "No, not that I'm aware of. If you're thinking of selling it, I'm afraid I can't be of much help. I specialize in land properties only. But I could suggest a good broker, if you like."

"Thanks. I'll keep that in mind." Olivia watched the mother and son walk through the crowded room, talking quietly. Nearby diners seem to be studying them, but Andi did not stop, though several people waved eagerly for her to come to their table.

"I wonder why he kept it a secret," Olivia mused aloud.

"Not a clue. But she seems to know her business. Since she specializes in high-end properties, you'd be in good hands. I still think you should check her out," Rafe said. "Don't jump into bed with the first person who makes an offer."

"You're right. I'll talk to several people before I make up my mind. Now what about dessert? That root-beer float was good, but I could use some coconut-cream pie."

By the end of dinner, five local residents had passed by the table. All of them stared curiously at Rafe, but they also glanced at Olivia with disapproval.

That was fine with her. At least things were equal now. She wanted them to disapprove of her as much as Rafe.

When they walked back to the car, Rafe leaned down and rummaged through the backseat. Olivia had been too distracted before to notice the clothes and running shoes in a pile.

"Sorry. I haven't gotten moved in properly. I didn't really plan to take the job here. I was going to travel for a few months, but Tom Wilkinson needed someone right away…and I couldn't refuse." Rafe gave a rueful smile, sweeping up a bag with napkins from a fast-food restaurant down on the coast road.

"You've been living on that? If I tell Jilly, she'll—"

"*Don't* tell Jilly. Whatever you do, spare me that. She's been sending me food at the station. The problem is, everybody else wants it. And Tom is looking thin. I've been giving most of it to him to take home."

Of course he would do that, Olivia thought. "I'm not a major-league cook like Jilly, but I can manage meat loaf and a creditable mac and cheese. I'll cook you something. There's no earthly reason for you to be living on fast food." She saw Rafe flush and push something onto the floor. Peeking over, Olivia saw a pillowcase wedged in the corner. She was pretty sure it was full of dirty clothes. "And you can give me those clothes to wash while you're at it. Once you finish moving in, you can take over cooking and laundry duty, but until then, I insist."

Rafe blew out a breath. "I keep meaning to get things set up at the house, but something always comes up. Still, the Laundromat downtown is fine. I wouldn't dream of—"

Olivia scooped the pillowcase up and moved it to her lap. "No more arguments. I'm taking this home and that's final." She drummed her fingers on the dashboard as they drove down darkened streets.

"Any idea when this power failure will be over? Was it a transformer problem or a weather problem?"

"We were told it was an equipment error. Somebody cut a line. They said to expect full service within six hours."

But that didn't make Olivia feel better, because her problem was not a simple equipment malfunction. "I still don't understand. If someone got into my attic, they had to use a ladder. Surely I or one of my neighbors would have noticed that."

"Not necessarily. I checked out the back porch. If you were agile enough, you could climb up that big apple tree and then jump to the roof of the porch. From there, it's possible to reach the dormer window at the back of the house. That would give you a pretty good vantage point to reach the attic."

Olivia didn't move, chilled by the picture Rafe had just painted. "I have to do something then. I hate to cut down that old tree but—"

"There's no need. One branch is enough. None of the others are big enough to stand on. I'll take care of it in the morning."

Olivia blew out a little breath. "Just show me the branch. I'll cut it down myself."

"With a shoulder still not healed?" Rafe shook his head. "Are you always this difficult, or is it just me that brings out the worst in you?"

Olivia stared out the front of the car, feeling the weight of his laundry in her lap. "Yes…and yes," she said, trying to hide a smile. "And thanks for dinner."

By the time they got home, Olivia had three voice messages waiting for her. The real estate agent named Andi wanted to swing by and check out the property for a price estimate. She said she had gotten the number from directory information and she sounded eager to move forward. Another message was from the mayor's wife. The third one was from the head of the bank. Both of them hoped to invite Olivia to lunch the following week. Olivia knew the real reason for the calls was to find out exactly what was going on between her and Rafe.

She decided to let them stew.

After she put away her coat, she went to make tea. "You don't have to stay here tonight, Rafe. I'll be fine."

He simply ignored her, moving to the back wall, where he tested the locks to the garage and back porch. "These things are too flimsy. I'll give you the name of a locksmith to call tomorrow to replace them. Now where's your security system?"

"What security system? I don't have one."

Rafe muttered under his breath. "You do now. That locksmith will get you set up. Here's the monitoring service I suggest." He scribbled a name and phone number on a small card near her phone. "This may be nothing, Livie, but you need to take it seriously. Get a security system set up and then use it. That means every time you go out you trigger it. When you're inside, you set it and keep the fob in your pocket. That's not a request. As your town law enforcement officer, that's an order." His voice was cold now. The look in his eyes made Olivia nod slowly.

"Okay. I will. But you're probably blowing this all out of proportion," she muttered.

She started to reach for the teakettle and was shocked to feel Rafe swing her around abruptly. His hands gripped her waist as he pushed her back against the wall. "Do you think I'm going to take *any* chances with your safety? Do you think I'm going to ignore this as a simple prank? I've worried about you every day since I left Summer Island. I thought about you and wondered how you were doing. I wanted to write, but I always tore up the letters. Most of all, I wanted to go back and change everything that happened between us." His voice was raw with emotion.

His hands tightened on her waist, and Olivia frowned at the sudden pressure. This made Rafe pull away.

His hands opened and closed at his sides. "You mattered to me. You always did. I think you always will matter to me, damn it. So don't treat this lightly and don't think I'll treat it lightly either," he said grimly.

Olivia cleared her throat. Her heart was pounding. Heat swirled through her face and became sensual awareness. She felt how close he was standing and caught his scent of coffee and aftershave.

What if she pulled him down and kissed him again? For real.

The naked hunger in his eyes told her that Rafe was thinking the same thing.

Olivia swallowed and then put a hand against his chest. "I'm not taking any of this lightly, Rafe. I'll… be careful."

"That's not what's bothering you. It's not what's bothering me either."

Her hand trembled. "You're right. But it's been a long day. I think we both need to sleep on this."

"I could sleep for a thousand years and it wouldn't make a bit of difference," he said hoarsely. He ran a hand along his neck and turned, tossing his jacket over one shoulder. "I'll sleep on the couch."

CHAPTER SIXTEEN

THAT WAS THE sane answer, of course.

Olivia knew that clearly. Getting a whole floor of the house between them was the best way to prevent any serious slips in judgment. But when she was curled in bed with the blankets tight around her face, sleep was completely impossible. How could she rest knowing that Rafe was one floor below her, and that he had been thinking of her all the time he was away in the Marines? How could she stop her feet from heading to the stairs so she could find out exactly where that last conversation would have taken them?

But Olivia was mature enough now to realize that simple sex with Rafe, as amazing as it might have been, would take them nowhere. She wanted more than an hour or two of pleasure. She wanted…

She couldn't put her finger on what she wanted. Her dreams had changed in the past weeks. She had also learned not to rely on anyone else to create her happiness.

But she was thinking about the old apple tree and moonlight dancing over Butterfly Cove and the strength of Rafe's lean body when she finally drifted off into troubled dreams.

OLIVIA WOKE UP half a dozen times in the next few hours. Something was close behind her, but she couldn't figure out what. In her dreams, she was on the old coast road and fog was moving in from a storm out at sea. The memory made her think of the storm and the car accident, but there was more at stake here.

She woke up, her heart pounding, her fingers digging into the blanket. The wind tossed pebbles at the big window overlooking the harbor. The noise must have woken her, Olivia thought. She listened but heard no other sounds. No one was in the house— no one other than Rafe, she reminded herself. She moved silently to the door and listened.

There was no sound. Just the stones, carried in the driving wind.

But curiosity locked her in its grip and she pulled a knitted shawl around her shoulders, moving silently down the winding staircase. She wanted to check on the house and be sure she had locked all the doors.

Then she saw Rafe, asleep on the couch.

His blue jeans were open at the waist. He wore nothing else, and Olivia saw the dark, chiseled sweep of his chest in the moonlight. The sight of him left her throat blocked. A sharp wave of desire made her knees go weak. She gripped the banister hard, listening to his low breathing. Only then did she realize Rafe was as restless as she had been. He lay tensely, his hands curved as if holding something heavy.

He muttered, and to Olivia it sounded like a low order.

She couldn't have turned away for any amount of money. Her feet moved down the steps, closer and closer, pulling her in a hypnotic spell as she struggled to make out what he was saying.

Another low order.

The words sounded like *target sighted.*

Something from the war. Some memory from Afghanistan, she thought.

Olivia couldn't turn away. She moved to the foot of the stairs, and with every step she was aware that she was bringing them both into danger and uncertain territory. She stopped, watching the rise and fall of his chest.

In a daze, she crossed the gleaming wood and then leaned down, captured by the fall of the moonlight and the clean citrus smell of Rafe's skin.

Claimed by yearning and bittersweet memories.

A board squeaked beneath her feet, and Rafe shot upright, circling her waist and yanking her down against his chest. Olivia gasped, the breath knocked out of her from the violence of his movement. He rolled her beneath him, his eyes dark with shadows, his body hard and impersonal.

Olivia knew she should have been frightened. But because this was Rafe and she had always loved him, she wasn't frightened. She didn't resist or make a sound.

She watched comprehension slowly fill his face,

saw his eyes narrow. One strong finger eased back a strand of hair from her cheek. She heard him curse softly. "What the hell are you doing here, Livie?"

"I...couldn't sleep. I heard a noise."

But he did not release her. "Are you okay?"

It took Olivia a moment to understand the question. He was worried that he had hurt her in his sudden force. "You mean, did you hurt me just now? You didn't."

A wave of air escaped from his locked lips. He seemed to be struggling to shake off dark memories.

"Rafe, I'm fine." She cleared her throat, feeling his thighs lock against her. "I heard a sound. You were moving in your sleep. That's all."

"That's all?" he repeated slowly. "I must have been damn noisy if I woke you up."

"You didn't wake me. I wasn't sleeping very well. I heard stones against the window, and I came down to check the doors."

Rafe rolled over and sat up quickly. "Was the noise from a window or from the attic?"

Olivia shook her head. She couldn't manage to find words, not when his jeans gaped open and she felt his skin warm against her arm. The harsh, masculine beauty of his body called out to her, and she shivered in intimate response.

What if they *could* go back? What if all the years of uncertainty and pain could simply fall away?

She reached out. Her trembling fingers moved along his chest, and the force of that simple touch made Olivia's breath catch. All her old, hungry memories came back and she realized then there had never been room for another man in her life. Rafe had filled up every part of it. There never would be another man in her future.

"Don't look at me that way, damn it." His voice was raw. "One of us had better be sane now. I don't think it's going to be me."

Her fingers locked on the long, finely knitted shawl. It seemed to give her strength and clarity. She had created every inch of the fine lace with looped and twisted threads of silk and alpaca. A voice whispered that she could create a future with Rafe from this moment, the same way she had worked the loving and careful stitches of the shawl. If they were very careful and very brave, it could happen.

"Do you want me to go? You want me to tell you that I don't want to be here pulling off your jeans until my skin melts all over you? Because I won't say that. I won't lie to you, Rafe. Tonight you said you'd thought about me every day since you were gone. Yet you never wrote and you never called. I tried to put you out of my life—and I almost managed to believe I had succeeded. But you were always there. You were a shadow in the twilight and a movement out of the corner of my eye at dawn. I saw you on the coast road. I heard your laughter on the beach." Olivia took a rough breath. "Now you're back and I'm not going to walk away from this. I'm not going to let *you* walk away from it either," she said flatly. "If you're too much of a coward to admit—"

He shot upright and in the space of a heartbeat she was flat against the wall, captured against the angry line of his body. "You're damn right I'm a coward. I've had too much time to think about what happened to us, Livie. We were oil and water. I was the bad kid from the wrong side of the tracks and you were the town's model citizen. We should never have felt anything for each other. But I'm not going to screw up your life again. The thought of giving you pain makes me a coward," he said grimly.

She stared back at him, her fists on his chest. "And you'll throw away everything we could have, all the future we could make together, because of the possibility that I might be hurt?" Anger began to burn through her. "Nothing is guaranteed in life. No weatherman, economist or spiritual adviser can give a certain answer about anything. I'm willing to stumble along, Rafe. We can work it out as we go. But if you're not interested…"

His hands opened, sliding into her hair; they tightened slowly to fists and his body locked against her. "Being interested isn't the problem, Livie. Feel what you do to me. I can barely think or breathe for wanting you." He pressed his thighs to hers and Olivia knew the full measure of his response. It was impossible to miss. "But I'm not offering you careless sex. I'm not interested in an hour here on the sofa. I want more. Do you understand?" He tilted her head back slowly and then sighed when his lips found the hollow beneath her ear. He goaded and searched, her name on his lips as he kissed his way lower. He kissed the pulse that throbbed at her throat. Then he leaned forward, resting an elbow against the wall, sliding his hand around her waist and pulling her against him.

Olivia didn't fight any part of it. She simply closed her eyes and followed the aching waves of sensation, knowing this was Rafe, this was the thing she had wanted for almost fifteen years, since she first understood what could happen between a man and a woman. She couldn't deny either of them its blinding conclusion.

"I'm not prepared, Livie." His voice was rough, raw with his effort at control. "I can't protect you. We need to stop here."

"I don't care about that. I want you, Rafe."

He stared at her, and his eyes were dark with hunger. Then he cursed. "You should care. You don't know where I've been or the things I've done."

"You're here now. You're with me. That's all that matters," she whispered. Her hands slid down, opening the waist of his jeans and Rafe choked out her name with a broken sound of satisfaction and anger. "We're not going to have sex, Livie. I'm telling you that flatly."

She didn't listen. She pushed the straining denim lower and searched the hard, muscled skin, finding her way by instinct in the moonlight. She felt him shudder and then her fingers closed along the fully aroused length of him.

She wanted him so badly that she almost cried out with the frustration of waiting. "Now, Rafe. I want you inside me."

His fingers fell, gripping her hands in their intimate caress. "Hell." He stood rigidly, his heart hammering for long moments. Olivia felt each beat, felt each bead of sweat on his forehead as he stared at her.

"Don't think, Rafe. Not now. Don't make me wait. I've waited my whole life for you," Olivia choked out, her voice breaking in its emotion.

"Honey. I never meant to hurt you. And I won't hurt you now," he said roughly. His lips moved to hers. The heat of their tongues joined as they took and gave pleasure in hungry movements. Olivia had the taste of him on her mouth and it drove her mad with need. She jerked blindly at his jeans and felt Rafe finish the job, so that he stood naked and aroused before her. Her breath caught at the beauty of his body and the unrestrained power of his response for her.

Her nightgown opened and fell to the floor, loosened by his deft fingers. All she wore now was the fine, knitted silk shawl that caressed her burning skin with the exquisite touch of a lover's fingers.

Rafe leaned down and kissed her through the fine silk. He found her hollows and teased the tips of her breasts and her aching thighs until Olivia couldn't breathe, couldn't think. She felt a breathless voice inside her, pleading for release, praying that she would finally know how her oldest fantasy was supposed to end. She wasn't prepared for the way his teeth bit at her earlobe. Her breath caught at the rough friction of his callused palms on her breasts. But he kept the whisper-light silk between them, watching her face with total focus as he made her skin burn with pleasure. In his unflinching honesty he let her see his own need in turn.

"You're the most beautiful woman I've ever seen, Livie. You were then. You still are." His hungry mouth whispered dark praise against her skin, sliding aside the silk scarf but never letting it fall, keeping it between them to fuel their blind desire.

"This isn't going to be fast and easy. Accept that or we stop right now. I've dreamed about this moment for too long to hurry this," he said harshly.

She couldn't frame a word that made any kind of sense. All she could do was nod.

"Well, then, let's make some history, honey."

Olivia's nails dug into his shoulders. She heard him give a little grunt.

"If it's good, you have to wait. And this is going to be far more than good." He curved her body backward, secure in his arms while he traced the line of her ribs, her stomach and the shadowed triangle between her legs. Olivia swallowed hard, unable to breathe as his fingers brushed gently across her aching skin.

And then the silk fell away. Instantly its light

warmth was replaced with his mouth. Rafe tasted and tongued her ribs, her breasts, until she caught back a moan of pleasure. She shuddered and raked her nails urgently over his shoulders.

But he didn't hurry. Not even when she pulled him down to kiss him, wet and blindly. His voice hardened with passion. "This is what I dreamed of at night, when the mountain passes were freezing and there was artillery fire in the distance. This is what I always wanted, and it kept me alive when nothing else could have. I'm giving you back those memories now, Livie. They're as precious as my life itself. They kept me from dying in a dozen ways and in a dozen dark hellholes. So let go, honey. Let me see you lose yourself in my arms and against the heat of my mouth." His voice turned raw. His eyes were chips of darkness as he gently brought his fingers inside her, whispering her name when she shuddered and gasped. Then her velvet skin closed around him, gripping tight while passion broke over her.

He was an expert lover, Olivia realized dimly. He read her eyes and her emotions, judging where to push her to greater pleasure. He gave her full honesty and took his pleasure the same way, hot and unhurried as he found a stroking path inside her.

It was nothing like what Olivia had expected. It was hot and raw and direct, blinding her senses. The way his eyes raked her skin left her embarrassed because she wasn't used to this kind of intimacy.

But it made no difference. She couldn't deny him

anything. Her eyelids fluttered. Her heart raced in a crazy dance as his fingers circled and withdrew, driving her up into a need that was never completely fulfilled.

"Please," she whispered, her voice shaking.

"Of course, Livie. All you had to do was ask me." His lips found hers. His hands worked their dark, dangerous magic against her.

And Olivia shivered blindly, lost in the grip of unimaginable joy.

Because this was Rafe. Because she had always loved him and always wanted him this way.

She whispered his name, drawing in the sight of his face and the passion in his eyes. She could feel the force of his focus and the care he was taking.

For a moment her old anxieties reemerged. They tormented her with angry doubts the way they had done for the past twenty years.

Who was she to think a man like this could love her or want her? She was too awkward, too anxious. Nothing had changed. She didn't *deserve* to be happy. She stiffened in his arms, and Rafe read the meaning of that movement instantly.

"Take this thing I'm offering, Livie. Don't think. Just take it. And then feel me. My hands. My mouth. Just let go. Do it now."

His rough voice melted over her, and suddenly the fear was gone. His mouth opened, nipping the sensitive line of her breast. His tongue followed, wet and circling and sure, driving her up into a blinding place she had never been before. When he muttered her name harshly, Olivia felt his fingers deepen their touch, opening against her.

He wants me, Olivia thought. *He wants us and everything we can find together.*

The knowledge made Olivia shudder. Then she fell, fell blindly, while passion and memories sang through her in a dark dance and a climax she could no longer resist.

CHAPTER SEVENTEEN

SILENCE.

Wind in the trees. The distant sound of waves crashing in the cove.

The old house creaked, full of memories in dark corners. Rafe felt Olivia's hands tremble as she leaned against him. He held her, half-propped against the wall, her body silver in the moonlight. Her hair fell over her cheek and he was certain he had never seen anything more beautiful. But where would they go now?

As if she had sensed his thoughts, Olivia's head tilted. Her eyes opened, half-dazed.

She cleared her throat. "I guess this is that part."

"What part?"

She took a slow breath. "Where you say this changes everything." She turned to face him, her eyes huge. "Go on. Say it."

"No." Rafe picked up on her mood. Her insecurity was returning, but he wouldn't let that happen. "I won't say that, Livie. Because good sex doesn't change everything. It's just the start. I want more."

Olivia's eyes darkened. "As in…a relationship?"

"Something like that." Rafe smiled slowly, tracing the line of her cheek.

Olivia was still wobbly, and she rested her arm around his shoulders for support. "But we agreed. It wasn't...supposed to happen."

"It *did* happen. Are you sorry?"

She swallowed hard. "No. Of course not. But where do we go from here? This is all—well, it's new to me, Rafe. But I guess you noticed that."

He slanted her face upward in the moonlight. "How new, Livie?"

She looked away. "Enough for this conversation to be embarrassing." When she shivered, Rafe draped her knitted shawl around her shoulders.

He slid his palm under her chin, his eyes intent. "How many relationships have you had?"

"Does it really matter?" Her voice was muffled.

"Oh, it matters a whole lot."

She gave a little shrug and reached for her nightgown. "A few. I forget."

"How many, Livie?" His voice was rough.

"I don't *know*. Three. Maybe a few more. Can we drop this subject now?"

"Fine. Where's your bedroom?"

"At the top of the stairs."

Rafe caught her in his arms, cutting her questions off cold. She felt her tension and awkwardness grow, as if the slow passion and surrender had been no more than a dream.

"You don't have to worry about intruders. I'll be right downstairs."

"You aren't…sleeping up here with me?"

"I think we both need a little space tonight. Besides, I need a clear head. If you're beside me, that won't be possible. And just for the record, I don't believe there were three men." Rafe pushed open her door with his foot. "I'm guessing not even two. Someday you'll tell me why there weren't more. You're a beautiful woman. Men must have been lined up at your door."

"Hardly."

Rafe slid her to the floor, his hands gentle. "We'll discuss that in the morning. It's going to be a long day. You'd better get some rest."

"I need a plan. So what is our plan?" Olivia sank onto the bed, her hair a dark cloud around her head. "Do we act like nothing has changed? Do we let everything turn moody and emotional? I just need to know."

"I'm working on a plan. Now get some rest. We have to leave early to visit that place up the coast. Tomorrow we can make sense of all this."

She looked at him and blinked. "Does that mean you're not going to…" Her fingers twisted at her waist. "That we aren't going to…"

"No, we aren't. Not tonight. I meant what I said, Livie. We're different now. I don't know about you, but I'm playing for keeps. I want more than a few hours of reckless sex on the sofa."

And he was going to get it, Rafe thought fiercely. This was the distant dream that had kept him focused on life during the grim decade he had spent surrounded by the violence and chaos of war.

Olivia looked confused—and a little wary.

"Trust me, Livie. This is the best way. Get some sleep."

Rafe had a sharp instinct that tomorrow could bring discoveries she wasn't going to like. Though he hadn't been a police officer for long, he had picked up a few things already. One of those was that you didn't keep a boat secret from friends and family unless you were doing something on that boat that you didn't want anyone else to know about. If that was true, Rafe would be right next to Olivia when she found out. She wouldn't face any painful discoveries alone.

He turned out the light and walked to the door.

"Rafe?"

"Right here."

"There weren't three." Olivia's voice was a whisper in the darkness. "Or two. There was only one man in my life. For all my life."

He stood in the doorway, feeling as if he had been kicked. He wanted to sink onto that big bed and teach her a wilder kind of passion. He wanted to wear the sweat of her body when he drove her over the edge.

But he didn't.

Tonight they needed to figure out where they had

come from and where they were going. They needed ground rules and a plan.

"There's only been one woman in my life, too. She's been in my blood so long that she's almost part of me now."

"Have you told her about this?" Olivia asked softly.

"Nope. I'm afraid I'll scare her off."

Olivia sighed. "I think you should tell her." Her voice was sleepy. "You never know. She might be tougher than you think."

THE OLD HOUSE creaked and settled.

Moonlight worked through sheer lace curtains. But Rafe didn't move, watching Olivia drift off into dreams.

This time he was going to do everything right. Rafe *did* have a plan, and seeing that Olivia Sullivan didn't get hurt was the most important part.

CHAPTER EIGHTEEN

PALE SUNLIGHT FELL across Olivia's face. She blinked, pulling the pillow over her head. Still half-asleep, she yawned, her body oddly relaxed as she stretched slowly. She couldn't remember the last time she had slept so well. And her dreams...

They had been silent, hungry, full of yearning images.

Olivia sat up sharply, remembering Rafe. *He* was what was different now.

All the things she remembered, the images that still burned through her head, had been far more than dreams. Last night—she had reached for her passion. And he had been expert and implacable in helping her to find it.

Her face flushed at warm memories of his callused hands sliding into urgent skin. The rough, hungry way he had said her name.

The way he had sensed her response and pulled her out of herself, encouraging her to take exactly what she wanted.

Dizzy with those memories, Olivia covered her face. It was almost too much to imagine. She had dreamed those moments again and again over the years, drawing comfort and hope from their hot, rich possibilities, and now that the reality was here it was too enormous to fit into her calm, organized little world.

Oh, yes, she definitely needed a plan for *this*.

She heard a light tap at the door and yanked the quilt up to her neck as the door opened slowly.

"Livie, are you up? We need to leave in an hour. I made coffee."

Olivia recognized the heavenly smell that had been teasing her senses. She sat up slowly. "Okay— I'm up. I'll be down in a few minutes."

"Is everything okay?" Rafe stood outside the door. He hadn't looked inside.

Olivia realized he was giving her the time and space that he seemed to put such value on. "I'm fine."

It was a lie. She was in turmoil. One part of her was delirious with happiness, determined to make sure that Rafe had the happy ending he deserved. But the dark, unhappy voice from her girlhood simply sneered. This *wasn't* going to work. It never did.

Olivia took a deep breath. No more negative talk. Her hands clenched on the quilt. First she needed coffee.

Then she needed a plan. "I'll get in the shower. Then I'll be right down. And then...I have a plan."

Actually, she didn't have a plan. But Olivia swore she would by the time she got downstairs.

MORE THAN A little giddy, she washed her hair, showered quickly and then stood, letting the water beat down on her face while she tried to come up with mature, sensible possibilities.

Only one made any sense.

They were going to have an affair. A dark, sweltering out-of-control affair. That's what they both needed. No soul-searching. No moral homilies or dreamy questions.

Just an affair. With no limits and no conditions placed on it by either of them.

She wasn't planning any further than that, Olivia decided.

With her eyes closed, she turned, searching for her towel. She met strong fingers instead.

"I've got your towel over here. That one fell and got soaked, so I brought you a new one."

Olivia's eyes were wide-open now. She was painfully aware of the long line of Rafe's body just beyond the shower curtain.

She discovered it was one thing to be rational when he was two floors below, but it was entirely different when he was standing close enough to touch. She watched his tanned fingers slide back the shower curtain and hold out a fresh towel.

"Is that coffee I smell?"

"Right here on the sink."

"Then forget about the towel. I need caffeine a whole lot more."

He gave a dry laugh. "It's not as good as Jilly's, but it's guaranteed to wake you up."

Olivia peered around the shower curtain. Rafe was

leaning against the wall, one hand in his pocket. His chest was bare, hazed with steam from her shower. Olivia was pretty sure that she lost use of half her brain cells when she saw the top two buttons of his jeans were unsnapped.

Hot possibilities hammered through her head, as seductive as the warm, damp steam playing over her naked skin. They had just put the space of a night between them. Surely that was enough time for reflection and calm.

There was no need to wait any longer.

The old Olivia, the awkward girl who had always thought too much and acted too little, would have stayed safely behind the shower curtain.

The new Olivia said *the hell with that.*

In one smooth movement she took the towel from him, swept it over his shoulders and circled his neck, pulling him toward her and kissing him with slow, searching heat. Her tongue played over his and Olivia smiled when his breath caught in a low, murmured curse.

His breath was ragged as he studied her face. "Livie, are you sure—"

"Shut up and kiss me."

And he did. The calm focus of the night before was gone. His hands slid all over her, damp with her dampness, and his mouth was hard, just on the edge of rough.

Olivia wouldn't have had it any other way.

She drove her nails along his back. She lifted her

knee and wrapped it around his thighs, pulling him against her. Rafe's eyes darkened. He picked her up, while she tightened her legs around him.

Slowly he pinned her against the steamy bathroom wall.

"Livie." He ground out the word hoarsely. "You know where we're headed. Any longer and we won't be turning back."

He was giving her a choice. A part of Olivia's dazed brain was moved by the thought. But the rest of her was irritated, frustrated by the delay. So she didn't bother to answer. She simply drove her body against him, slick, needy skin against slick, needy skin.

Olivia shuddered as she felt his jeans inch lower, pushed downward by the friction of their bodies. She heard the sound of her own breath, rough and fast as she raked her hand down his chest and then lower, into the gaping V at the waist of his jeans.

Touching him was heaven. Taking him within the circle of her fingers was the stuff of all her hot fantasies. Except Olivia was grown-up now. She knew exactly what those fantasies meant—and what would come next. She wanted *all* that.

"Livie, give me a minute."

She didn't want to give him a minute. Not a second. She needed this right now.

Then she realized she had said the words out loud. And to her shock, Olivia realized she didn't care a bit. She was tired of pretense. The need that held her, wrapped around the two of them, was all that mattered.

She felt him pull something from his pocket. His breath was harsh and labored. His jeans slid down and Olivia used her foot to shove them to the wet floor of the shower. She felt his body against her, chest to knees, chiseled with muscle. He was more beautiful than she could have imagined, and his need touched a lifetime of memories.

She took a broken breath and drove her body against him. She felt the hot pressure at her thighs, heard Rafe mutter, and then felt him push inside her. The taste of him was on her mouth and she felt the hammer of his heart beneath her hand, still pressed against his damp chest.

His arm locked around her waist. He slid the wet hair out of her face, his eyes very dark. "Look at me, honey. Look at me and know exactly what we're doing. I've wanted this longer than I can remember, and we're both going to have it now."

Olivia felt heat rip through her, swallowing reason and thought and planning. She wasn't ready, though she had thought she would be after all her years of fantasies.

She wasn't ready at all. Not for the heat. Not for the hint of pain that quickly gave way to a hot blindness as he moved inside her, deep and slow.

A wave of pleasure caught her, and she arched back in his arms, locking her hands on his shoulders.

She felt his lips at her forehead as he whispered her name and the world tore away beneath her.

OLIVIA'S HEART HAMMERED. Her breath was hoarse. Her legs locked around Rafe's waist as pleasure continued to spasm through her.

Even then Rafe didn't move.

He was too busy being a damn gentleman, Olivia realized. Even when he was deep inside her, so close to his own passionate release, he waited.

To hell with that, she thought.

She lifted her leg and pushed against him, shivering to feel the passion begin again. She drank in the darkness of his eyes at the moment that his control gave way. Olivia wouldn't give either of them time for more questions or obstacles. She gripped him with tight, intimate strokes and felt him lift her legs higher. "Livie, if I hurt you—"

"You're not. You're everything, Rafe. Just—don't stop."

He took a hitched breath. His hand opened on the wall, muscles clenched for control. Olivia felt him, smooth and hot and huge as he drove up, deep inside her, while fantasy wrapped trembling fingers around hot reality and their bodies became one, the way she had always dreamed they would.

When she looked at him, her heart seemed too fragile for all the emotions flooding over her. "Rafe," she whispered in one broken, aching voice.

His hand anchored her hips. "Right here, honey."

His hands were hard and sure as Olivia felt the pleasure rise to crest again. She was crazy with feeling him, crazy with waiting and all this was so completely unlike her that she should have been horrified.

Instead she was fearless. The hot certainty that this was Rafe holding her, taking her inexorably, made the last fiber of reason snap. Pleasure gripped her, their bodies wet and agile in each other's arms.

"Don't make me wait," Olivia rasped.

She felt the hammer of his heart. His mouth opened on her forehead. The dark, hungry words he said washed over her, and pleasure struck. Olivia rose in blind instinct, gripping his neck.

Rafe caught her hips and held her. His hands shook as he drove deep, caught with a hunger that had been too long unfulfilled. He speared his fingers through her hair, whispering her name.

Then he followed Olivia over the edge to his own shattering climax.

CHAPTER NINETEEN

STEAM SWIRLED THROUGH the quiet room.

Olivia took a slow, ragged breath and watched beads of water trickle down the tile wall. Her heart pounded. Her knees were ready to cave in.

She couldn't move a muscle. Their bodies were still locked, still pressed in intimate grip, and Olivia decided she'd like to stay this way forever.

Rafe's fingers trailed slowly over her shoulder. She felt him lean down and plant a kiss in her hair. "Are you ready to move?" he murmured.

"Give me a little time. A century or two should work."

His hand traced her cheek. "That's faster than I can." He caught her waist as she began to slide down the wall. "Is there something in the water here? Because that was—" Rafe laughed weakly. "That was like nothing I ever experienced. It's either the water or it's just you, Livie."

How was she supposed to answer that? And was this one of those moments when men rated their satisfaction? Olivia just didn't have the energy for it. "Is that a complaint?"

"Hell, no."

He slid their bodies together, letting the hot, wet friction stir in waves over Olivia's sensitized skin. "I'm so glad to hear it," she said weakly. Because her whole body seemed to be drained of energy, she hooked her arms around his head and let him hold her. The feeling of Rafe holding her was the best thing Olivia had ever felt.

He caught her leg with one hard hand, holding her steady when her knees grew weak. Even then, he was still inside her. She could feel the hot movements that followed his release.

His heart was still hammering. She felt it beneath her ear, and something about that made Olivia smile crookedly. So this was what sex with Rafe Russo, the Summer Island bad boy, was like.

Olivia had spent most of her girlhood wondering. A good deal of her adult life, too. Now she knew. She also knew that the reality was more amazing than anything she had ever dreamed about.

"I guess that's a game plan. It wasn't exactly what I had in mind, but I'm not complaining."

His lips moved to her hair, and Olivia heard his dry laugh. "It wasn't exactly what I had in mind either. But then I saw you and all that hot steam and I forgot everything else. It seemed like a good idea at the time. Hell, no man with a beating heart could have walked away from you, Livie. You tear my breath away."

"You always knew the right thing to say. I can see that hasn't changed."

"The way I feel about you hasn't changed. It never will," he said harshly. He ran a hand slowly along her leg and then anchored her waist. Carefully he brought her feet to the floor. When her knees gave way and she would have fallen, he held her upright.

Rafe took a rough breath and cursed softly. "We have to go, Livie. If we don't leave very soon, we're not going to get to the boat early enough."

She nodded, aware that this was very important. But for the life of her, she couldn't exactly remember why. The only important thing right now was the warmth of Rafe's body. "Right. The boat." She said the words slowly. If she worked hard, she might be able to remember the rest of it. "I'll go get dressed. Meet you downstairs."

Suddenly they heard a tapping on the floor below and the muted sound of voices.

Rafe's eyes hardened and he slid Olivia behind him. He grabbed his jeans from the tile floor and jerked them on. "Stay here."

Olivia opened her mouth, but she didn't argue. She realized that Rafe was in full threat mode. More muffled noises echoed from the stairway. Something scratched at Olivia's bedroom door, and it swung open.

Duffy, Jilly's white Samoyed, stood sniffing the air, studying the two of them intently.

"Livie, are you up yet? Walker and I are down here. We brought you breakfast. And coffee, too, I might add."

"Hell, how'd she get in?" Rafe's body seemed to lose some of its tension. But he looked acutely uncomfortable.

"She has a key. Don't worry, I'll go down first." Olivia took a long, lingering glance at the beads of water still trickling down Rafe's chest. Desire surged again, but she hammered it back ruthlessly. "You might want to button up your jeans and find a shirt," she said dryly. "Although I doubt that this situation will surprise Jilly very much."

Rafe stabbed a hand through his hair. "Shirt. Jeans. Roger that."

Olivia heard the confusion in his voice. Clearly, he had been hit as hard as she had been. She liked that idea very much.

She reached down for her clothes, folded on the edge of the bed and then called out to Duffy, "Did you come to see Aunt Livie? Are you ready for a run on the beach, big guy?"

The white dog barked loudly and then danced around Olivia in excited circles. She felt guilty when she realized there would be no time for a run or even a walk. She and Rafe would have to leave immediately if they wanted to beat Martin up the coast.

Without looking down, she shoved her blouse into her jeans and grabbed her shoes. "I'll be right down, Jilly," she called.

She glanced back at Rafe.

He was buttoning his jeans, but he seemed to sense her glance. Smiling slowly, he touched the tips of two fingers to his mouth. His dark eyes narrowed, running over her body.

And then he tossed her a little kiss.

Already head over heels, Olivia felt her heart drop even deeper into a dizzy, unsettling state that she was still not brave enough to call love.

"WALKER HAD to pick up more supplies at the hardware store and Duffy wanted a run on the beach, so I decided to come by and cook you breakfast. Where do you keep your—" Jilly turned around in the middle of her explanation, then stopped when she saw Olivia madly trying to tame the tangles from her hair. "Livie, what's going on?"

"Nothing. I'm fine. I'm perfect. Thank you for coming by to cook breakfast. The problem is, I have an appointment up the coast. We'll be late if we don't leave in five minutes."

Jilly frowned. "We?"

"Rafe and I. He thinks he should come along. We'll explain it all later," she said quickly.

Jilly walked across the room, shoved away Olivia's hands and studied the buttons that were completely mismatched on her blouse. "You and Rafe. Now that's interesting. Is he around here somewhere?"

"He's somewhere. Upstairs, I think. He came over early. He wanted to be sure that we weren't late."

"He came over early." Jilly cleared her throat. "Then get going. I have coffee in a thermos, and I made croissants this morning. Cream puffs, too. I'll pack them up for you to take along."

Olivia studied her energetic friend. This was a new level of hyper, even for Jilly. "Why were you up cooking cream puffs and croissants? It's barely seven-thirty now, Jilly."

Her friend shook her head mysteriously. "I guess that will have to wait." Jilly smiled as Rafe appeared in the doorway.

His jeans were buttoned, Olivia thought thankfully. And he was wearing a T-shirt.

But his feet were bare. She made a strangled sound, aware that Jilly was missing none of these details.

"Morning, Rafe. I brought you some croissants and hot coffee. Cream puffs, too. I couldn't sleep, so I got up to bake."

"Sorry to hear that you couldn't sleep, but those croissants are going to be great on our drive. Did Olivia tell you that we have to leave?" He glanced at the clock and muttered. "We have to leave five minutes ago, in fact."

After her friend walked outside, Olivia gathered up her cell phone and purse and locked the house in record time. When she crossed the front porch, she saw Jilly playing with Duffy on the lawn while Walker and Rafe stood on the driveway, talking.

"Sorry to run, Jilly. Thanks for all the food."

"No problem. Have a nice drive with Rafe. Just remember, you two are coming over for dinner tonight. I'm trying out a test menu." Jilly looked from one to the other, smiling faintly. "Don't be late. No matter how…distracted you are."

"WOULD YOU LOOK in on the house a couple of times today? Don't bring Jilly." Rafe's voice was low. "But bring Duffy. Let him run around and sniff."

Walker nodded, but his face was grave. "You want to explain why?"

"Not now. No time. We have to make this appointment. It's important, or I wouldn't ask." Rafe looked up at the porch, where Olivia and Jilly were talking. "Something's wrong here. I think it has to do with her father. Until I know, I'm taking no chances with her safety. Someone was in her house. The power was cut."

Walker's eyes darkened. "Understood. I'll swing by. I'll bring Duffy. Winslow, too. That dog doesn't miss anything."

CHAPTER TWENTY

OLIVIA COULDN'T KNIT. Too many possibilities and worries filled her head. She tried to calm her mind as Rafe drove through the quiet, twisting streets and then up the wooded coast. When she pulled out her current project, a lace shawl made of hand-dyed alpaca, the soft folds felt reassuring. "I suppose this could all get weird. I mean, people in town are watching us. They're…talking."

"Tell me about it," Rafe muttered.

"But let's forget about all that and enjoy each moment. If people have problems with us being together, then screw them." Olivia swallowed. "Did I just say that?" She looked off into the distance and smiled slowly. "I did. I just said that. And it felt really good."

Rafe slid his hand onto hers. "It sounded good to me, too. Just so it's on the table, I want a future with you, Olivia. It may not be neat and tidy and it may take us a while to figure out how we're going to manage it, but that's my game plan right now. A future. The one we've waited for for too long."

Olivia gripped his hand back. Because his touch was hard and strong, she faced a subject that she had been trying to avoid. "This boat of my father's.

You're pretty sure it's important because he didn't tell anyone about it. And that means…he was trying to hide something there. That's why you want to go along with me, in case there's a problem." She forced out each sentence, feeling a little dizzy, as if she was standing at the edge of a gorge and the land was falling away in front of her.

And she couldn't go back.

Rafe didn't answer. That told Olivia that she was right about the boat. "Okay. I'm ready for whatever we find. I think."

Rafe muttered something under his breath. Olivia thought it sounded angry, but she knew it wasn't aimed at her. "Aren't you going to knit? Jilly said you always knit."

Olivia didn't move. "Not today."

TWENTY MINUTES LATER they reached the address Martin Eaglewood had emailed Olivia. The dock was small, at the end of a nondescript little town. An unpainted pier ran down to a small cove with a dozen cars parked in the facing lot. A small trailer doubled as an office.

"This is *it?*" Olivia frowned. This wasn't her father's style at all. He liked luxury and brand names in everything he did. Status was crucial to him, and this place was depressing.

She started to get out, but Rafe put a hand on her shoulder. "I'll go get the key, Livie. Then we'll check out the boat together."

"But how can you get the key? I'm his daughter. Why would they give it to a stranger?"

"Because I'll explain that I'm a deputy with the Summer Island police and that I'm investigating a possible felony committed on the property." Rafe flashed his badge. "This opens a whole lot of doors."

"And you think there really was a felony committed here?"

"At the moment, I have no expectation of anything. I'm just doing what it takes to get us in and out fast."

Spoken like a seasoned soldier, Olivia thought. And she was glad to have him watching her back. "Okay. I'll wait for you. Just—don't take too long." Because she realized she might be losing her nerve.

RAFE WAS BACK in less than five minutes carrying a diagram that showed the location of every boat. As he walked beside Olivia, he kept his arm around her waist.

Comfort and reassurance, she realized. And she was intensely thankful for both.

When they came to the center of the dock, Olivia glanced down at the map and then up at the gray forty-foot boat docked before them. "This one?"

"That's the number. Your father had rented it for the past six years."

It looked unpainted. The deck was empty and the small windows were coated with grime.

No status at all. Somehow Olivia couldn't imagine her father ever putting foot on that deck.

"I'm ready. Let's go see what we can find."

Rafe moved ahead of her onto the deck. Olivia realized he was careful to stay in front of her.

She had a sudden awful thought. "There couldn't be a dead body or anything here, right? I mean—bodies go bad. It would…smell or something."

"Don't worry. No dead bodies. After a while you get to know that smell," he said quietly.

Olivia had another quick glimpse into the life Rafe had led for the past decade. She said nothing, but squeezed his hand. Then she followed him down the narrow steps to the lower rooms.

She rarely set foot on a boat because she got terribly seasick. Then Olivia had a strange thought. Her father knew she hated boats. He had always encouraged her to avoid anything to do with the water, reminding her how nauseated it made her. She wondered now if that was no accident.

When she looked up, Rafe was standing in the doorway of the small lower galley. His broad shoulders blocked her view. Olivia tried to look over, but he didn't move. "Rafe, what is it? What do you see?"

"Not much. Looks like nobody has been in here for a long time." He moved aside finally, and Olivia glanced around her at the single bed and chipped table. A small dresser stood beside a built-in cabinet with drawers, all the furniture cheaply made and showing signs of age.

No dead bodies.

Nothing horrible.

But there was gloom here along with something depressing. Olivia frowned. "Let's hurry. I don't want to be here any longer than we have to."

She walked past Rafe and swung open the door to the closet.

IT TOOK THEM less than ten minutes, working together, to examine every inch of the room. The only thing in the closet was a dry-cleaning bag with a quilt inside. Olivia recognized the blue-plaid design. It was definitely her father's. The plastic bag had the logo of Summer Island's only dry cleaner.

She glanced at the tag and saw that the invoice was dated almost two years before. "So this means my father hasn't been back here for two years? Is that right?"

"Probably. For now let's just look for information, rather than try to figure out what it means. You work better that way," he said slowly.

"He died barely a year ago. Why didn't he come back here? Do you think he…forgot?"

"I don't know, but it's part of the picture, honey. When we know that, we'll know everything else." Rafe was studying the small dresser with its built-in drawers.

"What's wrong? You've searched that dresser three times."

"Look at the bottom. There's at least a foot of

space there, but the drawer only goes down for about six inches. What about the other six inches?"

Olivia saw instantly what he meant. She leaned down and grabbed the handle and Rafe tried to stop her, but she shoved his hand away, yanked out the flimsy plywood drawer and looked inside. "There's a piece of wood in here. Thin wood. You could probably break it if you had to."

"Don't touch anything." The cold edge in Rafe's voice made Olivia frown.

He knelt down beside her, pulled on plastic gloves, and knocked the plywood carefully. They both heard a hollow ring as he tapped from front to back.

At the back the sound of the tapping changed. It grew muffled, because the space below was no longer empty.

Now that Rafe knew what he was looking for, he could work faster. He traced each side of the enclosure, searching for openings or metal springs. At the back-left corner, he found a small piece of metal jutting from the wood. When he pressed hard, the false floor of the cabinet gave way, revealing a gray metal box with a black lock.

Neither of them moved for long seconds. Rafe cleared his throat. "By all rights, we should be doing this differently. But you are his only remaining heir, so we're going to do it like this." Rafe lifted the metal box carefully and rested it on the dusty floor.

He studied the simple combination lock. "Any idea about the combination?"

Olivia shook her head.

"So it's a good thing I brought my trusty lock-decryption tool." Rafe reached into the canvas bag he had brought from the car and pulled out a narrow metal tube. He slide the end beneath the lock, twisted hard and the lock opened.

Then he looked at Olivia. "Are you sure you want to stay? I can do this. You can wait for me in the car if you—"

"Open the thing. Do it now," Olivia said grimly. Something felt wrong. She didn't understand anything about this place and she was determined to get answers.

Rafe nodded and opened the box, then lifted out a portable VCR player with a flip screen attached. It was an older model, but it looked nearly new, as if it had been well maintained. Next to it Olivia saw four video cartridges.

None of them bore markings of commercial releases. Their only marks were a neat set of dates marked in highlighter pen. The handwriting was her father's. Olivia recognized it immediately.

"Plug it in." Her voice was cold.

Rafe hesitated. "Olivia, you might not want to do that. Why don't you let me look at these first."

"He was my father and this was something he went to great trouble to hide. But I won't have any more secrets. I *need* to understand."

Rafe nodded slowly. He carried the player to the little table and chose one of the cassettes. He tried to reach the electrical outlet, but the cord was too short, so he leaned down, rummaging in his bag. "We need an extension cord. I have one out in the car. I'll go get it."

"Okay." Olivia sat down on the bed. She heard his feet tap up the stairs and cross the deck.

When she looked down, she noticed a closer outlet in the bottom of the wall, hidden behind the rickety desk chair. In growing impatience, she put the player on the floor, plugged it in and powered up the device. Everything seemed to work fine.

Then Olivia reached for the top video, slipped it into the player and pressed the play button.

CHAPTER TWENTY-ONE

OLIVIA SAT UNCOMFORTABLY in the dark room, waiting for the blank screen to vanish. Outside, she heard the sound of waves and seabirds. She wondered if Rafe had found his extension cord.

She also wondered why on earth her father had rented this boat and kept it a secret.

Then shadows began to move over the little flip screen. Olivia saw the grainy images change and resolve into white skin, dark gloves. She heard low, muffled laughter. Naked skin flashed by.

Her heart hammered as she recognized her father—with a woman who wore black gloves with metal studs. The gloves came down hard on naked skin, leaving a trail of blood. Olivia stared at the grainy images, frozen, not sure what she was seeing.

A hand touched her shoulder and she swung around with a gasp.

"It's just me, honey. You found an outlet?"

Rafe saw the screen and frowned. Then he moved in front of Olivia as the low laughter continued while leather and metal struck naked skin. A man's voice rose, pleading for more.

Her father's voice, in a way Olivia had never heard

it, broken and confused and weak. Olivia closed her eyes, too dizzy to stand up. Dimly she realized that Rafe had leaned down, flipping off the player.

"You should have waited, Livie."

"I saw the outlet and I thought I would try one of the videos." She gave a dry laugh. "How dangerous could that be?"

But the laughter became a bitter weight as she stared at the video and the dingy room. Sawyer Sullivan, the powerful mayor and shrewd real estate developer, had been a man of taste. But this was a different man entirely. How could you keep two lives separate and not go completely mad?

"I think we're done here," Rafe said flatly. "I'm taking you back to the car. I want you to stay there, Livie. I'll get everything from this room and bring it along with me."

"You don't have to be involved. This is…my problem."

"I've been involved since the first day I saw you. I think I stalked you as a grubby nine-year-old coming home from the library."

"I know. I saw you there on the steps wearing baggy jeans and carrying a baseball glove. I thought you were…cute." Olivia was pretty sure he had brought the subject up to distract her, but she managed a smile. She still remembered Rafe in those torn blue jeans, trailing home after her in the twilight.

She touched his cheek gently. "In case you didn't get the memo, you're not grubby now, Deputy. You're quite a hunk, as any woman will tell you. And I'm glad you're here because, frankly, this whole thing with my father and these videotapes is really… creeping me out." She tried to keep her voice light but failed. "Don't leave anything behind for someone else to find."

"I'm taking all of it, don't worry."

"I don't want to see anything more," she said stiffly. "But if there's other information in those videos that could explain what he did with his money… with *our* money—"

"I'll check them. Meanwhile, you probably should talk to someone. Talking can be good."

What she had seen could leave scars, Olivia knew. It definitely raised deep questions. Her father, always in control, always the dominator and the manipulator, had carefully hidden a life where he chose a very different role.

But she didn't want to think about that now. The thought of confiding in anyone except Rafe left her queasy. "Did he really…enjoy that? He was always so strict with me. Everything I did was wrong. My skirts were too short, my sweaters were too tight. But they weren't and I *know* they weren't, because Grace and Caro could wear the same kind of clothes." Her eyes hardened. "And then there were those things he said about you, about how you only wanted to be around me for sex. That I couldn't trust you."

Rafe finished loading up the videos and swung the big bag over his shoulder. He studied the room and then walked to the door. "He was dead wrong, Livie. And now we're done here. Let's go."

But Olivia couldn't move. She was trying to make sense of years of pain—her own and possibly her father's. "I hate that he had to do something like that. That he needed to be hurt."

Rafe slid an arm around her waist. "He didn't trust people very much, not even you. Maybe he didn't trust himself either. I'm sorry for him," Rafe said quietly.

"Why?"

"Because when you stop trusting, you stop living."

THE DUFFEL BAG was stowed in Rafe's trunk when Martin Eaglewood drove up in his late-model Lincoln. His smile slipped when he saw Rafe cross the pier.

The two men shook hands. Then Sawyer Sullivan's adviser walked back to Olivia. "I don't understand. You aren't coming to see the boat? Have you already been there?"

"We got here a little early, Martin. The man at the desk gave us the key."

"I take it that you didn't find anything worthwhile?"

"Just a dry-cleaning bag with an old quilt inside. It was from the Summer Island dry cleaner," Olivia said slowly.

The older man looked off toward the sea. "So

there was nothing else. This was a wild-goose chase. I'm sorry there wasn't anything in there to help you."

"So are we." Rafe leaned down and glanced at the backseat. "I don't see my cell phone. I must have left it on the boat." He started down the pier and then glanced back at Martin Eaglewood. "Why don't you come along, since you're here."

The tall man shoved his hands into his pockets. "Sure. Since I'm already here."

Olivia frowned as the two men crossed the dock. She was pretty sure that Rafe hadn't left his cell phone in the boat. There had been a hard look in his eyes when he left.

She wondered what he expected to find out from Martin Eaglewood.

THE TALL MAN with silver hair glanced around the boat. "This one?"

"That's what they told us." Rafe opened the door. "Go on downstairs."

Eaglewood seemed relieved as he glanced through the empty bedroom. "Nothing here. You're right. It doesn't look like anyone lived here."

Then he made a hard sound of anger as Rafe turned him around. "What are you doing?" he demanded.

"You knew about this boat. You knew about the rest of it, too."

Eaglewood cleared his throat nervously. "Okay, okay, I knew. Sawyer was into some kinky stuff. He always came here to the boat because no one knew him here. He figured it would be safe."

"How many others knew about this?"

"No one. Just me. He always wanted cash to pay for…whatever he needed. I got the cash for him and I didn't ask questions. That was the arrangement." The man rubbed his neck. "And if you're wondering if I was involved, the answer is *no*. I'm not into that stuff."

"Somebody else knew," Rafe said quietly. "The people who shared this room with him would have known."

"I guess so."

"His money vanished somehow. It would have been your job to trace where it went. I think you need to work harder on that. How many clients would you lose if Olivia Sullivan filed professional misconduct charges against you?"

Eaglewood's face went white. "Don't even talk about it. I'd be ruined. This business is all word of mouth."

"Too bad." Rafe turned to go.

"*Wait.* I—I knew something was going on here. I knew it was dark and that Sawyer didn't want Olivia to see it." He glanced back over the dock toward Rafe's car. "He wanted a son, you know? Someone to take on his real estate business. I never could persuade him that a daughter would be just as good. He brushed away any idea of working with her. And Olivia was always so polite, so smart, so…capable.

She just wanted him to show a little affection." He frowned. "I'm not sure Sawyer could." He ran a hand over his eyes. "So how can I help?"

"Needless to say, this stays right here in this room. For his sake and for Olivia's sake. But I'm counting on you to start digging. See if you can track who he spent time with. Where he traveled and if he had bank accounts there."

Eaglewood nodded quickly. "I'll try. Just...make sure she doesn't file any charges."

"Then work fast. Olivia and I are both getting impatient. When our patience wears out, you can expect a visit from me. And I'll be in uniform," Rafe said flatly.

"DID YOU FIND IT?"

"Find what?"

"Your cell phone." Olivia raised an eyebrow. "You said you left it on the boat."

"It was there, under the desk. I must have dropped it," Rafe muttered.

"You didn't forget your cell phone. It's here in the glove compartment. Why did you lie and make him go back there with you?"

Rafe tapped two fingers on the steering wheel. "You really want to know?"

"I want to know. More than that, I *need* to know."

When Rafe filled her in on the conversation with her father's financial adviser, her face went pale.

"Martin knew about this thing that my father did? He was involved, too?"

"He said he just supplied cash. My sense is he was telling the truth about that. According to Martin, no one else in town knew. Your father made certain of that. That's why he came here."

"He traveled twice a year. He said it was for business or political conventions. He never told me the names of anyone he met at these conventions." Olivia's fingers moved restlessly in her lap.

Rafe leaned over and took her hand in his. "We'll figure this out. Martin will see if he can track who your father had been involved with. Maybe it will lead us to where he put those accounts."

"If there *are* any accounts." Olivia sighed. "So what do we do now?

We. Rafe liked the sound of that. He liked being included in Olivia's future. He glanced back and watched Martin Eaglewood walk into the rental office. "We're done here. Martin is going to ask some questions, but you won't be coming back to this place, so now you should relax. Try this."

Rafe handed Olivia her knitting bag. He lifted her needles and project and placed them carefully in her lap.

Olivia took the soft yarn, but she didn't pick up her needles. "I need the truth, Rafe. It isn't just about the money. I need to know about my father's state of mind because he's part of me. He always will be."

And then she picked up her needles. When

her hands shook a little, she frowned and took a deep breath, starting over until the stitches moved smoothly. Rafe saw the skill and experience that went into each stitch.

"You're pretty amazing. Do you know that, Livie?"

She glanced up, surprised. *"Me?"*

Rafe touched her cheek. "Damn right."

Olivia didn't answer. Clouds were coming in as she stared south along the coast road, through the trees that hid Summer Island.

CHAPTER TWENTY-TWO

OLIVIA FROWNED AT the twisting road. Fog swirled, tangled in the dense branches of pine trees that hugged the cliffs. It was barely noon, but the sky had turned dark.

Olivia felt jagged and surreal, as if a part of her was here in the car, watching the breakers out at sea, while another part sat in the gloom aboard that depressing boat, trying to understand who her father had really been. Maybe everyone had secret lives, she thought. Did it really matter?

"The tape...it didn't shock you?"

"It wasn't illegal, Livie."

"But it *was* painful. Okay, I just made a joke." She let out a slow breath. "I must be feeling better."

"If you really want to know, what I felt was disappointment. Your father can't have been very happy if he was living like that, with two parts of him cut up and separated so completely. And if he wasn't happy, *that* affected you." Rafe frowned. "I never saw him act warm or encouraging to you, and I hated that," he said grimly. "I thought he might be different when I wasn't around."

"Not really." Had her father's distance and disapproval been so obvious? Had everyone in town watched her, hiding their pity?

Had Rafe pitied her, too?

RAFE WAS HUNGRY by the time they reached the little outdoor restaurant by the beach. He had worked here briefly as a teenager, and he knew the menu well. Though the owners were new, the place still made the best fish tacos south of Seattle. And you couldn't beat the view from a picnic table overlooking the cove. The restaurant wasn't flashy or pretentious, Rafe thought. He was pretty sure that Olivia would enjoy it.

"So explain this whole knitting thing, will you? I get the part about having finished garments that you've made yourself. I get the thing about choosing your own colors. But it's pretty expensive, right? When Jilly unpacked that shipment of yarn for the Harbor House, she told me a sweater in some of that yarn could eat up a whole paycheck."

This brought a laugh from Olivia. "She's right. There's a reason we call some of that stuff *crack yarn*."

"Just promise me there will be no laws broken. Otherwise I might have to come over and investigate." Rafe passed her a full plate with guacamole, chips and fish tacos. "This is another thing I kept thinking about while I was gone. Nobody can make guacamole like this. Don't tell Jilly, but I have the chef's recipe. I think this guy even grows his own peppers and avocados."

"My lips are sealed." Olivia toyed with a piece of her taco. "Do you like to cook?"

"I like to *eat*," Rafe said dryly. "Learning to cook was self-preservation."

"You're smart, much smarter than most people realize. You always tried to hide it growing up. You used to race up Main Street on your motorcycle and delight at all the angry faces. You got Cs when you could have gotten As. You played sports, and then you quit. All the other parents were furious and called you lazy. Or worse."

"Maybe they were right."

"No. You were *bored*. That was always your problem. All that rah-rah stuff with the cheerleaders and the pep rallies held no interest for you. So you jumped on your big motorcycle and roared away up the coast."

"Things were hard then. I got hard along with them," Rafe said quietly. He looked down, surprised when Olivia linked her fingers through his. And then she kissed his hand slowly.

Instantly all the desire was back, blinding him the way it had that morning. All it took was one look, one touch.

"I'd like to ask you one thing." Olivia's mouth was firm as she stared back at him. "I don't want you to look at me and see the mayor's daughter or the town good girl. I'm asking for you to look at me and see the woman I want to be, Rafe. There are things that I want to know about. Things I would *only* trust you to show me. And that's what I'm asking for. Because I trust you—I more than trust you."

Rafe didn't quite trust his voice to answer. "More than trust?"

"I love you. I always have."

Rafe took a deep breath, trying to process what she had just told him. "Sweet, wonderful Livie. You've always been the only woman in my life."

Olivia looked down at her tray and then calmly wrapped up her remaining food. "That was good. Can we go now?"

She didn't wait for his answer. But there was something very determined in the set of her shoulders, Rafe thought.

THE TEMPERATURE HAD fallen twenty degrees by the time they reached the turnoff for Summer Island. Heavy fog twisted through the dark pines and Rafe slowed for each hairpin turn. Olivia was half-asleep beside him, with his jacket over her shoulders.

Suddenly a truck whined behind them. She sat up with a start.

"What's wrong?"

"Nothing. It's just a truck." Rafe glanced into his rearview mirror. "But it's a truck driven by an idiot. This road is way too narrow to play chicken, and the fog sure isn't helping. What does he think he's doing?"

Behind them a dusty white truck moved back and forth, flashing his brights and trying to pass. Ahead of them the road curved sharply. As soon as they were beyond the curve, Rafe pulled sideways, and the white truck shot forward. As he passed, he honked loudly, nearly clipping Rafe's car as he shot into the fog.

"There's stupid and there's *dangerous*. I think that driver just slid into the dangerous category." Frowning, Rafe reached into the glove compartment for his emergency amber strobe beacon. He clipped in the power cable and put the strobe on top of the car. "I'm sorry, Livie, but we're in Summer Island jurisdiction here. That idiot is going to get somebody killed."

"Do whatever you have to do. He's driving really crazy now."

Ahead of them the white truck was skidding back and forth across the road. Waiting for a straight stretch, Rafe pushed up his speed, coming close enough that the amber beacon light had to be visible.

But the truck shot forward and vanished around the hairpin turn high above the ocean.

CHAPTER TWENTY-THREE

MOST PEOPLE LOOKED up nervously when they saw a cop show a badge outside their car. They managed to fake an expression of surprise and innocence. "Gee, is there a problem, Officer?" Never mind that they were going seventy in a twenty-five-mile-per-hour zone.

But this guy was very cool, Rafe saw. No eye contact. No wriggling in the seat. No sign of nerves.

Rafe scanned the interior and saw no firearms. No open liquor in view and no drugs evident. "License and registration, please."

Again there was no surprise or awkward attempt at humor. "In my glove compartment. I'm going to open it now."

"That's fine."

The papers were all in order. No violations noted. Rafe took his time, registering the details, looking for anything that could signal a problem. "Are you in a hurry, sir?"

This brought a quick snap of eye contact. "I don't know what you mean."

"You just passed me going upward of seventy on

a dangerous stretch of coastal road. That would indicate you're in a hurry."

"I didn't know you were a cop. And—I didn't realize I was going that fast either," the man added quickly. His fingers opened and closed once on the steering wheel.

"Something making you drive in such a hurry, Mr.—" Rafe checked the registration. "Mr. Connors."

"I'm going home. I've been away for six years, and I'm...pretty excited."

He didn't look excited, Rafe thought. He looked determined. Some of what he was saying was true and some of it sounded false. "Working in another state?"

"Yeah. The job situation here in Oregon sucks. I was lucky to get hired on down in San Diego."

Rafe had seen that bad economy for himself. Unfortunately, too many young people had to leave the coast to find work. The only major employers nearby were in the tourism sector, and that wasn't everybody's cup of tea.

Rafe scanned the inside of the car again. Everything was neat. Only a canvas backpack and a bottle of water. He felt the man's impatience, but there were no signs of fear or guilt. There were also no signs of alcohol, drugs or firearms. Nothing illegal at all.

Rafe decided to cut him some slack. After all, he knew how excited a man could feel going home after years away. "You have a woman waiting for you, Mr. Connors?"

"Yes, sir. I do."

"And she lives on Summer Island?"

"That's right."

"Then I advise you to slow down and drive safely so you can make it home for dinner," Rafe said flatly.

The man hesitated. "So I can go now?"

His eyes were relieved. Rafe picked that up, but not much else. "You can go. Here's a ticket for speeding. You'll need to take care of that on Monday morning." He handed a folded paper through the open window. "Enjoy your stay on Summer Island, Mr. Connors. And don't let me see you speeding again."

The big fingers opened and closed on the wheel again. "Thank you, Officer. I'll watch my speed. You can count on it."

Rafe watched him drive away. Then he called in the license and registration to the dispatcher. He wanted the citation on record, and since he didn't have his cruiser, he couldn't run the plates himself.

When he walked back to the car, Olivia was sitting up very straight, looking concerned. "Is everything okay?"

"Just fine."

"So what are we doing now?"

"We're going home. And then, Ms. Sullivan, I plan to cook you dinner."

RAFE WASN'T BROOKING any kind of argument. Livie was going upstairs to rest.

She looked surprised at his insistence, but her forced smile told Rafe that she needed a chance to regroup. He would give her the space to do that.

But first Rafe had to tell her something, and he knew it was going to hurt.

While she washed her face, he stood beside the bed and glanced at all the framed photos on her desk. Her whole past was in those pictures. All the laughter and all the memories of four amazing girls who grew up to be four amazing women. They had always planned their futures together, four friends with gigantic dreams.

Rafe was glad that Livie had friends like that. When you had friends like that watching your back, the world was a much kinder place.

When she was settled beneath a big quilt, Rafe sat down beside her and cleared his throat. "Livie, there's something you need to know. I didn't tell you before because it doesn't put me in such a good light. Your father doesn't look so good either. But I guess it's time you knew all of it. The fact is, he set it all up. It was his plan. But I could have said no." Hell, he was making a mess of this already. How was he supposed to explain?

"You could have said no to what? What did my father set up, Rafe?"

He ran a hand along his neck, trying to focus his thoughts. Going back into the dusty corridor of his memories was harder than he expected. "By every rule in the book, you should hate me. After all, I left you without a word of explanation. I stood you up on your prom night, something you'd been dreaming about for weeks. Everything was arranged. Your dress. Your shoes. Caro was going to do your hair. I remember all that and I know how excited you were."

Olivia frowned at him. "She did my hair up in a twist. I borrowed her grandmother's garnet necklace. Then you didn't come. I sat by the front door for three hours and you never came." Olivia looked away. "My father said…he told me that you said proms were for kids and you didn't have time for that."

"I said nothing like that, Livie. He lied." Rafe's voice hardened. "The truth is that I did a stupid thing the night before. I went out driving with some friends, and one of their brothers showed up, talking about a way we could make a whole lot of money. There was a car—all we had to do was drive it to Portland to a friend's garage. He would pay us each a thousand dollars. It was just a lark, he said. And we agreed."

Rafe shook his head. The disgust was still with him. "Except it was a *stolen* car and we were picked up. And that was my second arrest, Livie. The first time—"

"You stole a pack of Cokes off a truck at the loading dock. I know all about that. It wasn't important."

"I'd broken some windows, too." Rafe cleared his

throat, but the bad memories weren't so easy to shake off. "I was very stupid then, Livie. I needed someone to knock sense into me. The second time I got into trouble, it was the real deal. That car we drove had been used in an armed robbery that very morning. And that meant all of us were suddenly accessories in a felony."

"But *you* didn't know that."

"The police didn't see it that way. And your father, who happened to be the mayor, didn't see it that way either. He came to see me in jail and told me he had a solution. I wouldn't do time and he'd keep my record clean. In return, I was going straight to Portland. I would stay there for a month until I turned eighteen. Then I was going right into the Marines. I wasn't to come back to Summer Island or to try to contact you. That was the deal, Livie. I was angry and I was frightened and I was stupid. So I said yes."

Rafe had expected her to flinch or be angry. What he didn't expect was her sigh. She slid her fingers through his. "So *that's* what happened. That's why you didn't come that night and why you never called me," she whispered.

"I couldn't. If I did, your father said I would go right to jail. My friends would go there, too. So I did just what he said. I hated the way it would hurt you, but I did it anyway. I was a kid and I was stupid."

"He didn't give you much choice. At least I know the details now. My father seemed so happy that whole year. He was smug. I understand why. He had managed to separate the two of us." Olivia turned and picked up the one framed picture of her father on her nightstand. She frowned at it for a long time and then turned it over, leaving it facedown on the table. "He didn't want me to be happy. He didn't want me to be strong or confident or curious. Then I might leave and have a life without him. He couldn't accept that possibility," she said coldly. "If there was a meeting or a party or an interview, he told me to stay in the back and be quiet. He told me no one wanted to hear what I thought because what I thought didn't matter to anyone. He said that my only value was as his daughter. There, I said it. I never told anyone that before." Her voice shook. "And you know what the worst part is? After a while, I believed him."

Rafe looked down, furious. How could any father say something like that to his own child?

"He didn't care about me. He wanted to be powerful and have people do what he told them. I think he was afraid of letting anyone get close to him. Maybe the only way he could was…by giving up his control the way he did in that video." Olivia stared at the pictures, at the one picture turned facedown. "I'm glad you told me, Rafe. It was a terrible choice that you had to make. And it sounds exactly like something my father would do. If you had told me then, I would have run away, Rafe. I would have gone anywhere you wanted and never looked back."

"You were fifteen, Livie. I was broke and in trouble. What kind of life could I have given you then?

You would have ended up pregnant and I'd have landed in jail." Rafe's voice was harsh as he turned their linked hands over and then raised her palm to his lips. "No, your father was right that time. I needed to go away and become a man. You needed to stay here on the island and find someone who could make you happy."

"But I didn't find anyone. Not once." Olivia's eyes glistened. "Not until now. And we've both grown up, Rafe. We can handle hard choices when we need to." She took a deep breath and then smiled at him. "I think it's about time we got this thing right."

Her fingers tightened. She pulled him toward her.

Her breathing was fast and Rafe felt the heat of her skin. He wanted to give her more time. He wanted her to be clear when she chose whatever came next. He didn't want the shadows of her father's choices to hang over their lives any longer.

But it appeared that Olivia was as stubborn as ever. She slid her hands over his shoulders. "This is my choice. I want you in my life and beside me on this bed. Touch me, Rafe. I'm ready for whatever happens next. My father is not going to ruin this."

Rafe was pretty sure there were a lot of reasons that he should stand up and walk out of the room.

But his heart wasn't in it.

His heart was right here, with Olivia. So he slid down over her, feeling her instant response. And Rafe let his heart lead for once instead of his mind, while Livie matched him heartbeat for heartbeat, need to need, so fierce and honest that she broke his heart.

And then she made it whole again when she took him deep inside her. Rafe followed, and he didn't look back. *You can't stop trusting and you can't forget your dreams,* he thought. And this was the only dream that had ever mattered. For a long time the Marines had been his home. He had made his closest friendships there and had learned how to become a man amid the dust and the gunfire and the fear.

Now Rafe left behind his pain and regrets and replaced them with all the pent-up passion of a decade, watching Olivia shiver, her eyes hazed with shock and delight at the hot touch of his mouth and his tongue.

He took her there in the silent house, feeling the weight of hard memories burn away into brighter dreams, while the last sunlight brushed the winding streets and glinted over the old coast road.

CHAPTER TWENTY-FOUR

FOR A LONG time Rafe simply watched Olivia sleep.

When she twisted restlessly, he ran a hand over her forehead until she sighed and drifted back down into dreams. Even asleep, she curled toward him, searching for his warmth.

Rafe felt something slide in beneath his distance and his cynicism. The thing felt fragile and raw, newly sprouted. He was pretty sure it was a sense of peace and security and homecoming, the first time he had felt those things in his troubled life.

He stood up carefully. He found his clothes, dressed and padded down the stairs. He was pretty sure he had a crooked grin on his face.

She was going to be ravenous when she woke up, and Rafe had the answer for that. Chipotle macaroni and cheese with roasted poblano guacamole and freshly fried corn chips.

Jilly was a master chef, but Rafe had his own skills. He had made enough money to survive during those weeks before he had joined the Marines, working at little restaurants along the coast where you were always paid in cash.

Down in the kitchen Rafe stood silently, taking in

the order of the room. All the tile counters were pristine. Canisters were neatly labeled, and the counters shone. Everything was in its place.

He flipped a dish towel over his bare shoulder and studied the contents of the refrigerator. He hated fast food and he liked the idea of taking care of himself. He was going to enjoy taking care of Olivia now.

The refrigerator was full of food marked with dates and ingredients. Rafe smiled at Olivia's clear handwriting on the labeled bags.

He rummaged through the well-stocked pantry and then pulled out pasta and spices. He found dried peppers and added them to the pile.

He didn't indulge in false modesty. His chipotle macaroni and cheese was irresistible, and he was going to love seeing Olivia's face when she tasted it.

TWENTY MINUTES LATER water was boiling, the cheese was grated and freshly roasted peppers lay on the counter, filling the house with a dark, smoky scent. Rafe took down the good crystal he found in a cabinet, along with blue-and-white china plates and real damask napkins. He set the small table by the big picture window carefully while the pasta cooked. In a cabinet near the pantry he found a merlot that would stand up perfectly against the heat of the macaroni and cheese.

He stiffened as a shadow crossed the front porch. A key jangled at the front door. Rafe drew back into the pantry so he couldn't be seen.

The front door opened. "Livie, are you home?" The shadow formed into Jilly, who strode through the foyer and stopped in the doorway to the kitchen. She frowned at Rafe and then eyed the food on the counter. "Are you *cooking?*"

"Why? Is it a capital offense?"

Jilly moved into the room. "The way you do it could be."

"Do all chefs have an ego the size of Montana or is it just you?"

Jilly smiled at him. "Yes."

"Livie's upstairs asleep. She had a tough day." Rafe turned away to stir the pasta, which had begun to boil.

"You really can cook, can't you?" Jilly moved closer, looking over his shoulder. "Macaroni and cheese? With roasted poblanos?"

"The poblanos are for the guacamole. I'm using chipotle in the macaroni and cheese."

"Very nice. I just may steal that." She leaned back against the counter, scrutinizing Rafe from his bare feet up to his bare chest and tousled hair. "This is interesting. You were here this morning when we arrived. Now you're cooking in the kitchen, barefoot, as if you own the place. I'm going to take that as a sign that things between you and Olivia are no longer casual. Because if not, you shouldn't be sleeping with her."

"Who said that we were—"

"Get real, Rafe. You think I couldn't tell something like that?" Jilly frowned at him.

Of course she could tell. All Olivia's friends would be able to tell, Rafe thought grimly. "It's serious, Jilly."

"Glad to hear it. It took you two long enough. But I'm only going to say one thing to you. If you hurt Olivia or betray her trust in any way, I'll kick that hunky ass of yours all the way up the coast road and over to Portland. Is that understood?"

"It's understood. But I'm not going to hurt her." Rafe stared hard at Jilly. "Exactly the opposite."

After a long time Jilly nodded. "Glad to hear that. It's about time she had a man to watch her back."

And then with her usual mercurial change of moods she swung around, studying the ingredients on the counter. "So you really did learn to cook while you were gone. When did this earthshaking event occur?"

"News flash, Iron Chef. We lowly mortals can stumble along in the kitchen when we have to."

Jilly touched the dishes lined up neatly beside the row of spices that Rafe had assembled. "You can do more than stumble along. Is that your recipe?"

He nodded.

"Okay, now I'm curious. Are you going to share it with me?"

Rafe made a big deal of considering it. "I might. If you share your Mayan cinnamon and chipotle brownie recipe with me."

Jilly crossed her arms. "I'll think about it. But that brownie recipe is going to make me a whole lot of money when I get my webstore set up." Her smile faded. "Not that I'll be having brownies for a long time." She stopped abruptly and looked away.

"Why not? What's going on?"

"Never *mind*," she muttered. "Forget I said that."

"Spill the rest of it, Jilly."

She sighed and paced the kitchen. "I wasn't going to mention it until tonight. The fact is— Oh, hell. I'm pregnant, Rafe. I just found out. And I'm terrified," she muttered.

"I don't understand. You don't want a baby?"

"Of *course* I want a baby. I'm thrilled and Walker is over the moon at being a father. But I don't think this baby that we're making will want *me*. I'm no good at maternal stuff. Nurturing is beyond me. Playdates and birthday parties would terrify me. How could I possibly be a good mother?"

Rafe waved a hand, cutting off her breathless litany of expected failures. "Stow it, Jilly. You'll be the best mother on Summer Island, you idiot. You'll have the best Halloween parties and the most exciting sleepovers. You'll be the cool parents that all the other kids wished they had."

Jilly brightened considerably. She gave a mock punch to Rafe's chest. "You're kidding, right? Wait— if you're kidding, don't tell me. Because that's probably the nicest thing anybody's ever said." She frowned and ran a hand through her hair. "And if you'd stop distracting me by being so nice, I would remember to be angry. You two were supposed to come over for dinner, remember? Everybody should be there shortly. They're expecting you to show up, too. That's why I came over to see what was going on when you didn't call. Grace and Noah will only be in town tonight. Then Noah has to go back to San Francisco, and I really want you to meet him."

"I'll try, Jilly, but Olivia had a tough day. We found some things out on the boat, and she has got a lot to think through."

"What kind of things?"

Rafe shrugged. "You can ask her. I know it would be good for Olivia to talk to you about it."

"It sounds serious."

"It's as serious as she'll let it be. Myself, I think it's nothing so bad. But I'm not Olivia. I've always thought she was a little bit fragile. Now I don't think she's fragile at all. I think under that quiet facade, she's one tough woman. But she needs her friends, so stay close, Jilly. With what's going on in your life, everything is going to change. You four always watched out for each other. You're going to have to do that now more than ever," Rafe said slowly.

There was a movement behind them in the doorway. Olivia stood in her nightgown, a long knitted shawl wrapped around her shoulders. Even fresh from sleep, with her hair tumbled around her shoulders, she looked elegant and sexy as hell, Rafe thought.

"I hope we didn't wake you up," Jilly said quickly. "I was worried when you didn't call, since I expected you two for dinner tonight. Grace and Noah are already there. Caro and her grandmother came, too, along with the baby. But if you don't feel up to coming…" Jilly let the words trail away.

"I'm really sorry, Jilly. I forgot all about it." Olivia slanted a look at Rafe. "Did you tell her?"

Rafe shook his head.

"You wouldn't. You're honorable that way." She walked slowly across the room. "It's one of the reasons I love you so much," she said quietly. And then she rose to her toes and kissed Rafe slowly.

When she turned around, Jilly's eyebrow rose. "If you two lovebirds can manage to get dressed and finish your dinner, we'll expect you at the Harbor house for dessert. In one hour."

Jilly glanced at Rafe's bare chest and shook her head. "Do me a favor. Don't ever get your picture taken like that in the kitchen. Bare feet. Bare chest. Tight blue jeans. Sweet heaven, I'll have no business left. Every woman in the world will want your mac and cheese, if they see you cooking like that."

Rafe muttered darkly. "If you'd get out of here and give us some peace and quiet, we might manage to finish dinner in time to get to the Harbor House."

Jilly flicked her hair at him. "Enjoy the chipotle. Something tells me you'll be generating your own kind of heat in here first."

After Jilly left, Olivia moved to the stove. "It

smells amazing. And I'm ravenous." She looked at the formally set table and the dishes on the counter. "I can't believe you did all this while I was asleep." She smiled self-consciously and then wiggled away when Rafe ran a hand over her waist and down her slender hips. "None of that, Deputy. If we get started, you'll distract me. Then I'll never get my food." She slanted him a look under her lashes.

"All you have to do is ask, honey." Rafe's voice was husky. "Why don't you go sit down while I get this into the oven. Then I'll open up that bottle of merlot I found in the pantry."

"Feeling quite at home. I'm glad to see that, Rafe. Because for as long as I have this house—you should make it your home." She watched him assemble the casserole and slide it into the oven. "But why was Jilly so edgy, as if something was up?"

Rafe glanced back at her. "Not sure I follow."

"Did she tell you something?"

Rafe didn't answer, his face expressionless. Jilly wanted to break the news tonight. He had to respect that.

"It looked important." Olivia's eyes widened. She ran across the room and grabbed Rafe by the shoulder, knocking wine over both of them. "She's *pregnant!* It slipped out, didn't it? Jilly can't keep a secret about anything for long."

Olivia beamed up at him, so pleased with her detective work that Rafe couldn't find it in his heart to lie. "You aren't supposed to know. She wants to announce it tonight. She's also worried that she'll be a terrible mother."

"Jilly? She'll be fantastic. They will be *great* parents. I'll bet they'll have the most popular house on the block."

"That's exactly what I told her. But you know how Jilly likes to worry."

"You know us all so well." Olivia studied his face for a long time. "Sometimes I forget how close we all were back then. We used to go to the beach, to climb on the cliffs."

"Better not forget it. I know all your secrets, starting with grade school. And now if you'll stop distracting me, I'll get this into the oven so we can take our wine out on the porch and watch the last of the sunset."

Olivia moved close behind him and kissed his shoulder. Then she kissed the hollow beneath his neck and the center of his hard chest. "I love you, Deputy Russo." The words held absolute certainty. "I guess I've loved you since you stalked me at nine. So can we please get it right this time?"

Rafe Russo's Crowd-pleasing Guacamole Recipe

Forget about salsa.
This knocks salsa out of the competition. Try it with chips. With rice. With lettuce wraps. With English muffins or black bean soup or chili. As a topping on salad or hamburger.

The ingredients are limited, but be sure the avocados are newly ripened and with no bruises. It's all about the avocados! And please—only white onions. Not yellow. Not red. Definitely not Vidalia.

Ingredients

3 ripe avocados
1/2 medium white onion, chopped fine
1 poblano pepper
2 T freshly squeezed lime juice
1/2 tsp smoked sea salt
Chopped cilantro for topping

Chop white onion and put aside.

Dry roast uncut poblanos over a grill or in a cast-iron pan for about five minutes until blistered and black, turning often. (Remember— no oil.) Place cooked peppers in a paper bag until cool, and then peel away the black areas of the skin. Cut peppers and remove seeds. Chop coarsely and add to onions.

Mix in salt.

Cut avocados in half, remove skin and mash slightly, leaving chunks for texture. Toss with vegetables. Add fresh lime juice and mix well.

Sprinkle with cilantro—and enjoy!

Optional: add 3 T chopped fresh tomatoes and crumbles of freshly cooked bacon. Serves 3-6, depending on the appetite.

CHAPTER TWENTY-FIVE

THE HARBOR HOUSE was lit up brightly when Olivia and Rafe parked outside. Small Christmas-tree lights were draped across the front porch and a big autumn wreath hung at the freshly painted wooden door. Bright red geraniums ran along the top of the porch railing. The house looked alive again, glowing with good energy and fresh life, Olivia thought.

Through the open windows she could hear laughter and the clink of glasses. A baby cried and was quickly comforted. Olivia heard Duffy bark, followed by the sound of Jilly's good-natured commands to the dog to be quiet and come sit down beside her.

It was chaos. It was noisy and unpredictable.

It was friendship in all its shapes and sizes. The noisy house welcomed her in, wrapped warm arms around her the way it always had growing up, when Olivia had no real home of her own except the cold house and even colder father who had never really made her feel welcome.

She looked up, feeling Rafe's arm slip around her shoulders. "So what do you think? Will it pass muster for the opening?"

"It looks incredible. You four could never tackle anything simple, could you? You always had to dream big. And you got it right this time. My guess is the parking lot will be overflowing from the first hour you open."

"I hope you're right. If I were a tourist driving by, I'd definitely stop in. We're working on special promotions for knitters. We may even get some visitors from as far away as Portland."

"Oh, I think they'll come from a lot farther than Portland," Rafe said slowly. "Let's go in. Jilly's brownies are calling to me. I'm going to get that recipe out of her somehow, mark my words. After all, with a big thriving enterprise like the Harbor House, you need to keep your local law enforcement satisfied."

Olivia ran a hand across his chest and smiled darkly. "Satisfaction is very high on my list. You can be certain of that."

Rafe stopped at the doorway. The smells and the noise and the bustle and the laughter hit him with almost physical force. He remembered the derelict outline of the Harbor House, full of graffiti and broken windows as he had seen it, growing up. Every few years things would look better; new owners came, and then they went. Businesses started up and businesses failed.

But this venture would succeed. He could feel it in his gut.

Because these women cared. They would stay the

course. All this bustle and laughter and commitment were what he had fought for on the other side of the world. This was what he had come home to find.

But his philosophical musings were forgotten the second the door opened. Caro bore down upon them. Her grandmother followed, carrying Caro's wriggling child. Jilly's white dog jumped around Rafe in circles, thrilled by the new arrivals.

After the noisy hellos, Grace introduced the man she was going to marry. Noah studied Rafe gravely as the two men sized each other up.

Noah held out his hand. "Welcome back to Summer Island, Deputy Russo."

"Nice to be home. And call me Rafe. Hard to believe that things haven't changed very much back here. When you're where I was, you got the feeling you were at the end of the world. Time stops over there. You're sure that nothing will be the same when it's over."

Noah nodded. "I know what you mean. There's a fellow in D.C. who sends his regards. He said to tell you the hats are still green and the beer will be cold. I suppose that means something to you."

"Yes, it does. Tell him to keep his head down." Rafe rolled his shoulders. "Whatever happens, you can count on Jilly to cook a fantastic meal," Rafe said gruffly.

Grace and Olivia had been talking, and now Grace turned to Rafe. "Welcome home, Rafe. It's been too long. And, Olivia, we have a surprise for you."

Grace moved back a step while Noah lifted a big framed picture.

Rafe saw that it was an architectural rendering of the Harbor House, captured in an exquisite pen-and-ink sketch. He recognized Olivia's signature at the bottom. The details in the sketch left him speechless. She had captured the grace and dignity of the old house perfectly.

"We're going to hang it in the front foyer. Everybody needs to see your work, Olivia."

Olivia flushed. "I don't—know what to say."

"Say that you'll knit more sweaters for the yarn shop, and I'll be satisfied. Your samples will sell a lot of yarn."

Olivia laughed. "I'll get right on it. I already have six different projects on my needles right now, but who needs to sleep?"

"Don't worry, Jilly will probably kick me out of the kitchen any day now. After she does, you and I will go knit samples together." Grace leaned closer. "Jilly has her new food empire all mapped out. Luckily, she's going to use the internet this time around." Grace held up a plate to Rafe. "What do you think?"

Rafe turned the plate slowly. "One cappuccino brownie, one cinnamon-chipotle brownie and a slice of banana-cream pie. How did you know what I like, Grace?"

"Easy," Grace said. "You always had a soft spot

for sweet things." She studied the bustling room. "This is the first time we've gotten everyone together here."

"If you ask me, the four of you have worked a miracle. I still can't figure out how you managed it."

"That's what Noah keeps saying." Grace moved closer to the tall man and slid her fingers through his.

"You're going to have at least four people staying here, I can guarantee that." Noah slid his arm around Grace's waist. "My father tells me he's bringing the whole family to visit next month. They'll be some of your first guests. My mother has heard a lot about Jilly's cooking and she can't wait for a one-on-one cooking class."

Walker tapped a knife on a glass.

Jilly and Walker moved to the front of the room, and Walker held up his hand. "Sorry to interrupt my wife's excellent desserts, but if you'll sit down, we have a few things to say. No, don't look bored. It's the price of admission for having Jilly's brownies. You have to listen to a story."

There were a few mock groans.

"Stow it. Jilly has an announcement."

Walker looked ready to burst with pride, Rafe thought. And if he was ever lucky enough to have a child with Olivia, would he look that same way?

Rafe figured he probably would.

Jilly glanced around the room slowly. Then she turned to Walker. "I never thought I'd come back to Summer Island. I had bigger plans for things I could only do in big cities. But one night I met a man in a little airport up in a little mountain town and I fell in love. Well, the truth is, I fell in love with his *dog* first. So where are you, Winslow?" A big dog cut through the crowd and sat beside Jilly. He rubbed his head against her leg. "You see what I mean? This guy is a real heartbreaker." Jilly rubbed Winslow's head and then took a deep breath. "The other thing is—when Walker and I decided to make our home here in Summer Island, it was because of you. The Harbor House is our home."

There was another round of applause, and Jilly slid her hands into Walker's. "The last thing we wanted to tell you is that…we just had the results. We're crazy excited. I'm terrified, too, but Walker tells me that's normal."

"Terrified about what?" This came from Caro's grandmother, seated and holding Caro's now-sleeping child.

Jilly looked at Walker. "You tell them."

Walker rubbed his jaw and smiled slowly. "Jilly's pregnant. We wanted all of you to know about it first."

Whatever Walker would have said next was drowned out by shouted congratulations and wild clapping. Glasses of champagne were held high, and crystal clinked.

Jilly went beet-red. Walker looked a little flushed, too. Olivia was pretty sure her heart was going to explode with happiness at any second.

Because these were the people she loved most in the world, she thought she wanted to make her own announcement now. She wanted to say that Rafe was home to stay, and she and Rafe were together now, the way they had always hoped to be.

She didn't know exactly what their future would be, but they would be together, figuring out the challenges every step of the way.

A cell phone chimed quietly. Olivia glanced up as Rafe reached into his back pocket, pulled out his phone and scanned the number. There was a faint narrowing of his eyes.

He looked at her, smiled and said, "I have to take this."

Then he walked away, cell phone to his ear.

"Anything wrong?" Jilly moved next to Olivia. The two watched Rafe disappear into the kitchen.

"He got a phone call. Probably nothing."

Olivia was still waiting five minutes later. Rafe had not returned.

Grace moved next to Jilly. "Where is our local law enforcement officer? Those brownies are going fast."

"Rafe's in the kitchen," Jilly said thoughtfully. "He got a call. Probably some paperwork at the station."

Rafe walked over to Walker. The two men spoke quietly.

"Wonder what they're talking about. How to align your tires or clean your distributor cap?"

Rafe saw the three women staring at him and

crossed the room. "I've got to go. Tom Wilkinson called. There's a little problem down at the station. I should be back in an hour. Why don't you stay here with your friends, honey. I'll come back and get you when I'm done."

"Of course. Do what you need to do. Just a friendly warning, though. If you take more than an hour, those brownies will be gone."

Rafe touched her cheek and then frowned when his cell phone rang again. He took the call and turned away toward the door. Olivia heard him repeat a number before he closed the door behind him.

She didn't move, struck by a cold wave of fear. But she wouldn't cave in, not the way she had before. She was surrounded by her friends, and Rafe knew what he was doing. She wasn't going to let her mind be derailed into dark possibilities.

Walker cleared his throat. "Those brownies are going fast. I think I'll bring more from the kitchen."

When he moved away, some instinct made Olivia follow. She saw him cross the kitchen and keep right on walking, out to the side porch. Rafe was there, standing next to his car. The trunk was opened; she could see a long metal case inside.

Walker glanced down as Rafe opened the case. Olivia couldn't make out what was inside.

"What is it, a burglary?"

"Domestic disturbance. I don't know how long I'll be. Can you take Olivia home? I don't want her to be alone tonight."

"Don't worry about Olivia. She'll be fine here. You need some help?" Walker asked. "Noah and I can tag along if you want."

"Better not. Official jurisdiction and all that." Rafe closed the big case.

Walker nodded. "Got it."

Olivia thought she felt a silent message pass between the two men. Cold wind brushed her face like icy fingers. Then Rafe was gone.

Olivia stopped Walker at the steps. "What did he say?"

Walker frowned. "He had something to do at the station."

"No, he said there was a domestic disturbance. And I heard him say a number. Ten-forty-seven." Olivia stared at Rafe's retreating car, her face pale. "I've been studying the police codes. I wanted to know what they meant since I was seeing Rafe. Ten-forty-seven means armed with firearms. That's bad."

Walker didn't say anything.

Olivia turned around, her face set. She found her purse and walked over to Jilly. "Can I borrow your car?"

"Of course you can, but where are you going?"

"I'm going to be there. In case...well, just in case."

Walker moved a step in front of her. He shook his head. "Olivia, you can't go there. This is a police matter. It will be dangerous."

Olivia pushed his hand away. "I'm not a fool. I'm not going to get close or be a distraction. I just...I just want to be there in the distance." She stared at Jilly, her eyes pleading. "Can I borrow your car?'

Jilly looked at Walker, who muttered a curse. "Hell. If you're determined to go, I'll drive you. But only under these conditions. You do *exactly* what I say. No noise. And you do *not* leave the car. Not under any circumstances."

"Fine. Now can we go?"

Walker touched Jilly's cheek, took a deep breath and slid the car keys into his pocket. "Make sure that I don't regret this, Olivia." His voice was very hard.

Olivia barely heard him.

CHAPTER TWENTY-SIX

HE WAS HERE and yet he wasn't here.

Rafe felt the cool wind on his face, smelled the musky perfume of pine needles. The Oregon coast was a universe away from the drifting dust and acrid heat of Afghanistan, but violence felt the same, no matter what patch of ground you stood on.

This time the threat was at home, close to those he loved. Rafe didn't allow himself to think about that now.

Tom Wilkinson looked sick, his features pale and drawn. The dispatcher had pulled him away from therapy at the hospital, and pain lines were etched on his face. "You have your equipment?"

Rafe nodded.

"Good. Here's the situation. It started as a domestic dispute. Husband just got back from prison. Wife seeing another man. Things went south fast. There's a three-year-old child in there," the sheriff said coldly. "One of our men went in twenty minutes ago. He hasn't reported back. Shots were fired and we think the deputy may be wounded."

Rafe nodded. Domestic disturbances were the worst, volatile and totally unpredictable. With a child involved, everything became a nightmare. He said nothing else, moving around the car and opening the trunk. He pulled out his big case, which carried the sniper rifle he had used through two tours of duty in Afghanistan.

He had hoped to put this part of his life behind him for good. He had done enough killing in the drifting desert dust.

Rafe assembled the equipment expertly and then scanned the dark hillside. He narrowed his focus to a tunnel. Only three things mattered now.

Threat. Terrain. Resolution.

As he worked, he let the noises of the night play around him. He absorbed the sounds of the wind and the distant crashing of waves at the coast. Then he looked at the sheriff. "I'm going to need secure vantage. There's a clump of shrubs to the right of the driveway—0300." He used the military location designations as a habit.

Wilkinson nodded. "You won't be visible from the house. There are no streetlights in that area either. It's a good spot. For the record I'm authorizing you to use lethal force. I've tried to reach the man inside for ten minutes. He never answers. We know his wife is inside and we know there's a child involved. Our time is running out. Unless you hear differently, if you have an opportunity then take the shot."

Rafe felt the world still. He felt the cold barrel of the rifle beneath his fingers, felt the wind in his hair.

He felt the terrible weight of life and death settle on his shoulders. There was no room for error.

He stood motionless. "I want to make this clear. I'm to take the shot. Is that right?"

Tom Wilkinson nodded curtly. "Take him. The nearest SWAT team is forty-five minutes away. We don't have that much time. It's on you, Rafe."

"Understood." Rafe would not shirk the responsibility, no matter how unwelcome it was.

"Follow me." The sheriff gripped his side as if it hurt. Then he waved Rafe forward into the woods.

"THIS IS TOM WILKINSON. How are things going in there? I'd like to speak with you."

There was no answer from inside the darkened house. Somewhere Rafe heard the faint cry of a child as he took up a position along the slope. Through a window at the stairwell he could see movement in the room, but he couldn't pick out figures.

He needed to be closer.

"I'd really like to talk to you." Tom's calm voice went on, and Rafe knew he was trying to establish contact with the hostage taker while getting an update on the situation inside. "Do you need anything in there? Food? Water? Is anyone hurt?"

Just as before, there was no answer.

Rafe moved quietly up the deep hillside, focused on that small window and what it could tell him. He heard the sound of something heavy dropping and then the frightened cry of a woman.

Whatever was going on inside that house could explode into violence at any moment.

Rafe crawled to the window and sank flat. He eased a set of night-vision goggles into place and waited for the scene inside to grow clear.

In the green flare of the goggles, he made out two figures in the middle of the room. The smaller figure was locked into place, a shield in front of the man. This had to be the hostage. Rafe studied the room, looking for any other movement or figures.

The child cried again, sounding cranky and frightened and tired. The sound seemed to come from an upstairs bedroom.

Tom Wilkinson kept on talking, his voice calm and deep next to the front door. "Maybe if you told me what you want, I could help you. I can't do anything to help if you don't talk to me. Are you good with that?"

Rafe saw the big figure fling the woman around. He heard her muffled cry of pain.

Silently, Rafe eased open the window. His primary duty was to protect the hostages. Somehow he had to separate the man from his wife and child.

"Look, I'm putting a case of Coke near the front door. I brought you some pizza and some tacos, too. It's all I could manage on short notice, but I figure you must be hungry. The pizza is nice and hot. It's here on the porch, whenever you want it. I'm going back to my car now. Just so you know."

Rafe's mouth twitched. Tom Wilkinson looked

and sounded like a man who didn't have a care in the world, like a law enforcement officer who was a little short on brains. But Rafe knew that this was exactly the right thing to say. He had lowered the threat level and offered something to the hostage taker without being asked.

The man inside didn't answer, but Rafe saw the two figures move awkwardly toward the door. The woman was still locked tightly against the man's chest, but Rafe saw her lean against the wall, nearly falling as the man opened the front door slightly and then grabbed at the food outside.

He swung the door shut immediately, then leaned down, clearly searching through the bags that Tom had left.

The woman was too close. Rafe still did not have a clear shot. He let the wind move over him and felt the cold metal beneath his hands while he waited, deep in a zone of focus that could last for hours.

"You got the food. That's good. If you want anything else, you just tell me. All you have to do is call out. I can hear you."

Suddenly the woman spun around, staggering toward the back of the room. The man charged after her and Rafe saw his hands swing out in a slashing blow.

Her scream of pain was cut short as the man struck her again and then again.

She seemed to stagger. The man struggled to hold her and then half carried her along the wall. With her still locked against him, he leaned down and seemed to be digging for something on the ground.

Rafe heard the unmistakable sound of a round being loaded into a chamber.

"*Talking's done.* I'm going to kill her." The man inside shouted at the front door, "I'm going to kill her and then I'll kill that kid of hers." His voice was hoarse with exhaustion and fury. "You listening out there, Pop? That's what I'm going to do. There's not a damn thing you can do about it."

From his position near the window, Rafe could hear the woman's low, broken sobs. Somewhere in the house a child continued to wail.

Rafe didn't move, waiting for a clear shot.

The man inside shouted at the front door. "It's too late."

The wind whined. Seconds became hours.

The man raised an arm. "She didn't wait. Another man lives here. Their house now. Their kid, upstairs howling. It's *her* fault that they're all going to die. I told her what would happen. I told her to wait." The words reached a crescendo of fury. "Say goodbye to all of them. To that deputy, too, back in the closet, bleeding out." He swung the woman around, wrenching her neck sideways as if she was a doll. "I told you to *wait!*"

The words echoed through the house as the man struck again.

This time the woman twisted, kicking upward in

blind anger and desperate fear, and the man's hold broke, just for a moment. The two figures separated.

Rafe relaxed his shoulder.

Hands calm. Body floating. A heartbeat became a lifetime.

And then he took the shot.

OLIVIA WAS IN the front seat when she heard a man yell from inside the house, then the terrified cry of a woman. Something thumped hard. Another scream.

Why didn't they do something? Anything?

A rifle split the silence. Two fast shots. *Boom-boom!*

Olivia's hands locked in her lap.

A woman keened. Wind gusted through the woods as a police car passed without lights or sirens. An ambulance pulled up behind Walker's Jeep.

Tom Wilkinson and two officers broke through the front door and went in.

WALKER SAID NOTHING when the emergency team brought a stretcher down the driveway with a woman and a child.

Police radios chattered. Two officers walked quickly toward the house.

Olivia sank back and closed her eyes.

She heard Rafe's voice, absolutely calm. When he walked onto the porch she forced her locked fingers to relax. He was unharmed, a rifle in his hand, some kind of goggles under his arm.

She looked at Walker. "I don't understand."

Another gurney came out the front door. Walker started the engine.

"Did Rafe fire those shots?"

Walker frowned at the stretcher. "We're going. Neither of us should be here, Olivia."

CHAPTER TWENTY-SEVEN

THEY DIDN'T SPEAK on the drive back to the Harbor House.

Walker glanced at Olivia every few minutes to see how she was handling the situation. Her face was very pale. But she looked thoughtful, even calm.

Walker figured that she had a whole lot to be thoughtful about.

When they pulled into the driveway, it was hard to process the return to the normal world of friends and laughter and trust. The lights were on in the big house. They could hear music and dogs barking and an occasional roll of booming laughter.

All of it seemed a million miles away from the grim scene they had just witnessed in the woods.

"I saw Rafe's rifle before he left. And that's the sound I heard." Olivia didn't look at Walker. Her eyes were very dark and seemed to shimmer. But she was holding it together. He liked her a lot for that.

"Olivia, I can't say whether or not—"

She raised one hand impatiently. "No, don't say anything. You don't have to. I was there and I heard everything you heard. I'm just walking through this for myself. I'm trying to give it clear meaning. For

Rafe—that's important. I know that he was in the Marines in Afghanistan. It was some important job, but none of us back here had the details." She looked down, staring at her fingers in her lap. "I can't even imagine what that must have been like. How do you put those memories away and come home to start a normal life again?"

Walker sat unmoving, his hands on the wheel. She had pretty much said it all. Though she had not asked, he could tell her from personal experience that it was nearly impossible to forget the gunfire and the sweat, the screams and the fear. You did it day by day, minute by minute. You put your boots on the ground and you kept walking forward. There was no secret decoder ring to help, no easy shortcuts. Rafe had hard work ahead of him.

Walker turned off the engine. He knew that Olivia was thinking hard, trying to come up with answers to questions that she didn't even know how to ask.

Walker decided the best thing he could do was listen.

"He'll have paperwork to finish. I think he may need some time to think about tonight. So I'll give him that time." She sat up straighter, looking very determined. "I'll give him twenty-four hours. Not a second more."

She had made up her mind. That was a very good thing. There was serious chemistry between Rafe and Olivia. Anyone within a mile could feel the sparks when they were together.

But change could be brutal. It had taken Walker years, and in the end he had succeeded because of Jilly's courage and absolute refusal to accept anything less than the best for the two of them.

Walker prayed that Rafe and Olivia would find the same trust together.

Neither of them moved, listening to the engine click and pop and the waves crash down in the cove. "I think that's a good plan, Livie. Give him a little space."

She nodded slowly. Again something shimmered in her eyes. "I don't think I'm up for a party right now. Do you think you could drive me home?"

Walker nodded. He understood that it cost you to hold things together when emotions were hammering at you, screaming to take control. "Of course I'll drive you home. But Rafe doesn't want you to be there alone."

"I'll be fine. He's making a lot more out of this than he should."

Walker shook his head. Rafe Russo was a careful man. If he thought that Olivia should not be alone, he was probably right. "I'll go with you. I'll call Jilly and tell her you weren't feeling well. She'll understand."

But the night seemed restless and full of unanswered questions, offering no peace. As they drove through the winding streets toward the heart of town, the moon rose over the horizon, shimmering through the trees and painting the cove silver.

There was light now. But it didn't make Walker feel any better about the things he had seen. Men were capable of great violence. It was far easier to believe in hate and to assume a threat.

Walker didn't choose to live that way now. It was a struggle, but he had managed it with Jilly's help.

He had to wonder if Rafe had the courage to make the same leap of trust in his future…and if Olivia was strong enough to help him.

THE FIRST THING Olivia did after they got home was check the phone messages.

Nothing.

Then she checked her cell phone to make sure Rafe hadn't called.

Nothing.

She hadn't expected either, but it was still a disappointment. She made Walker a cup of tea and started a fire in the fireplace so the house would be welcoming in case Rafe turned up. She knew little about law enforcement, but she figured it would be late when Rafe finished. He would have official paperwork and maybe some kind of formal interview with Tom Wilkinson before they could close the case.

She heard Walker outside on the back porch, his voice low and calm. She guessed he was talking to Jilly, saying as little as possible about what had happened, assuring her that everything was fine.

Olivia sank into the big wing chair by the fire. As she had a thousand times before, she reached into her big felted wool bag and pulled out her knitting. The smooth strands slid through her fingers, offering comfort and distraction and the certainty that new things could grow no matter how bad the world became.

In a week or two weeks there would be a finished shawl in that bag. Olivia planned to give it to the hospital for patients awaiting chemotherapy treatments. She tried to knit one thing a month for the hospital. Sadly, they always needed more.

She forced that thought from her mind, along with the memory of the two booming gunshots. As she focused on the complicated lace chart, her fingers slipped into their familiar rhythm, and Olivia felt the dim echo of welcome from other women in other times and places. Through these stitches they shared their own comfort, hard-won in times of war and famine, in religious intolerance and political unrest. Somehow those women had survived to pass down their patterns and all their skills to generations they would never see.

Olivia would survive, too.

THEY HAD FINISHED one pot of tea between them. Walker insisted on making Olivia a sandwich and more tea. He had barely put the kettle on to boil when car lights appeared in the front driveway. A door opened and closed.

Jilly appeared at the front door, looking very determined. Walker must have gestured to her, because she vanished before Olivia could say anything.

Olivia kept right on knitting. She desperately needed the comfort it brought her.

Dishes rattled. She heard a faucet turned on and then turned off, then low, murmured questions. When Jilly finally emerged from the kitchen, Olivia saw she had her own knitting bag. Without a word Jilly walked to the chair at the other side of the fire, sat down and began to knit.

"You don't have to stay, Jilly. I'm...fine."

Jilly nodded. "Of course you're fine. I know that. You're the strong one. I always knew that, Livie. But I'm staying just the same."

Olivia knew there would be no point in arguing. She also knew that with one short call, Grace and Caro would be here within minutes also, if she asked. But she didn't need to talk or discuss or analyze tonight. She simply wanted to *be*.

As stars rose against the deeper shadows of night, wool moved through skilled fingers. Knitting needles clicked and danced. In that slow, measured rhythm of nerve and hand, Olivia found the courage to accept whatever changes would come. She had a clear idea of her future and the person she meant to become. She had touched the shadows of her own heart, faced her own fears and knew she would never be happy without change.

Tomorrow, she told herself.

Tomorrow it would all begin.

CHAPTER TWENTY-EIGHT

RAFE SAT AT his desk, papers in a neat stack in front of him. He had been briefed by Tom. He had given an oral report to a state investigator, stating that he'd pulled over the man on the highway, but seen no evidence to detain him. There would be more formal investigations in the days that followed. Now he was glad for the distraction of the official paperwork to be completed.

When he finally looked up, two hours had passed. He hated to call Olivia this late, but knew she would be waiting to hear from him. He didn't want to leave her in limbo.

But something had changed. Rafe felt the cold presence of death and the weight of responsibility for the thing he had done.

He didn't want that to touch Olivia's life. He had promised himself that he would keep her safe, and now he had done the opposite, bringing *his* world, with its violence and uncertainty, directly into a line of conflict with hers.

He stared at his cell phone a long time, frowning. Then he took a deep breath and dialed.

She answered on the first ring.

"Rafe, are you okay?"

"I'm fine." He considered his words carefully. He didn't want to lie, but he couldn't reveal very much of the truth either. "I'm stuck here at the station. I've got a lot of paperwork. It was…a busy night."

The silence hung. She started to say something but stopped.

Rafe frowned. He didn't hear voices or laughter or music. "Are you still at the Harbor House? Did everyone go home?"

"I got tired. Walker drove me back. I'm here now with Jilly. We're knitting."

Knitting with Jilly was good, Rafe thought. He didn't want her to be alone. "Is Walker there, too?"

"He's here. So…are you coming over?" she asked.

"I'm stuck here for at least another few hours. I think I'll head back to my place afterward. I'll call you tomorrow."

The silence seemed to hang, heavy with uncertainty. "Olivia?"

"I'm here. It doesn't matter how late you finish. I'll be here. Come by."

"I think tomorrow is better." Rafe needed time alone. The ghosts didn't go away just because the job was done. This was something he had to manage by himself. "We'll talk tomorrow, Livie. Get some rest."

"You, too," she said quietly.

She hung up first.

THROUGHOUT THE NEXT day Olivia kept herself very busy.

A locksmith had come, and she now had a sparkling new alarm system that she had to remember to use.

She didn't really think she needed it. Probably it had just been squirrels up in the attic. But she was willing to humor Rafe.

Meanwhile, there were the little bits and pieces of her life to focus on. She sent out more résumés and job applications. She made follow-up calls for old applications that were pending. She returned books to the library and politely suffered through a drawn-out interrogation by the lady in front of her in the line, a former neighbor. Everyone wanted to know about Rafe.

Was she seeing him? Were they serious? Was Rafe going to stay on Summer Island or was this just a temporary job?

Olivia hid her irritation and said they would have to ask Rafe those questions.

She put air in her tires. She restocked groceries. She went to pick up a package left for her at the post office.

At every stop, someone had a question about Rafe—and about her relationship with him. She was beginning to think she was in a fishbowl. No one had ever questioned her like this before. Olivia realized she had never been half so interesting until Rafe had come back from Afghanistan.

Bad boy + good girl = hot gossip. She told herself to get used to it.

SHE CAUGHT THE sidelong stares and the raised eyebrows at the grocery and the pharmacy and the small local bookstore. When she went to the bank, one of the tellers asked her if Rafe Russo had opened an account yet. If not, the bank would welcome his patronage, assuming he was planning to stay.

Olivia wanted to snap back that it was none of his business what Rafe planned to do with his money. But because she was always polite, she forced a smile and said she would pass on the message.

She wanted to discuss all of it with Rafe so they could share a laugh at the town's avid curiosity. But she heard nothing more from him. And the silence began to dig at Olivia.

When six o'clock came and went, she called Rafe's cell phone.

It went directly to his voice mail. She left a brief message and told herself it was nothing. He was still busy from the events of the night before; no reason to bother him with additional phone calls.

Two hours later he called her back. He said he wanted to come by, if it was convenient. There was a distance to his voice. Always hypersensitive where Rafe was concerned, Olivia caught the change immediately.

She was certain that something had changed when he stood silently in her front foyer, turning his service hat between his fingers, looking as if he had something important to tell her.

She didn't think he would talk about his job or what had happened in that darkened house. It was an official police matter, and she wasn't supposed to know about it.

She forced a smile. "I hope you got all your paperwork finished? Tom shouldn't keep you this late. But I have fresh brownies in the oven. I can make you some tea."

Rafe stood stiffly by the big stained glass window. Light played over the hard lines of his face. "I'm going to pass on the brownies, Livie."

"Okay," she said slowly. "What about tea?"

Rafe shook his head. The distance in his eyes was growing. He studied her face intently, as if he was trying to memorize the shadows and curves.

As if he wouldn't be seeing her again for a while.

Fear, anxiety and irritation churned inside her. But Olivia wouldn't let them take control. She kept her breathing slow and measured and walked into the kitchen, forcing him to follow her. She poured herself a cup of tea and filled another cup for him, then sat down at the small table. "Are you going to tell me or are you going to make me ask?"

Rafe leaned against the counter. "Is it so obvious?"

"To me it is. You've got something to say, so say

it." Olivia felt the fear burn deep, carrying the old insecurity. But she refused to go back to what she had been. They would face this problem head-on—whatever it was.

Rafe turned his hat slowly in his hands. "I came by tonight to talk to you, Livie. I didn't want to call. I thought it would be better like this. In person."

Olivia felt the room contract, a cold weight on her shoulders. She told herself to breathe. Whatever he said, she could deal with it. "So now you're here. Tell me about this important thing."

"It looks like I'm not going to be staying on here. Tom told me today that he had lined somebody else up for the job, someone who took a leave of absence two years ago. He thinks that will work out better. It's a small community and he thinks a local man is a better fit for the force."

Olivia blinked, trying to understand exactly what he was saying. "You're leaving? I don't understand. I thought you liked it here."

Rafe nodded thoughtfully. "It's a good job. I'm just not sure that I'm the best man for it. We both know I've got some history with this town. A lot of people have long memories. Tom thinks that it would be better if I took a position in a different place, somewhere that I would be starting fresh."

Olivia shot to her feet. "That's ridiculous. This town should welcome you with open arms. So what if you have a past? Everybody has a past."

She spun around, searching angrily for her cell

phone. "I'm giving Tom a piece of my mind. I can't believe he told you something like that."

"Don't, Livie." Rafe's voice was harsh. "Tom was only doing what he thought best. I think it's best, too."

"So you're kicking the dust off your feet and getting the hell out of Summer Island, is that it? The little town has bored you already. After all, there's no point in staying. I'm certainly not enough to hold you," she said coldly. "I'm certain you can get a dozen better jobs than this one with your skills."

Rafe's eyes narrowed. "What skills are you talking about?"

Olivia caught her mistake and shrugged. "You've got a lot of combat and field experience. Those should be valuable."

Rafe nodded slowly and then put his hat on the counter. "I've had some offers. I talked with Tom today. We both think it's for the best."

Olivia kept her face expressionless. "So that's it? You just dropped by to tell me you're leaving. Hello. Goodbye. It was nice to know you."

Rafe frowned. "Olivia, don't—"

She shot to her feet. "*Don't* tell me what to think or what to do, Rafe. And don't think you're walking out of my life with only a lame explanation. I won't make this easy for you. If you wanted it *easy,* you should never have come back here," she said fiercely.

Rafe took a deep breath. One hand rose as if reaching toward her, then dropped to his pocket.

"You're right." He cursed softly. "I thought it would work out—I thought there was a way. But now I see it's impossible. The longer I stay here, the more trouble I will bring you."

Olivia crossed her arms and stood up straighter. "Because you shot a man? Because that was your responsibility and you handled it?"

Rafe's eyes narrowed. "How do you know about that?"

"Because I was there. I made Walker take me. I knew what that police radio code meant and I saw the rifle in your car. That's what you did in Afghanistan, isn't it? And it's what you had to do again here." She stared at him, seeing the shadows under his eyes and the lines of exhaustion that hadn't been there two days before. "Tell me the truth, Rafe. We can't build any kind of future without that."

He nodded slowly. "It was a skill I hadn't known I had. When I came back here, I thought that was behind me. Except it never will be. I won't pull you into that world, Olivia. It's not a place you should know about."

"You did the right thing, Rafe. I have no question about that."

"You don't know about any of it," he said harshly. "I thought I could make this work but I can't, Livie. I'd end up hurting you again. I refuse to let that happen. It's over," he said quietly. "You deserve a prince and a fairy-tale ending." He picked up his hat. "All I can give you is shadows and bad memories. Let it go. Believe me, it's best like this." He moved closer, touching her cheek lightly, carefully.

And then he took a step back, his eyes turning distant. "It's best like this. I know it. In a week or a month, you'll know it, too."

Olivia heard the words as if they came through a long tunnel. She couldn't seem to move.

I won't, she thought. *You're wrong.*

His feet echoed across the room. She heard the door open. "I won't believe that," she said. "I'll never believe that, Rafe."

But he had already gone.

CHAPTER TWENTY-NINE

IT WAS THE *right thing to do.*

Rafe told himself that over and over the following day. He had never fit in here as a boy, and now he was back from a war zone with ten years of baggage.

He clenched his hands and tried not to remember Olivia's pale, rigid features. This was the right thing to do.

He hadn't heard from Walker or Jilly. That meant Olivia had not spoken about this with them. Probably she had seen the good sense in what he had told her. He didn't want to hurt her again, but a clean break now was infinitely preferable to a slow, seeping wound.

Meanwhile, as he went about his business, Rafe registered every sidelong glance, every suspicious question. There was a protectiveness about Olivia that was impossible to miss. When he went to the café for food, he saw the averted eyes and heard the whispered conversations.

Yes, leaving Summer Island was *clearly* the right thing to do.

Tom had been against his plan to go, but once Rafe made it clear that his mind was made up, the sheriff had reluctantly agreed. At the end of the day Rafe would be on the road, headed south or east or anywhere but Summer Island.

He heard the sound of car horns and raised voices outside his window. Brakes screeched loudly.

The traffic was bad today. That was strange, because there were no special events that he knew about.

Feet clicked down the hall from his desk. Low voices. More honking outside.

Rafe heard pebbles tossed against his window. Frowning, he moved around his desk and glanced out. Then he blinked and looked again.

Cars were backed all along Main Street. People milled around, looking up at the police station. Then they turned to stare at the big red BMW convertible pulled over the curb, halfway onto the grass. The shiny car had blocked the sidewalk to the police station.

Rafe saw who was driving the red Beemer and muttered under his breath.

Olivia? Why was she sitting on the hood, staring up at his window? And whose car was that?

"Where's a police officer when you need one?" she called out, clearly oblivious to the disturbance she was creating. "I'm talking to you, Deputy Russo. I'm pretty sure that a few laws have been broken down here. So why don't you step away from your desk and come do your civic duty? Take me into custody."

Rafe ran a hand over his eyes, telling himself he wasn't seeing this.

He turned to find Tom Wilkinson in his doorway. The sheriff cleared his throat and pointed toward the street. "Someone's calling you, Russo."

"I heard."

"Then maybe you'd better go deal with it. I can't have a car parked on our front lawn. She's blocking the whole street now."

Rafe shook his head. "So what do you want me to do about it?"

The sheriff hooked two fingers in his belt. "If she's broken the law, I'm counting on you to arrest her, Deputy Russo. Now get moving."

Him? Arrest the town good girl? The boy voted most likely to screw up his life? No, Rafe would talk some sense into Olivia Sullivan for her own good.

There were more cars and more people gawking when he opened the front door. He elbowed his way through a growing crowd. Once he came around the corner of the building, Rafe saw why.

Olivia was lying on the hood of the Beemer, wearing a raincoat. Her feet were bare and her brightly painted red toenails moved up and down as she bounced her leg impatiently. When she saw Rafe, she gave a brilliant smile and sat up.

Her raincoat gaped open. Rafe was pretty sure she was only wearing a lacy bra and bikini panties underneath.

Before he could ask what the hell she thought she

was doing, Olivia sat up and crossed her legs, looking very pleased. "Well, at last. I'm glad to see our local law enforcement on the job. I'm pretty sure I'm not supposed to be here on the front lawn. And do you see that carton of Coke in my front seat? I just stole it. So you'd better arrest me."

Rafe felt the people around him push closer, trying to hear. He heard someone whisper, "Isn't that Olivia Sullivan? Why is she in that raincoat with no shoes?"

He pushed through the crowd and leaned over the car, frowning. "Livie, I don't know what you're trying to do, but—"

"Do? I'm *trying* to do my civic duty. I'm a dangerous criminal. I should be taken into custody immediately."

"Hell. Come off the hood of that car, Livie." Rafe kept his voice low in a vain hope that the people around him couldn't hear.

"Why should I come off the car? I just spent all my money to buy it. I had a perfectly good Volvo. But it's so…bo*rrr*ing." She dragged out the word and gave a little laugh, studying her red toenails.

That's when Rafe heard the slur in her voice. "Olivia, have you been *drinking?*"

She tilted her head and considered the question. "Yep, I have."

Rafe frowned. "How much have you been drinking?"

"Two bottles of beer. One glass of wine." She

stared at the tree next to the spot where her car was parked. "I tried some vodka. Didn't like it. So I had two glasses of champagne next."

Rafe winced. She was going to have one helluva hangover the next day, which would serve her right. And she didn't fool him for a moment. "I'm not going to arrest you, Olivia. I'm going to take you inside and give you black coffee until you sober up. I'll have someone drive this car off the sidewalk while we do it."

She shook her head. "No, you won't." Still smiling, she pulled a key out of the pocket of her raincoat, which was now gaping open with a dangerous view of her slender thigh. As Rafe watched, the key disappeared into her lacy bra. "Not unless you come and get it."

Behind Rafe someone chuckled.

"There's more, Deputy. I've got rented DVDs in my car. They're three months old and I never paid any fines. I've got library books that were never returned, too. Some of them were my father's. Do you know he borrowed a Tom Clancy book back in 2003 and never returned it? Can you believe that? The town mayor and he didn't return his library books." Olivia half slid off the front of the red BMW, landing on her bare feet right in front of Rafe. She dug one red fingernail into his chest. "So what are you waiting for, Deputy Russo? *Arrest me.*"

There was more low laughter around Rafe.

He leaned closer. "Damn it, Livie, I'm not going

to arrest you. Now where did you put your shoes? It's cold out here. You're going to catch pneumonia."

"Don't feel a thing. Must be the champagne. Or the Glenfiddich that I found in the pantry."

"Glenfiddich? You never mentioned that," Rafe said curtly.

"Forgot." She turned slowly, her hands outstretched. Rafe saw way too much naked thigh when she did it. "It feels wonderful. Like little bubbles dancing into my brain. If you really want me to back the car off the sidewalk, then I can—"

Rafe stopped her quickly. "There's no way you're getting behind the wheel of anything. You're way over the legal alcohol limit."

"I guess I am." Olivia glanced down, trying to peer into the top of her bra. "I'm not sure where the key is. Why don't you have a look?"

Rafe pulled the raincoat tight around her. "We're going inside."

"So you're going to arrest me?"

She was still smiling at him radiantly when she swayed and wrapped one hand around the mirror of the shiny new car, trying to stay upright.

Rafe caught her before she fell. "Come on."

But Olivia wasn't done. She smiled up at him, touching his cheek. "That's nice. Thank you." She glanced over his shoulder and frowned at the tall man behind Rafe. "There's no need to look so angry, Mr. Howland. I know you don't like Deputy Russo. You've been telling everyone that he's mean to animals. And it's all because when Rafe was in fifth grade he threw a balloon filled with water at your cat. That stupid tomcat chased us all over town. He clawed our feet and jumped off a porch at us. He even bit Jilly. If you ask me, that cat was the one breaking the law. But it makes a better story the way you tell it, I guess."

Olivia pointed a finger at the woman standing next to Roy Howland. "You don't like Deputy Russo either, do you, Mrs. Long? I think it's because your daughter had a crush on him all the way through high school. Deputy Russo wasn't interested, so your daughter stole a pack of cigarettes from the cash and carry and blamed it on Deputy Russo, didn't she? Too bad everyone saw her take the cigarettes. You never forgave Deputy Russo for that, did you?"

The tall woman flushed bright red and stalked away.

Rafe knew exactly where Olivia was heading with this and he didn't want her help. "Don't fight me, Olivia. We're going inside."

"I've changed my mind." She wriggled, struggling to get free. "I want to stay right here. I want to drive my car off your front lawn—but I can't find my keys. They're in here somewhere." Olivia twisted sharply, trying to reach into the front of her raincoat.

Sweet heaven, what would she do next? He thought about having one of the other deputies take her inside for coffee. That would be safer. But Rafe didn't want anyone else touching her.

Not now or ever.

"Are you going to put me in a jail cell? I've never seen one."

Rafe caught back an oath. "No, I'm not taking you to a cell. I'm going to dump you into the back of my cruiser. Then I'm going to drive you home and make you drink about two gallons of coffee."

Olivia made a slow pout. "Coffee? Don't want any of that."

The avidly curious crowd parted in front of Rafe as he carried Olivia around to his cruiser. He was congratulating himself on getting the situation under control when he felt her wriggle against him. One leg rocked in the air. She gave him an innocent smile.

And the smallest thong bikini Rafe had ever seen dropped down onto her toe, swung in the air and then went flying over his head.

He made very certain that the raincoat didn't slip again. With a wave of relief he dropped her into the backseat of his cruiser. "You are now in official custody, Ms. Sullivan," he said gruffly. "*My* custody. And it's going to be one helluva bumpy ride."

CHAPTER THIRTY

OLIVIA LOOKED AROUND her with interest. "Good. I should be." Then she wrinkled her nose. "It smells funny back here. Did you know that?"

"Sometimes people throw up. Usually when they're drunk like you are." Rafe slid into the driver's seat, threw the locks and started the car. "I know exactly what you're doing. It's a bad idea."

"I don't know what you're talking about," Olivia said airily. She leaned back in the seat, and the raincoat skidded down her shoulder, revealing all of her neck and a good part of her lacy pink bra.

Rafe scowled at her in the rearview mirror. "The raincoat. Close it up, Olivia."

She looked down and shrugged. "Aren't you going to put handcuffs on me? I could be dangerous."

Rafe rolled his eyes. "The only danger here is that you might throw up all over the backseat," he muttered.

"Possible." Olivia frowned. "I'm not feeling so good now."

Rafe glanced back at her in concern. "How bad is it?"

"I'll survive," she said in a very small voice. "I

hope." She looked out the window as Rafe turned off the main street. "Aren't you going back on High Street, past the police station? People should see you doing your civic duty in arresting a dangerous thief."

Rafe muttered under his breath and ignored her.

OLIVIA LOOKED WORSE by the time he parked in her driveway. Her face was pale and her eyes were closed. She had one hand open on her stomach as if she was sick.

Rafe opened the door and lifted her out carefully. Even though he knew it was dangerous to touch her, he swung her up into his arms and carried her up the front steps. "How do you feel?"

Her answer was unintelligible. Her eyes fluttered once, and she might have muttered his name. Then she was out cold.

If he hadn't been so angry, Rafe might almost have laughed.

He still had her house key, and he juggled her against his arm while he unlocked the front door. He put her down on the couch while he went to turn off the alarm.

When he came back, Olivia was propped awkwardly on the sofa, peering at him. "Where am I?"

"You were at the police station. Now you're at home."

"Are you going to extract a confession of all the things I did?"

"I'll skip the interrogation," Rafe said dryly.

"Your punishment will be the mother of all hangovers tomorrow morning. Hasn't anybody ever told you not to mix hard liquor, beer and champagne?"

Olivia rubbed her forehead. "Seemed like a good idea at the time." She tried to stand up and swayed dangerously. Rafe lunged and caught her waist.

"Hell. What am I going to do with you, Olivia?"

Her eyes closed. Her head fell against his chest and she wriggled closer. "Anything you want, Officer," she whispered.

GRIMLY RAFE CARRIED her up to bed and slid her under the covers. There were a whole lot of things he wanted to do to her. He wanted to shake her and then talk some sense into her. He was trying to do the right thing, but she wasn't helping.

He couldn't take his eyes away from her red nails as she lay in the middle of the big white bed, deep asleep, one hand under her cheek. In the silence Rafe felt something shake free deep inside him, the ground shifting hard beneath him. There had always been a bond between them, even when he was nine and she was barely seven. How could he walk out on her now, when leaving felt all wrong?

He rubbed his neck and sat down in the big wing chair by the picture window. Through the tall trees outside he could see the moon caught on dark branches.

That morning everything had seemed so clear. He had known exactly the right thing to do.

Now nothing seemed clear.

On the bed Olivia moved suddenly. She twisted sharply, saying words that he couldn't make out. Rafe sat down beside her and took her hand. "It's okay. Just a bad dream."

Her fingers tightened. She seemed to be pushing something away from her face, almost like spiderwebs. Then her eyes opened.

She stared at him for what felt like an eternity.

"You're here. I'm not…dreaming? Or just drunk?"

"I'm here—even though I shouldn't be. That was a crazy thing you did, Livie." Crazy but wonderful, Rafe thought. And by breakfast, everyone in town would be talking about it.

Her eyes hardened. "It had to be done. One of us had to be sensible."

He had to smile at her skewed logic. "If you can call it sensible. But I'll be honest first. I think I might have made a mistake."

She raised an eyebrow. "No kidding."

"Whatever I did was to protect you, Livie."

"I don't see it that way." She stopped and swallowed a sound of pain. "You were right. Those mixed drinks pack a punch."

"Are you okay? Does your head hurt or your stomach?"

"Everything hurts. I'll never drink again."

Rafe eased her back onto the bed and pulled the covers up around her. "That's a relief. We'd have a permanent traffic jam on Main Street if you did. I'd never get anything done."

She looked interested at that. "I thought you were leaving."

"So did I. I keep trying—but it always feels wrong."

Rafe was done attempting to argue sense into her. If she was crazy enough to put up with his life and all its shadows, who was he to argue?

Olivia closed her eyes and slid her fingers through his. "About time," she mumbled.

"But we need some ground rules, Livie. There are things you need to understand, things I have to face. It's going to take me some time to deal with that," Rafe said slowly. "And then we have to consider the future. As it happens, I put away a fair amount of money while I was in the service. There was nothing else to spend it on, so I saved it. Back then, a good portfolio actually made money."

Olivia just stared at him. "You're rich?"

"I wouldn't call it rich. Comfortable maybe. But I can help you while you get your finances sorted out." His voice fell, grew husky. "So I will help you. It's not open to question."

She started to argue, to tell him that she could manage quite nicely by herself. Rafe saw the stubbornness fill her eyes.

Then she sank back against the pillow, one hand to her forehead. "I'm sure there's a reason to argue with you about that, but it can wait until tomorrow. It's starting. That thing you told me about."

"Remorse? Or did you change your mind about me?" Rafe had wanted her to be reasonable, but it would be unbearable if she cut him adrift now.

"No, you idiot. The mother of all hangovers. And I think…it's getting worse."

He leaned down, scooping her out of bed. "I'll get you into the bathroom. Then I'll go down and fix you a special tomato juice drink. It always did the trick for me in the service."

"Did you get drunk a lot?"

"Honey, you *don't* want to know."

She took a deep breath. When he looked down, her eyes were bleary, but filled with certainty. "I love you, Rafe Russo. I've loved you for most of my life. Don't you *ever* forget that. And if you ever walk out on me again, I'll murder you. I'll do it with my drafting pen. Understand?"

Rafe raised one eyebrow. "*Drafting* pen?"

"Damn right."

"You have my promise, honey." He felt absolutely clear about his future and hers. She belonged right here in his arms. "I may be reckless, but I'm not crazy. I've loved you for most of my life, too, Olivia Sullivan."

"Good." Olivia's eyes closed. "Now how about that tomato juice thing you promised me…"

EPILOGUE

Summer Island
Late afternoon

THEY CAME FROM six states, not just Portland. They came in limousines and taxicabs and on motorcycles. Somebody even drove a golf cart.

By the time the sun was heading down on the day of its grand opening, the Harbor House was filled with people and a traffic jam snarled the coast highway.

Some people said it was making the town into a noisy, chaotic mess. Most of the others said it was a jolt of life and a godsend to the local economy.

Rafe Russo, the new acting sheriff during Tom Wilkinson's medical leave, said that the town council needed to widen the coast road fast because his deputies were already too busy to direct traffic all day when cars were stuck in line for the new café and the popular little yarn shop.

The town council, after some intense debate behind closed doors, agreed.

"HAS ANYONE SEEN LIVIE?"

"Over there. She's talking with her real estate

agent, I think." Jilly pointed over her shoulder vaguely. "I think she's finally got an offer on the house. Walker, honey, we're almost out of iced coffee over here."

"Coming right up."

Jilly blew him a quick kiss as she reached around him. "By the way—did you get that cash register to work?"

"All fixed." Walker caught her waist and turned her around. "Take a break for ten minutes. Grace is handling the cash sales now. Caro's grandmother will take over in here."

"But—"

"No arguing. We agreed."

Jilly blew out a breath. "Right. This is totally… wild, isn't it?"

Walker leaned down and calmly whispered, "I told you so."

OUTSIDE ON THE back porch Olivia and the real estate agent weren't talking about how to get the best price for her house. An offer had already been given and accepted. The house would be sold in a month.

Olivia felt nothing but relief to know it was done.

But the real estate agent, Andi Moore, had pulled Olivia around to a quiet part of the yard near the side fence. "I can't take this any longer. I need to tell you the truth. My son was the one up in your attic. I sent him in there after I turned off your electricity. He—

he was supposed to find something in your attic. It was a key."

Olivia blinked at her. "You did that?"

"There's no good way to say this, so I'll just jump in. Your father and I—we were involved, Olivia. For the last nine years of his life. We met in Los Angeles or Chicago or New York. He was very private that way. He wanted to spare me any gossip. I loved him…deeply. But he was a difficult man. He had trouble showing emotions. And I think…there were many things he did not want to share with me. But that was fine. The time we had together meant so much."

Olivia swallowed. "You were…lovers?"

"And we were very, very good friends." Andi laughed. "We were old, but we weren't ancient. You don't have to look that surprised."

"I'm sorry. It's just…a shock. He never mentioned you to me."

"He valued appearances. Maybe too much. But your father worked very hard to become a success, Olivia. He liked order. Control. Did you know that he was adopted? In and out of foster homes. He was sent back after he'd been adopted twice. He never said much, but I think those experiences made him very hard inside."

Olivia sat down in the sunlight, her iced tea totally forgotten. "Adopted? He never told me that, but he didn't tell me much anyway."

"I don't think anyone knew. He was proud of his

image and his success. He wanted people to think of him *that* way, not as someone who'd been abandoned as a baby."

"I can understand that. He would never want pity."

"I know he was hard to understand. He could be very distant…even sometimes cruel. But I loved him and I believe he loved me. So at the end, when he was getting more and more confused, I told him he should go to you and ask you for help. He refused. We argued, but he always refused." She looked away. "Then he asked me to do something for him and I agreed. He said there was a key in the attic. He said you should have it. There was something he had forgotten and that you should know about it."

Olivia couldn't seem to move. "In my attic?"

The agent pressed an envelope into Olivia's hands. "He couldn't write by that point. It was about a month before he died. So he told me what to write and I wrote it down for him. It's all in here. I should've told you sooner, but…I wasn't sure how. And coming from a complete stranger, I thought…well, I didn't know what you would think."

She stood up stiffly. "About the house, I got you the best possible price. I'm not accepting a fee either. I refuse. That's for your father. And it's an apology for the way I bungled this whole thing."

Olivia saw that the woman was trying hard not to cry. She reached out and squeezed her hand. "I only wish I'd known. I'm sorry he never told me. He had so many secrets."

"He was proud of you. He told me that when you wrote him from Italy. He kept some of the photos you sent him. I know he didn't show it, but he was proud in his way. I hope you will believe that."

Olivia took a slow breath. She began to believe. It didn't change everything. But it helped her accept who he was.

"Thank you. It matters, believe me. Why don't you come inside?" Olivia said on impulse. "Jilly has her barbecue almost done…"

"No, no, I'm going. You're much too busy here and my son has a gymnastics competition down at the high school in an hour. But…stay in touch, will you?"

Olivia nodded. "I'll be right here on the island. Rafe and I will be looking for a house soon. Nothing huge. Maybe up on the hill, next to Caro."

"In that case I'll keep an eye out for a property for you. I think…yes, I may have something in mind already." Andi squeezed Olivia's hand and stood up. "Thank you for not being angry—and for understanding a little."

Feeling bewildered, Olivia looked up as Rafe walked down the steps.

"Livie, somebody wants to buy all that cashmere yarn. Jilly said you would know where it was." He hesitated, looking at her closely. "Is everything okay?"

"FINE. PERFECT, ACTUALLY. I'll go get the yarn right now. Somebody wants to buy *all* fifteen balls of it?"

"That's what I hear." Rafe watched the real estate agent walk away. "Was there a change in the offer for the house? Don't tell me the deal fell through already."

"Not at all. In fact, Andi thinks she may have a house for us up on the hill near Caro. There's more, too." Olivia slid the envelope into the pocket of her hand-knit sweater and smiled slowly. "It can wait a little. I'll—I'll tell you later."

"It's good news?"

"Yes. I think it will be." Olivia stood up and slid an arm around his waist. "Let's finish up inside. We should be closing in forty-five minutes. We'll help with the cleanup, and then I'll meet you down at the cove." She kissed him with slow, teasing bites that made Rafe's eyes darken.

"I'd rather go now," he muttered. "This is a zoo."

"The price of success, Sheriff Russo."

"*Acting* sheriff," Rafe corrected.

"Maybe." Olivia smiled broadly and walked toward the house. "You bring the champagne and I'll bring the blanket, Sheriff."

IT WAS OVER an hour later before they could get away. Olivia was tired, but she was singing inside, pumped with the success of their grand opening. She knew there would be months of hard work and uncertainty before the business was secure, but the beginning was better than she could have dreamed.

Down at Butterfly Cove, Rafe was already waiting, one hand on the ladder to the tree house at the top of the high dunes. Olivia saw something shine in the branches, where a dozen Mason jars had been strung up as lanterns. Rafe climbed up the ladder to light the first one when he saw her.

Her heart seemed too full for the love that swept through her as she felt a circle of dreams slide into place around them.

He had come home after too many years of shadows.

So had she.

Something darted over her shoulder as she crossed the dunes toward the beach. A second orange blur followed.

Olivia looked up in surprise as bright wings fluttered around her head, fine but supple, with a strength to fight Pacific gales.

The monarchs had come back to the cove, stopping for red clover and goldenrod and milkweed to fuel their long journey to the fog-swept groves of Northern California.

The air seemed to flash with wings, golden and orange around her. One circle was complete, Olivia thought in awe as the small, hardy travelers looped in graceful spirals around her, full of magic.

And now another circle was about to begin....

* * * * *

AUTHOR'S NOTE

Thank you for joining Olivia and Rafe on their twisting journey through sadness and loss—back to home, friends and love. With the Harbor House open at last, all the Summer Island friends are going to be busy!

So is the new acting sheriff. Old secrets never stay hidden, and Rafe has vowed to keep the island and those he loves safe.

I hope that Summer Island's magic continues to touch you as it has touched me. In its fog-swept coves and quiet streets friendship runs deep, and the love of good yarn runs even deeper. Olivia will be creating new patterns for the Island Yarns shop, and you can find all the details at my website—www.christinaskye.com.

If you were intrigued by Rafe's guacamole recipe, check out the Southwest recipes on my website. I have a secret twist on Rafe's version. Yum! Don't tell Jilly.

You can find all the techniques and how to make the special ingredients at christinaskye.com. While you're there, check out my favorite chai tea recipes, too. I haven't forgotten knitting—or crochet goodies either.

As summer sunlight fades into winter storms, the Harbor House will shelter old friends and new strangers, drawn to its bright windows. Four strong women will fight to protect what they love most. And their remarkable men will be right beside them. Their stories will continue....

I'll be watching for you down at the cove.

With warmest wishes,
Christina

REQUEST YOUR FREE BOOKS!

2 FREE NOVELS
FROM THE ROMANCE COLLECTION
PLUS 2 FREE GIFTS!

YES! Please send me 2 FREE novels from the Romance Collection and my 2 FREE gifts (gifts are worth about $10). After receiving them, if I don't wish to receive any more books, I can return the shipping statement marked "cancel." If I don't cancel, I will receive 4 brand-new novels every month and be billed just $6.24 per book in the U.S. or $6.74 per book in Canada. That's a savings of at least 22% off the cover price. It's quite a bargain! Shipping and handling is just 50¢ per book in the U.S. and 75¢ per book in Canada.* I understand that accepting the 2 free books and gifts places me under no obligation to buy anything. I can always return a shipment and cancel at any time. Even if I never buy another book, the two free books and gifts are mine to keep forever.

194/394 MDN F4XY

Name		(PLEASE PRINT)	
Address			Apt. #
City	State/Prov.		Zip/Postal Code

Signature (if under 18, a parent or guardian must sign)

Mail to the **Harlequin®** Reader Service:
IN U.S.A.: P.O. Box 1867, Buffalo, NY 14240-1867
IN CANADA: P.O. Box 609, Fort Erie, Ontario L2A 5X3

Want to try two free books from another line?
Call 1-800-873-8635 or visit www.ReaderService.com.

* Terms and prices subject to change without notice. Prices do not include applicable taxes. Sales tax applicable in N.Y. Canadian residents will be charged applicable taxes. Offer not valid in Quebec. This offer is limited to one order per household. Not valid for current subscribers to the Romance Collection or the Romance/Suspense Collection. All orders subject to credit approval. Credit or debit balances in a customer's account(s) may be offset by any other outstanding balance owed by or to the customer. Please allow 4 to 6 weeks for delivery. Offer available while quantities last.

Your Privacy—The Harlequin® Reader Service is committed to protecting your privacy. Our Privacy Policy is available online at www.ReaderService.com or upon request from the Harlequin Reader Service.

We make a portion of our mailing list available to reputable third parties that offer products we believe may interest you. If you prefer that we not exchange your name with third parties, or if you wish to clarify or modify your communication preferences, please visit us at www.ReaderService.com/consumerschoice or write to us at Harlequin Reader Service Preference Service, P.O. Box 9062, Buffalo, NY 14269. Include your complete name and address.

ROM13R

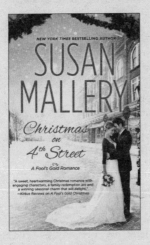

CHRISTINA SKYE

77659 THE ACCIDENTAL BRIDE	___ $7.99 U.S.	___ $9.99 CAN.
77608 A HOME BY THE SEA	___ $7.99 U.S.	___ $9.99 CAN.
77209 CODE NAME: BIKINI	___ $6.99 U.S.	___ $8.50 CAN.

(limited quantities available)

TOTAL AMOUNT	$ _____
POSTAGE & HANDLING	$ _____
($1.00 FOR 1 BOOK, 50¢ for each additional)	
APPLICABLE TAXES*	$ _____
TOTAL PAYABLE	$ _____

(check or money order—please do not send cash)

To order, complete this form and send it, along with a check or money order for the total above, payable to Harlequin HQN, to: **In the U.S.:** 3010 Walden Avenue, P.O. Box 9077, Buffalo, NY 14269-9077; **In Canada:** P.O. Box 636, Fort Erie, Ontario, L2A 5X3.

Name: _____

Address: _____ City: _____

State/Prov.: _____ Zip/Postal Code: _____

Account Number (if applicable): _____

075 CSAS

*New York residents remit applicable sales taxes.
*Canadian residents remit applicable GST and provincial taxes.

(H) HARLEQUIN® HQN™
™ www.Harlequin.com